THE SINS OF THE FATHERS

Mirador Publishing
Mirador
Wearne Lane
Langport
Somerset
TA10 9HB

The Sins Of The Fathers

By

Curtis Moon

Other books by Curtis Moon

The 21st Century Crusaders
Sentimental Journey
Secret Place
Beyond The Blue Horizon
Searching For Patrick
Fast Wings Of Destiny
A Thing Of The Past
Syria-Gyra
Royal Dissent
Sixth Book Of The Holy Bible
Otherwise Engaged
The Only Thing
Damage Limitations
Sins Of The Fathers
Days Of Old

CHAPTER ONE

The sad news heralded a bad day! The office was filled with gloom; everyone was depressed. The death of a reporter was always felt deeply by all those who worked on the newspaper... from messenger boy to the chief editor. Death was not new to any of us. We wrote about it every day. But such matters related to other people ...the general public... not to the writers who communicated the news. Certainly not to the main three reporters... Petrie, Barnaby and Savage. They called us the "hot-shots"; reporters with a high-reputation who had been writing for the newspaper for many years. Now we were down to two; and even less than that, because Barnaby had been injured in a road accident and had broken his leg.

Petrie and I had joined the newspaper at the same time many years earlier. We were not only colleagues but good friends. In time, he became a war correspondent while I took on a multitude of indifferent activities. Now he was dead. When I read the initial report sent through on the facsimile machine, all the anguish inside me frothed over. I was angry ... furious... filled with despair. 'Bastards!' I shouted across the office. 'Shot him in the back! Shot my best friend in the back! God... you knock your guts out trying to make a living by reporting the news and some trigger-happy fool ends it in one second with a single shot from a Kalashnikov rifle. No time to pray. No time to say goodbye to the wife and kids. No time for messages to relatives or friends... nothing! What a waste of a life!

"I'm going places, Bellamy!" he once told me. "I'm going places. Just you wait and see! Hang on to my shirt and you'll be in for a great ride!" Well he went places all right, ending up in a ditch in some God-forsaken country with a bullet in his back. How could anyone in the world shoot an innocent man in cold blood? Surely they must have seen he had a pen in his hand and not a gun! But then he was shot in the back. The cowards! He wasn't wearing a uniform. Jesus! Couldn't they see he wasn't wearing a uniform! Were they blind? We all know that ugly things happen in the heat of war which are best left unsaid and forgotten... but to shoot an unarmed man in the back when he's not wearing a uniform is way out of line! I hope they rot in hell!'

The occasion was so sad that even Ted Flanders, my bad-tempered, miserable, ulcer-ridden editor whose sole aim was to expose current situations operating against the public interest to sell more newspapers, wasn't around to shout at the staff. Nonetheless, he managed to sneak in to leave a memo on my desk... to cover a story. I fumed even more when I read it. It had been given initially to Barnaby. However, a relayed message explained that the luckless reporter had been struck down by a taxi, an act which removed him from all worthwhile activity, causing him to lay prostrate in a hospital bed suffering a broken leg and internal injuries. Despite his brilliance in the newspaper field, Barnaby had been proved to be a reprehensible liar many times in the past in order to avoid seedy assignments. A man with a silver tongue, he had the ability to draw on the most remarkable tales which poured smoothly from his misbegotten lips. On this occasion I gave him the benefit of the doubt because if he turned up on the following week fully fit I would surely break one of his legs myself! Whenever Flanders sought a replacement for him, it always fell to me to cover for him. In the heat of the moment, I offered no token of sympathy to my colleague... albeit he was probably painfully hospitalised. For the time being, my mind was wounded and bruised by the news of the sudden death of my dear friend and colleague, Jeff Petrie. He would be hard to replace on the newspaper; there was no one with whom to compare him in real life!

Flanders used Barnaby and myself as his trouble-shooting squad. It was the equivalent role of a commando in the army, or a professional in the S.A.S. There were times when it became really rough out in the field. The editor had developed this idea on his own and often boasted about its value, efficiency and success to the Chief Editor. His argument stressed that sales of the newspaper had risen fairly steeply in the past ten years, and there was no reason to challenge him on the issue. However, neither Barnaby nor I ever felt it was anything special... other than for the editor to gain himself another promotion point with his superior. We were chosen to undertake the most hazardous and difficult tasks to entertain millions of readers who would probably use yesterday's paper to light the fire, empty the ashes in the hearth, wrap refuse in it, eat chips from it, or use it for some other mundane purpose. News items were quickly expendable.

Barnaby never seemed to care if an assignment was tough or perilous. He seemed to thrive when danger lurked in the wings. I was far more concerned about my own welfare... being a coward at heart... but then every job had its risks. There was no rhyme or reason to dwell on the possibility or probability of personal danger. Personally, I had no pretensions of longevity. A long life meant little to me. I wanted only to live for today and relax in comfort by myself whenever the opportunity arose.

It was an hour later when Ted Flanders returned to his office. He stared at me through the window and then buzzed me on the telephone.

'Why am I not blessed with good reporters?' he demanded, although I knew he didn't mean it. 'I gave you an assignment early this morning and you're still sitting at your desk. What the hell do you think you're doing?'

'I'm writing the obituary of Jeff Petrie, if you must know!' I wasn't going to take any guff from him on this particular morning. 'Anyway, it's not an assignment as such. Your memo doesn't make sense. Maybe you should go back to night-school to learn English!'

He was shocked at my brazen attitude. Normally, we tolerated each other without being rude. Today it was different.

'You're upset. Well that's understandable. Look... come into my office and have a drink. We'll run through it together.'

I pressed the cross-bar on the telephone gently a couple of times to cause a clicking sound without cutting him off. 'I didn't quite get that, Ted!' I complained falsely. 'Couldn't hear you.'

The editor replaced the receiver and emerged from his office with an old-fashioned expression on his face. 'All right,' he said tiredly as he approached my desk. 'Don't push me too hard, Jimmy.!' He put out his arms which he rested on the desk and leaned across towards me. 'This assignment's a piece of cake. I'm just testing it out for a story.'

My ears perked up suspiciously at the ostensible simplicity of the task. 'Details, Ted. Details!' I tried to stifle a yawn as he droned on.

'A certain amount of turbulence in Eastern Europe. That's the trouble.'

'Are we talking about the weather, German European reunification, or what? You're not making sense.'

'It seems that a group of young people have conceived an idea that sounds sinister. We ought to take a look. If it's correct, there could be major problems. I want this paper to be the first one to publish the story. It all started here!'

I yawned loudly, unable to repress my feelings any longer. 'Is this going to be one of those kite-flying assignments where you end up screaming how expensive I am and what a waste of money it was to the paper?'

He seemed to be staring into the distance, not having heard my tirade.. 'The information concerns some people who organised themselves into a group a while ago, waiting for the agreement on German European reunification. Now the time is ripe.'

'Ripe for what, Ted? Reunification's not going to take place. Europe's in a hell of a mess.' It occurred to me that perhaps Flanders had been overworking and needed a vacation. The continued pressure of editing a major newspaper had caused him to become jaded. He needed to take a holidaya.!

'I'll tell you what they're ripe for!' he rattled sharply. 'The group's been growing secretly over the past thirty years and now has a core membership exceeding a hundred thousand people. You may also be interested to know it has links with twenty other countries in Europe and that each one has about the same number of recruits. If you take account of all that, we may be talking of two million people ready to form a clandestine United States of Europe. And many of them are fairly young. Am I getting through to you?'

'How come they're young people?'

'Because most of them are. That's what I hear.'

'But the European Community is in full flood. Why would anyone want to form a separate group covering the same countries?'

'That's one of the questions I want answered. So get the cobwebs out of your mind and come back to civilisation. Petrie's gone. No amount of remorse will bring him back. The public want to read the next edition of the paper. We can't stand on ceremony.'

I ignored his comments as so much rhetoric. His words swiftly reinforced the myth that he had no heart at all. The paper was his life... his only interest... nothing else mattered.

'Does this organisation have a Head Office? If so, where is it located? Who's in charge? Where can I get hold of them?' From habit, the questions began tripping off my tongue as my brain raced to learn more.

'Who knows who the Fuehrer is these days?'

In that single word... the term Fuehrer... Flanders caused the whole of modern history to erupt in my mind like an active volcano. I was too young to have been through the previous holocaust, but the evidence was there to witness in pictures, films and documents which had etched themselves on my mind. Could it be that those who had forgotten the warnings of their parents and grandparents were going to make the same mistake again?

'Are you still there, Jimmy? Is the light still on in there?' he continued sarcastically as my mind drifted back through the past.

I tried to marshal my thoughts with regard to the concept. I was relaxed, having shifted into low gear over the past week mulling over trivialities. It felt as if it needed a winch to haul me back to the real world. 'Is your source reliable?' I managed to say after a short while.

'I think so. He's never let me down before. If you can find a good story in it, I'll owe you a favour. That's a promise.'

I laughed loudly as he stood erect. 'When did you ever do me a favour, Ted? When you're in trouble, I'm the only person you can really fall back on. How bad is Barnaby anyway?'

He paused for a moment, pulling on his jaw thoughtfully. 'You weren't in the centre of London last evening driving a taxi, were you?'

'What's that supposed to mean?' I asked. He was intimating nonsensically that I might have created the accident which put the reporter in hospital.

'Never mind!' he snapped. 'Just don't stretch this one out like elastic. I don't want to have to explain the high cost to our illustrious Chief Editor.' He turned on his heel and went back to his office.

When it came to greetings and farewells, Flanders was not the best conversationalist in the world. Too many years of service in the newspaper profession had taken the varnish off his etiquette. At least for once he refrained from using indecent and blasphemous language.

I was too tense... too upset by Jeff Petrie's death to work that day. I couldn't even finish his obituary and had to pass it on to a colleague for completion. I drove into the Surrey countryside and sat on a park bench. In solitude, I reflected the indifference and intolerance of human-beings towards each other in war, and the futility of chasing ambition which often failed without warning so that ideals collapsed like a pack of cards. The sun was dipping over the horizon and I felt quite miserable. There were bad guys everywhere these days, and I often wondered what went wrong... and where would it all end. The strange view filled my mind that the planet on which we live is purgatory itself... that we passed through a life and ended here waiting to be transferred to Heaven or some other place. Alternatively, we may have arrived in Hell itself. Whenever I read the items in the daily newspaper, I considered the latter concept the most likely!

* * * * *

I left to start the assignment early next morning. For the time being, Petrie was out of my mind. A thick cumulus of cloud hid the sky and it began to drizzle. As the traffic grew thicker, my patience began to wear thin. When I came close to the Capital I started to recall the irritation and frustration experienced throughout the rest of the year. London was an awful place in which to work, with its never-ending stream of cars, the icy-cold unfriendliness of the people, a consistent buzz of background noise from the traffic, and air pollution which seemed prevalent everywhere. The traffic congestion ensured I would be late which was a bad beginning to the day. Long lines of vehicles were slouched in traffic lanes without budging for long periods, purring softly in their static positions. The rest of the journey was bound to continue in the same vein. I edged my car on to the kerb and climbed out, placing a piece of cardboard under the windscreen wipers to declare that it was out of action. My eyes scanned the mass of vehicles in despair until I saw a vacant taxi. Cab-drivers in London knew every inch of the Capital. If I was going to get to my destination quickly, a taxi would be the only realistic method. My mind was so preoccupied that I failed to notice a tall man climb from a large black limousine nearby. He moved towards me swiftly to grip me fiercely by the arm.

'This way, Mr. Savage!' he ordered briefly, pulling me towards the limousine.

I stared at him in astonishment. I had been standing on a major highway leading into London when a man I had never seen before took a tight grip on my arm and called me by my name. Curtly, he invited me to travel in his car and projected me in that direction.

'Who are you?' I managed to blurt out as a spark of fear welled-up inside me.

He opened the rear door of the car. 'Get in!' he ordered. He loosened his grip and pushed me so that I fell on to the back seat. The door was closed firmly behind me. He settled into the front seat and turned to look at me. 'You're in no danger, Mr. Savage. Your presence is required urgently, that's all.' He opened a window and place a siren on the roof which started to wail like a screaming banshee. The vehicles in front edged sideways to the kerb to give way, and the limousine sped forward.

'Who wants to see me so urgently... and why?' I asked, as the car forged through the thoroughfare of scattered traffic.

'You'll find out soon enough, ' he replied flatly.

I weighed up all the pros and cons. I wasn't being held prisoner... well not yet, at least. Nor was there a gun pointing at my head. 'This is all rather bizarre, isn't it?' I pressed, not expecting an answer. 'All this cloak-and-dagger stuff!' The tall man ignored the question. 'You know my name so you obviously know I'm a reporter with The Daily Post. Why couldn't you have telephoned me at the office?'

'I obey orders. The three wise monkeys, Mr. Savage. I don't see anything, hear anything, or say anything. It makes life much simpler.'

There was a long silence and then I decided to see what would happen if I tried to escape. I placed my hand on the door handle, ostensibly with the intention of diving into the road, even though the car was travelling at a reasonable speed, but it was locked and didn't give an inch. 'Don't mess about!' scolded the driver, witnessing my abortive attempt to liberate myself. 'It'll all be revealed to you. If you'll only be patient.'

The car turned into Westminster Square and headed towards the car park of the House of Commons. The expression on my face showed my surprise as my eyes ran over the building. I could hardly resist the obvious statement. 'This is the House of Commons!'

The driver failed to respond as he stopped the vehicle and waved a hand to usher me out. I stepped out of the car anticipating a rush of people ready to descend upon me without warning, but, to my relief, nothing happened. I followed him into the building and we walked down a long corridor. He stopped outside a heavily-panelled door and paused for a moment. Then he rapped on it loudly with his gloved hand before turning the handle and squeezing his head inside, taking great care to shield the identity of those in the room from my curious eyes. Shortly, after a muffled discussion, the driver pushed open the door and motioned me to enter. I obeyed hesitantly and had hardly crossed the threshold when the door slammed shut behind me.

There were five people in the room seated around a large polished table, and they stared in my direction. By the way they looked at me, I felt like something that the cat had dragged in! A tall, thin man, dressed smartly in a starched white shirt, a black jacket and pin-striped trousers got to his feet as I entered.

'Good morning, Mr. Savage!' he greeted amiably, taking my hand which he pumped up and down. 'My name's Maitland, Personal Assistant to the Prime Minister.' He pointed to the others at the table. 'May I introduce Miss Grayson, Technical Adviser on Defence matters, Lieutenant-Colonel Topham, also Defence, Sir Peter Cavenham, Home Office, and Mr. Jacobs, State Security. Please take a seat!'

Maitland turned on his heel and left the room by means of a side door which he closed behind him. I stared at the faces of the others with a high degree of suspicion. After all, I had been abducted and was being held prisoner in the House of Commons. It sounded fastidious and, if I ever divulged what had happened, no one would believe me... certainly not Ted Flanders my editor! There was one other matter which set off a red warning light in my head. How did I know these people were genuine... that they were the people Maitland purported them to be? I had never heard of any of them before! For a short while I stood perfectly still, and then decided that attack was the best form of defence. 'Perhaps one of you would be kind enough to explain why I've been abducted by such an eminent group of people.'

'Come now, Savage!' chided Sir Peter, finding the remark amusing. 'Nothing like that! We're inviting you to attend our meeting. There's an element of urgency and the need for absolute secrecy. Life doesn't always fit into neat little boxes, you know.'

I gave him a jaundiced look. 'Does this happen often? Inviting people here in this fashion?'

The Lieutenant-Colonel snorted at the insubordination. 'Dashed awkward!' he muttered reticently. 'Dashed awkward for everyone!'

Miss Grayson looked at me appealingly. 'You're quite right. We ought to apologise for causing inconvenience,' she ventured. 'Please sit down and listen to what we have to say. I'm sure you'll understand our difficulty.' She was a very attractive woman in her early thirties, with blonde hair, blue eyes and a very trim figure. The clothes she wore seemed to be a little too avant-garde for a civil servant. I took her advice and sat down, waiting for someone to give me an explanation but, to my annoyance, they all remained silent.

'I didn't know we had an organisation known as State Security?' I thrust pointedly, looking directly at Jacobs. He treated the question as rhetoric, staring back at me coldly without uttering a syllable. The silence continued until my ears seemed fit to burst as my heart pounded away loudly. 'Look... I'm not an impatient man normally,' I shouted angrily, 'but I would appreciate it if someone could tell me why I've been brought here... and what's going on!'

Sir Peter played with a pencil for a few moments, having doodled continuously since I entered the room. 'The P.M. will be here in a moment. I think he'll wish to discuss the matter with you at first hand. If it's any comfort to you, we're all waiting on him.'

I turned to Jacobs looking for someone to wound. 'I suppose you're MI5 and all that!'

'MI5!' snapped the security man. 'This is not a James Bond film, Savage!'

It was left for me to survey the room until something interesting happened and I decided to maul them in the meantime. 'State Security, Home Office, two from Defence and, on top of that, the Prime Minister. It's all very intriguing. Do you have a dossier on me... or a detailed curriculum vitae?'

'Don't be so damned conceited!' snarled Jacobs. 'You're here to do a service for your country. I suggest you stop speculating and cut out the chit-chat!'

I had the greatest respect for the person who appointed him to State Security for, in my view, a job of that description needed personnel who were extremely unpleasant and very hard. Jacobs fitted the bill perfectly... he was an extremely nasty man. 'A service for my country!' I repeated sarcastically. 'Well that's interesting. You see, a funny thing happened to me on my way to the City this morning. I was abducted for my country.'

'You were not abducted... ..' began Sir Peter, but his sentence tailed off as Maitland returned through the side door followed by the Prime Minister.

Everyone rose as a token of respect and the Prime Minister waved his hand for them to sit down again. They all obeyed except for Maitland who stood at the side of his superior as though prepared for action.

'Good morning, Mr. Savage!' greeted the Prime Minister, glancing briefly at the faces of those attending. 'First of all, please accept my apology for the method by which you were brought here today. Believe me, it was unavoidable. It's not the policy of this government to abduct people to the House of Commons, but on this occasion zealousness overcame caution. Please forgive us.'

I stared into the eyes of Sir Peter with a smirk on my lips at the Prime Minister's confession. However, he chose to look up at the ceiling tiredly as though bored with the proceedings.

'We're faced with a serious situation brought to our attention recently and we ask for your help,' continued the Prime Minister. 'Would you outline the details, Mr. Jacobs?'

The State Security man cleared his throat. 'The activities of every society, group, organisation, faction or agency in this country are examined regularly to protect the rights of citizens and to prevent unlawful and unauthorised intervention in the affairs of the nation. Although the government has no intention of imposing control on any section of the public, law and order must prevail. The riots in Liverpool, Bristol, Bermondsey and Tottenham, in the past, were prime examples where situations almost got out of control. At the same time, we monitor the activities of certain groups abroad to assess in advance whether action is required to prevent terrorist or other activities against the public interest. That's the role of State Security. Would you like to carry on, Sir Peter?'

The Home Office official drew his eyes down from the ceiling to stare directly at me. 'In normal circumstances,' he began, shifting slightly in his seat, 'it's sufficient to monitor without taking action. Information has reached us, however, of another element which has formed itself into something more serious... not only in this country but all over Europe. We believe your editor was able to learn of International Three Thousand, an organisation recruiting young people whose policy it is to overthrow all the governments in Europe. One can only assume they intend to created a United States of Europe counter to the existing system. In a single word, Mr. Savage, we're talking of anarchy and revolution.'

I sat silently, allowing the words to filter through my mind. They must have tapped Ted Flander's telephone to realise The Daily Post was going to intrude into their clandestine world. 'What information do you have?' I asked innocently.

'None at all!' retorted Lieutenant-Colonel Topham bitterly. 'My office only heard about this last week. It seems to be a very secret society. Perhaps that's the most disturbing thing about it. We've checked with a number of other European governments but they know little about it either.'

I shrugged my shoulders listlessly and shook my head from side to side. 'I understand what you're telling me, but how is my newspaper involved? I mean, you have all your own intelligence agents. What can I do?'

'We're asking you to volunteer for this task,' confided the Prime Minister. 'It's a matter of urgency and top priority. We're concerned that if we go through normal channels, those in control of International Three Thousand would be driven underground, and they might also accelerate their plans. That's the last thing we want to happen. However, if a nosey newspaper reporter starts to make enquiries, they may not suspect that anyone else knows about it. It would give us time before they spur themselves into action. The government requires a full report no later than thirty days from now... with details, locations and other information so that action may be taken in the interest of the public.'

'Tell me,' I requested humbly. 'Do you know why it's called International Three Thousand?'

Sir Peter shifted in his seat again as he came to the rescue. 'You may recall that Adolf Hitler told his nation the Third Reich would live for a thousand years. Well, this organisation is following a similar route. They intend to start their antics now, with the aim of changing Europe before the year three thousand anno domini. A thousand years. It rings a bell, doesn't it?'

'I'm afraid we shall have to insist on 'D' notices at the present time with regard to publication of the story in your newspaper,' continued the Prime Minister. 'In effect, Mr. Savage, this meeting never took place and none of us has ever seen you. Equally, you have never seen us, and no one is to be told anything... not even your editor. As you make inroads into this assignment, perhaps you would care to contact Miss Grayson. She'll appraise us of your progress in the field.' He stood up as if to leave and Maitland moved aside the chair. 'Before I go, I would like to thank you for your assistance. I'm sure you recognise the importance of your role and the service you'll be giving to your country. Thank you very much... and good luck!'

The others stood up as the Prime Minister left the room. I wondered if he was going to meet another person like myself to deal with urgent matters of a similar nature. The mantle of government at its highest level assumed many different roles. Sir Peter picked up his papers, including his doodles, shuffled them into order, and then stalked out of the room without saying another word. Lieutenant-Colonel Topham followed in his footsteps. Jacobs stared at me as though I was his prey and he was about to eat me. Then his face softened a little.

'Don't rush your fences,' he advised. There was silence and then he moved closer to speak to me confidentially. 'If you want, you can have Gates to help you. But it has to be unofficial.'

I expressed my gratitude with an element of surprise in my voice, assuming that Gates was the tall chauffeur who had abducted me. Perhaps Jacobs wasn't quite as nasty as he appeared to be at first sight. At least he was trying to help. I stared at him as he walked out of the room, presuming that, because of his attitude, he was probably the loneliest man in London... perhaps in the whole country!

'I suppose you think we're all afraid of our own shadows?' Miss Grayson's voice sounded smooth and interesting.

I glanced at her and smiled. 'Sometimes I think I'm in a zoo looking at the human-beings caught up in the web of civilisation, in the same way I watch the antics of chimpanzees. When you look at it in that light, it's difficult not to laugh.' She began to smile at my misdirected philosophy although it wasn't really funny at all! 'You better let me have details where I can contact you. How about dinner this evening? I know a nice little place where we can discuss everything in detail.'

She scanned my face for a while before making a decision. 'Very well, Mr. Savage. Collect me at eight o'clock.' She delved into her handbag to produce one of her business cards which she handed to me. 'The official address is on the front. My home address is on the back.'

'Do all your cards have your home address on the back? I mean, someone in your position... it could be dangerous.'

'Isn't life much more fun when it's dangerous?' she retorted. She looked at me with a slight smile at the corners of her mouth. I felt a warm glow move inside me and told myself she was only a pretty woman... a technical advisor on defence matters... nothing more. She was simply my contact with regard to information.

Outside the House of Commons, the traffic seemed to be moving much easier and I hailed a taxi to take me back to my car. When I reached the office, Ted Flanders was in his usual bad mood. The last time I saw him smile, there was a flash of lightning and a crack of thunder. He was standing in the office in his shirt-sleeves, almost dancing with rage.

'Where the hell have you been?' he shouted at the top of his voice. He cast his arm across the desk, sweeping papers and office paraphernalia to the floor in a very bad temper. I remained silent because he wouldn't believe me if I told him the truth. I decided that the words offered by Gates earlier in the day would suffice as an answer. 'I don't see anything, hear anything, or say anything,' I told him calmly. 'It makes life much simpler most of the time.'

His reaction was unprintable, failing to accept my comments in the right spirit. All I know is that when I reached my own office and closed the door behind me, the silence was deafening. On the desk stood a photograph of myself on a beach during my vacation. It seemed to be a million miles away. I toyed with the events of my first morning back at work and measured it against the quality of life. 'Was it worth it?' I asked myself. 'Was it all really worth it?'

CHAPTER TWO

The East End of London had always been one of my favourite haunts. I had an affinity with it. Perhaps it was my humble upbringing in the docks area which took me back to my roots. There was simply the comfortable feeling that it was my second home. The people were so natural in their attitude and behaviour; no side, no affectation, no innuendo. Life continued in reality without false hopes, high ambitions or feelings of grandeur. At one time, the territory became a slum of enormous proportions where the pitted and scarred brickwork of old crumbling buildings erected in Victorian days was commonplace. The streets were littered with stray refuse left to rot in the open, and a miserable stench lingered everywhere. In recent years there had been a change of heart by local planners who had turned the dock area into a wealth of offices, building giant monoliths, each with a thousand eyes for windows, staring out over an area where new replaced the old and the streets were clean. For me, the faint odour of the past still remained in my nostrils.

I had arranged to meet Calvin at the Dog and Duck in Backchurch Lane that afternoon. He was invaluable to me... one of the best informers I ever had the good fortune to groom in my stable. The value of his services to the newspaper had been considerable over the last five years, yet the results had paid him rich rewards. Calvin reminded me very much of the late W.C. Fields, the old music hall entertainer. His voice sounded the same and his attitude to life was identical. I could always imagine him imitating the great comedian saying: "When you wake up in the morning, smile... best to get it over with right away!" or "If at first you don't succeed, try again, then quit ... no use being a damn fool about it!" Calvin weighed about twenty-two stone and sat precariously on a stool at the saloon bar in the public house. He was a person who could be termed in the vernacular as a "know-all" and I, with hand on heart, could attest I had never seen him shift from the stool. It amazed me how such an indolent grossly-overweight person, who hardly seemed to move his body could amass such a lot of knowledge concerning the criminal world... but Calvin managed to succeed! In fact, the only actions I recalled about him was the movement of his lips as he spoke, which was very limited, and the automatic swing of his right arm when he raised a glass of beer to his mouth, which occurred often. As I entered the Dog and Duck, his eyes scanned my face without blinking and his expression was unmoved. It was as though he knew the reason for my visit and was ready to negotiate for the information. I went to the bar to stand close to him and ordered a drink.

'Not now! Not here!' he muttered through his lips which hardly moved. 'Take your drink and sit in the far corner!'

I looked about the room casually but no one was there except for a young couple gazing into each other's eyes romantically at one table, and an old codger smoking a briar pipe at another. Nonetheless, I followed the instruction and took my drink to the far corner to wait until it was my turn to be counselled. Within a short while, a seedy thin individual with an unshaven face and an ill-fitting suit entered and walked up to Calvin. He whispered something into his ear and the fat man's lips moved to ask a number of questions. After a few minutes, Calvin removed a bundle of bank-notes from his pocket, peeled off a few, and handed them to the other man who left the inn quickly. I wondered how the fat man knew someone was going to offer him information at that time. He seemed to have a crystal ball working inside his head. I had to admire him, for while he sat immobile on a stool all day long drinking beer, I had to race round the country like a lunatic, under pressure, with very short deadlines, writing stories for a bad-tempered editor. He waved a hand at me without looking in my direction and I walked over to the bar, drink in hand, trying to act casually without drawing attention to myself.

'Comes to mind,' he said slowly, as W.C. Fields used to do, 'that you have a great story on your hands. If only you can get a decent lead.'

'What story is that?' I challenged, testing him.

'Comes to mind,' he repeated, 'that many young people, in this country and others, are becoming very bad boys. They're not playing the game.'

'How come you know?' I asked with an element of frustration in my voice. The issue was a secret at top-level yet he seemed to know all about it. I felt as though I was the last one at the end of the line to hear of it.

'You're lucky, it's not going to cost you this time, my friend,' he continued. 'All my chickens are coming home to roost, and I'm in a good mood.'

It didn't sound good to me. Calvin never gave favours to anyone for nothing. He made his living by passing on information from that single stool... and his tariff was high. If he was willing to offer something freely, it was tantamount to the fact that he couldn't help. 'All right, what's my lead?'

'Igor Strogoff. Know the man?'

'Never heard of him!'

'Look him up in some of those newspaper files of yours. Igor Strogoff!'

'How do I get in touch with him?'

'Comes to mind there's a meeting at the People's Palace in the Mile End Road this evening at seven thirty. You might consider attending.'

I swallowed the rest of my drink and then nodded. 'All right, Calvin. I'll be in touch.'

'You do that. I'm interested to know the outcome.' He swung his right arm into gear to lift his glass as I left. I glanced back at him momentarily, still thinking of W.C. Fields. Somehow I could hear him say: "Comes to mind, I exercise extreme control... I never drink anything stronger than gin before breakfast!"

Calvin was a real East End character. Everyone knew of him but few had ever seen him... not unless they visited the Dog and Duck. For my own part, I wasn't sure whether to be grateful to him or not. The lead he had given me was hardly promising and I had a feeling in the pit of my stomach it was going to be a dead end. But beggars couldn't be choosers... it was all I had to go on. So I returned to the office and looked up the files to find some details about Strogoff. The newspaper had masses of background information in files or on microfilm. This time the data was scant indeed.

I thought about the assignment very deeply over an early evening meal, forgetting I had promised to collect Miss Grayson for dinner. I couldn't help it. When faced with a tough problem which seemed impossible to resolve, I had to grasp opportunities as they emerged. What wasn't excusable was my omission to ring her about it.

* * * * *

The People's Palace was once an old-time music hall... used mainly for burlesque and amateur dramatic performances. In recent years, it had become vacant, available to anyone wishing to rent it, for meetings or for some other purpose. It soon fell into decay and this was likely to be the last meeting as the property had been sold to an agency which intended to build a university annex on the site. As I approached the building, I noticed a crowd of people queuing for admission. I sauntered past, glancing at the posters pasted on the wall which advertised a meeting for peace, progress and prosperity. It seemed to me there were an awful lot of people willing to attend this tentatively innocuous event which would normally attract little interest in the East End of London. The depressed areas usually spawned a ready market of television 'soap' addicts rather than pseudo-political observers. To my astonishment, the queue appeared to lengthen as time progressed, causing me to consider the matter more deeply and to ask myself a number of questions. Why were all these people so interested? How did they become aware that the meeting was going to take place? What was going to happen inside? And where were the police? There was a lot which didn't add up!

I went to the back of the queue noticing with trepidation that each person was being screened before being allowed to enter the building. At first, I presumed the minders, bouncers, or the management were checking to determine if anyone was carrying weapons or explosive devices. But then I realised there was something more sinister. As I neared the entrance, I could hear each entrant mention a figure and a letter. The minder would mutter the word 'Region' and the next person in the queue responded. We shuffled along a little further and the person in front of me answered '4B'. I retorted '4C' and my heart beat faster before I found myself projected forward by the man behind me into the hall. It seemed that every individual attending had been invited to the meeting... each one representing an area identified by a code number. It was my good fortune that no one held a clip-board checking off each location, otherwise I would have been in deep trouble. One could only presume an uninvited guest would be sent packing especially as the minders appeared to be men of substantial brawn. As a devout coward, I had no interest in falling foul of any of them and only the bravest or most stupid person would insist on the right of attendance against the wishes of such sentinels.

The large auditorium was only partly filled and I decided to take a seat about one-third of the distance from the stage. More people filtered in and a young woman took the seat next to me, placing a small suitcase under her seat. I stared at her with concern, considering that she might be harbouring an explosive device in the case. Hosting a great deal of discomfort, as well as feeling a total stranger among people who were true members, I sat back in my seat and waited for the curtains to open, wondering why Calvin had suggested my attendance here. In a short while, the sound of an old scratched record, playing a march, crackled over the loudspeaker system, then the curtains opened to show a committee of four men and a woman sitting behind a wooden trestle table on the stage. Behind them, some large coloured placards had been erected as a backcloth bearing key words relating to Peace, Integration, Progress and Unified Prosperity. The Chairman rose and welcomed the audience, explaining he would introduce a special international celebrity later on, and he proceeded to run through the agenda. The peripheral speakers talked generally about the unification of people and countries in Europe, international peace, and world accord. I listened with a modicum of interest, trying not to yawn, and kept an eye on the young woman beside me lest she made a sudden move to open her suitcase. Eventually, after an hour of tiresome deliveries, the Chairman got to his feet and proudly announced the celebrity.....Igor Strogoff!

As soon as the name was mentioned, I sat upright in my seat wondering what had been in Calvin's mind when he gave me the lead. The newspaper files identified him as a Russian criminal who had escaped from a labour camp in Siberia. It was a claim to fame in its own right because only a very small number of prisoners fleeing from those vile, remote camps in the snowy wastes had ever survived. Once through the barbed-wire fence of the compound, an in-mate had to face of journey of several hundred miles, battling against the fiercest elements of nature... ice, snow and blizzards! It was necessary to avoid death from exposure where no shelter existed, food was unavailable, and wolves and bears prowled for prey. One of the serious perils was snow-blindness, and the only protection from the cold was the clothing worn at the time of escape. Despite that, having avoided recapture by the guards, who made an exhaustive search over a wide area, Strogoff managed to survive. However, it had been at great personal physical cost.

The large gathering waited patiently to see the honoured speaker and they remained unusually quiet for a while until the slender figure appeared on the stage and limped slowly towards the table. There was a crescendo of applause and then the hall fell silent. The audience observed the tense sombreness of his dress, for he was clothed in a black suit, a dark shirt and black tie, all of which contrasted sharply with his thin white face. They stared at him silently, compulsively, aware of the aura of the man whose very presence seemed to induce a sensation of fear... as though Count Dracula were alive on the stage! His predecessor, a fat arrogant man, had rampaged at the table, thumping and banging his fist regularly on the wooden panels. Strogoff, however, merely strode quietly to the centre of the stage in ominous silence, causing all petty murmuring to stop as he arrested complete attention. He became a magnet, forcing his audience which stared at him with awe, and they shuddered inwardly at the solemnity and the ability with which he held them... as if control occurred by means of mass hypnosis. Confronting them, his face was set like a death-mask... gaunt, with deep dark eyes, an exceptionally short straight nose resembling the face of a skeleton, and his fingers were black through frostbite. It was all so vivid that one woman emitted a muffled gasp into her handkerchief, shuddering spasmodically as though someone had stepped over her grave. Strogoff stood immobile without blinking at the bright floodlights, and still he remained silent. Yet so keenly did he hold their interest by his appearance alone that no one's head turned away and no mouth moved to utter a word. Finally, when the pregnant pause had lasted so long that people could hear their hearts beating loudly in their eardrums, he gripped the lapels of his black jacket and moved the thin line of his lips to speak.

'Comrades, I welcome you to this meeting to impress upon you some of the problems of your conventional way of life, and how it affects each one of you.' His voice was piping and rather unpleasant to the ear. 'Admittedly, equality is a rare state, and perfection cannot be established overnight. It needs much time, much effort and a great deal of concentration to create the economic and environmental atmosphere needed to improve the fate of mankind in a hostile world. We have the annals of history to remind us that separate governments ineptly pursue pernicious policies counter to the public interest. They mismanage countries, encourage wars, seek personal power, create chaos, and waste both the working efforts and the taxes extracted from the people they pretend to govern. How long can we sit back and accept the actions of well-meaning fools who are spearheaded into power through the actions of convention? Under the guise of democracy, any idiot can be projected into politics in one of the political parties. They become puppets of the political machine to represent a region of the country. To what ends? Have any of you met your Member of Parliament? I met mine yesterday and I can tell you he doesn't have a clue what's important to you. In the name of democracy, you may not have even voted for him. Is this the kind of government for the people? Is this the kind of system we need? And how does such waste and abuse of authority relate to all the separate governments in Europe... all of which are exactly the same?

I stared at the speaker sullenly, admiring the gall of this man to preach dissidence in a foreign land. It was obvious he was being supported financially by some organisation, agency or political body... which I assumed to be International Three Thousand. I wondered how quickly he would change his views if someone else paid him more. The paradox was strange. Strogoff would be arrested as a criminal if he returned to his native land yet, as a speaker for a splinter group in a foreign country, his authority reigned supreme. He droned on for another twenty minutes but I lost interest and fell deep into thought. I sensed an ugly feeling in the pit of my stomach which was a very accurate weather-vane for bad situations. There was something terribly wrong about this meeting but, for the moment, I couldn't put my finger on it.

'Believe me,' continued Strogoff, 'this country has been shored-up with a false economy operated by self-interested politicians from money borrowed internationally to hide the weakness of the currency. Practically all European governments are involved in this charade and the common man has no idea of the crimes currently perpetrated at high levels of business and government. I assure you, if there was not so much good work to complete here, I would have no hesitation but to return to my own country to enjoy the spirit of equality existing there.'

'Liar!' The word cut through the hall like a hot knife through butter as the young woman next to me burst into life. She rose from her seat and waved a clenched fist at the speaker. It confirmed my intuition she would do something irrational or dangerous. A buzz of comment could be heard floating across the hall but Strogoff ignored the heckling and continued speaking.

'There is a view that imperialism offers success in its policy towards freedom... '

'Liar! Liar!'

The interruption could not be ignored this time and the speaker's nostrils flared as he halted in annoyance. 'Do you wish to make a point, comrade?' he invited unwisely.

'You're a liar, Igor Strogoff!' accused the woman at the top of her voice. 'They would be delighted to have you back in your own country to arrest you as a criminal!' There was a stunned silence in the hall. 'I know all about you. You're a criminal who escaped from Schemlaya labour camp in Siberia. How they would welcome you back to face a firing squad! Perestroika or glasnost... it makes no difference!'

Strogoff motioned to some men at the back of the hall. 'Get her out of here!' he shouted. 'I will not have people trying to use subversive tactics to destroy the essence of this meeting!' He turned to the audience. 'Do you see how the authorities use their agents to control the freedom they insist you enjoy? They have fifth-columnists everywhere!'

'He's bluffing!' countered the woman. 'He can't go back because he's a criminal! You can check it out for yourselves if you don't believe me!'

By this time, a number of men were converging in on her from all sides. They were being well paid to keep order and now was the time to account for their value. I expected her to reach under her seat for the suitcase and blow the auditorium into smithereens but that was either the fear or fantasy flooding my imaginative mind. Within seconds, the men reached the spot and hauled her roughly into the aisle against her will. She struggled and lashed out feebly as they inflicted blows to her face and body. I cared little for her political beliefs but I couldn't stand by to watch her being beaten by two morons who enjoyed brutally savaging a helpless woman. I uttered some words of protest loudly which had no effect whatsoever and, before realising what I was doing, I had leapt from my seat to protect her. My only means of attack or defence was an element of Kung Fu previously taught to me by a master of martial arts during an assignment in the Far East some time ago. I was extremely rusty but my actions took the men by surprise. For a few seconds they were held at bay as the woman climbed painfully to her feet. However, there were too many of them to fight off and I recall being forced to the floor to suffer spasms of agony which shot through my body. Before I could find my feet again, I was dragged down the aisle towards one of the exits and propelled violently on to the pavement outside. On gathering my senses, I picked myself up and brushed down my clothes. The woman had been thrown out with me. She got to her feet and began to hammer on the door with her fists. It was opened by an enormous man with a flat nose and a cauliflower ear who told her, in no mean terms, how he would react if she didn't leave immediately. She kept demanding the return of her suitcase only to suffer the fate of having the door slammed in her face again. In the end, she turned to me disconsolately. 'Thanks for your help anyway,' she said gratefully and started to walk away. 'I hope they didn't hurt you.'

'Hey!' I shouted, limping painfully as I moved in her direction. 'You can't just leave me here like that!'

'Are you hurt?'

'Well... no... not really.'

'Then what do you want... a certificate of merit from the Women' Institute for services over and above the call of duty?'

'I want to know what was in the suitcase, that's all.'

'Nothing much,' she responded sadly. 'Just everything I own in the world.

Now I've only the clothes I stand up in.' Her cynicism did nothing to mask her anger.

I decided she must have information of one kind or another to help me in my quest. 'You sound as though you're broke with nowhere to stay. If that's the case, you'd better come back to my place.'

She turned on me savagely like a tiger ready to pounce. 'What the hell do you take me for?'

'Look,' I explained placidly, trying to calm her down. 'I'm a newspaper reporter. I had a tip to come here this evening to listen to Strogoff. I'm doing my job, that's all.'

The tone of my voice seemed to establish reason and she bit her lower lip for a few seconds. Then she nodded. 'All right, we'll talk, but if you lay a finger on me you'll be sorry you were ever born!'

I tried to keep a serious face. She was a delightful person; the toughness was only a facade. 'What's your name?'

'Carrie Fisher.'

'Well fear naught, Carrie Fisher. I'm Jimmy Savage. You're in good hands.' I hailed a taxi cruising along the Mile End Road which took us back to my apartment. After ushering her inside, I showed her the kitchen, inviting her to make some coffee and sandwiches. It was my intention to keep her occupied until she settled down. In the meantime, I would telephone Miss Grayson. The thought struck me in the taxi that I was with the wrong woman at the right time. It was necessary for me to apologise. By the time I had completed the call, arranging to see Miss Grayson at another time, Carrie emerged from the kitchen with a tray which she placed on the coffee-table. She sat in a large armchair while I lounged on the settee. I noticed that she had a nasty bruise on her cheek. I knew how she felt because the right-hand side of my jaw felt extremely tender.

'Where do you fit into the Strogoff scene?' I asked casually, hoping she might explain the reason for attending the meeting.

'With Strogoff? Nowhere really. I was once engaged to a man who spent his whole life pursuing political criminals. He was too young to get involved after World War Two ended but it didn't stop him from making it his life's work. He went to Israel to learn the tricks of the trade from the masters. Now he operates in this country with the undying aim of finding war criminals.'

'What's his name... this ex-fiance of yours?' The assignment was beginning to grow in stature and I wasn't sure I liked it. It was becoming apparent that many individuals and groups lived within a grey area of life, controlling the thoughts and actions of others ... completely beyond the knowledge or control of anyone else. Most people had heard of the CIA, MI5, the KGB, Majestic, and certain other foreign agencies which interfered deeply with world affairs in one way or another... .but small groups and private individuals... well, it really wasn't on!

'They call him The Rooter. It's because he has a classic record or rooting out certain undesirable elements who he turns over to those governments who seek them.'

'What sort of undesirable elements?'

'In particular, he has a hatred of Nazi and neo-Nazi organisations because his parents were killed at Dachau concentration camp. They managed to send him to their family in Britain just before the war broke out. He'd only just been born. They intended to follow him but events overtook them. He'll hunt down anyone who intends to suppress the people of any nation, and he's totally against extremism of any kind.'

'What's his real name... and how do I get in touch with him?'

'Not so fast, Mr. Savage,' she returned cautiously. 'I know nothing about you. Not yet anyway.' She was wearing blue denim jeans and reached down to her left ankle. When she stood up again, I was staring into the muzzle of a small automatic pistol. Suddenly, her presence in my apartment took on a sinister role. However much I loved writing and being a journalist, I didn't want to yield my life for it. Nor did I wish to miss out on a scoop because of some remote cause of which I knew nothing. If only Barnaby hadn't broken his leg I might be on my way to reporting something less hazardous. 'Please lay face down on the settee!' she ordered politely, which gave me a tiny ray of hope, for dangerous bandits were never courteous. I complied quickly and she removed my tie to secure my hands behind my back. Then she moved the standard lamp from the corner of the room to fetter my feet with the cord.

'Is this really necessary,' I grunted, knowing that I was wasting my breath. There was no response but I could hear her opening the drawers in the bedroom dressing-table and also those of the desk in my study as I waited in discomfort. She returned shortly and, to my surprise, untied my hands and feet.

'I'm sorry,' she apologised, as I rubbed my wrists gently. 'One can't be too careful. I had to make sure you really were a newspaper reporter and not someone from a political organisation with sinister ideas.'

'Are you going to play any more tricks like this?' I asked in mock annoyance.

She laughed and relaxed again in the armchair. 'The real name of The Rooter is Jack Berg. If you want to contact him, I'll get him on the 'phone. If he wants to give you his telephone number afterwards, that's up to him.'

I found my cordless telephone on the floor near the settee and pushed it across to her. 'There's no time like the present,' I remarked, urging her to make contact. She dialled a number and spoke to Berg, telling him about Strogoff and the incident at the People's Palace, then she threw the instrument to me. Normally, I do my best work face to face with people. Everyone has a personality of their own and it reflects, giving off vibrations which I tend to pick up. I disliked using the telephone on such occasions because the impact is generally negative and clinical. 'Can we meet and talk?' I asked the man at the other end of the line. It was a short crisp conversation and we agreed to meet on the steps of St. Paul's Cathedral the next day at six o'clock in the evening. He tempted me by mentioning a secret meeting he wanted me to attend, insisting he would tell me more about it when we met. I was pleased with Berg's direct attitude. He sounded ready for action, like other East Enders, with no side, affectation or innuendo.

When the call ended, I discovered that Carrie had gone. For a moment I believed that she had slipped through my fingers and left the apartment. When I went into the bedroom, however, I found her sitting in the bed with the covers pulled up to her neck. 'What are you doing here?' I asked stupidly, wishing I had bitten my tongue rather than make such an idiotic comment.

'A friend in need is a friend indeed,' she commented with a smile touching the edges of her lips. 'I reckon I owe you a favour for saving me from a fate worse than death.'

I shook my head slowly from side to side. 'You don't owe me your body,' I told her. 'I'm disappointed in you, Carrie. I thought you were a decent young woman with a lot of integrity. Do you always offer yourself to any man who helps you?'

She bridled at the assumption. 'That's a rotten thing to say!' she snapped angrily. 'I haven't slept with anyone for over a year.'

'Jack Berg?'

She hesitated for a moment. 'Yes, if you must know. It was Jack Berg! Look, you don't have to make a big deal out of it. If you feel nauseated or find me repulsive I'll sleep on the couch.' She paused to check my reaction. 'There are two reasons why I'm waiting for you in this bed. Firstly, I never knew it before but getting beaten up seems to turn me on. I heard that it sometimes happens to people who witness a murder.'

'And the second reason?'

'I find you very groovy... and from the look of this place you obviously live alone. I'm warm, tender, feeling really turned on in this bed. The rest is up to you.'

I smiled at the simplicity with which she regarded life. It would be a pity to refuse the offer and disappoint her. Within twenty seconds I had stripped off my clothes and moved into the bed alongside her. She had a fine slender body, not well-endowed, but seasoned with the freshness of youth. A raging passion welled-up inside me as our naked bodies merged. For a moment, as lust flooded my brain, I felt the urge to take her firmly in my arms and relieve my frustration in a brutal manner. Then I thought about the many opportunities we would have to share a tender kind of love together if I behaved myself and acted sensibly. Against my better nature, I kissed her gently on the lips, neck and shoulders before turning away to reach for the remote control of the television set. 'Look, I can't take advantage of you in this way,' I told her in the form of an apology. 'Believe me, I want to very much, but Channel Four has dedicated this week to the memory of Humphrey Bogart and I'm following it closely. Last night they showed Casablanca. Tonight it's The African Queen.'

I pressed the switch and tuned-in to the appropriate channel as she lay back on the pillows with a broad grin on her face. 'I think I've heard everything now!' she laughed. 'How dare you prefer Humphrey Bogart to me!' She put her arms around my waist and started to kiss my body in many places, rubbing her hands firmly over my flesh and down my spine. It was all too much for me. Although The African Queen wouldn't be shown on television for another four years or more, it would have to wait. While the pain of punches inflicted on my ribs earlier that evening took their toll, I conceded I had a much more pressing engagement with a very lithe, willing, attractive woman! It served Barnaby right! To the victor go the spoils! He could rot in hospital for all I cared... while carnal lust swept through me with an attractive woman waiting for my love in my bed!

CHAPTER THREE

We awoke very late the following morning. It was the first time I had slept so long for many years. However, Carrie had been very demanding and we didn't really get to sleep until almost four o'clock. She made breakfast but it would be more correct to say it was eaten nearer the time normally reserved for lunch. I resolved some of her immediate problems by opening one of the wardrobes widely to offer her a selection of clothes my wife had left on her swift flight from our marriage. Fortunately, both women were of similar size so that Carrie was able to discard her old jeans and her worn woolly jumper and I was delighted to see her so pleased at the result. We relaxed during the afternoon, sometimes in each other's arms, until it was time to meet The Rooter.

Berg was not the kind of person one remembered. He could easily be missed or forgotten... even in a small crowd of people. Short, thin, with sparse hair, even at his young age, he was poorly dressed in a shoddy anorak and wore thick tortoise-shell spectacles which rested on the ridge of a long narrow nose. Above all, he gave the impression of being totally insignificant. I couldn't understand what Carrie had seen in the man to bring herself to consider marrying him but she was a generation ahead of me and that gap in time made all the difference. We climbed the steps of St. Paul's Cathedral where she introduced me to the man. I shook his limp hand and wondered whether the effort of meeting him was worth all the trouble. Carrie thought otherwise and she made a huge attempt to glorify the record of her former fiance.

'You wouldn't believe how he secured the vital information which led to the capture of Heinrich Mauntner, the Nazi war criminal!' she gushed, much to the young man's embarrassment. 'There was political pressure preventing the man from being extradited to Israel, so Jack worked out a very audacious ruse. He served papers on Mauntner to attend the Crown Court on a specific day relating to his plea to remain in Britain. Jack sent two men dressed in police uniforms to collect him. They drove him to the court in a police car and ushered him in.'

I drove deeply into my memory banks to recall the case but the index file of my mind drew a blank. 'I don't remember what happened to Mauntner,' I admitted, still racking my brains.

'Of course not,' she continued enthusiastically. 'He wasn't taken into the court itself but to a large room in the next building through an entrance of the Crown Court. Jack arranged for it to be fitted out exactly like a courtroom and he employed actors to take the roles of the judge, jury and witnesses. They were all paid well so that the incident would remain a secret. As a result of this "hearing", Mauntner broke down and gave information on five other Nazi war criminals, as well as numerous details previously absent from historic files. Jack had him sedated and taken to London Airport where he was put on an El-Al flight to Israel. That's where he is at the moment. It saved the British Government a lot of money and everyone was satisfied... except Mauntner, of course.'

I stared at Berg with an element of surprise. He didn't seem the kind of person who would get results of that kind. He had abducted a war criminal, tried him in a false court, obtained information sorely needed, and had flown him from Britain without the authorities realising what was going on. 'What would have happened had you been caught in the act?' I asked him.

Berg smiled as if he knew the answer to all the secrets in the world. 'Mr. Savage,' he began, almost insolently, 'one of the rules of the game is that you never do anything unless you're absolutely positive you're not going to get caught. The doctrine is that when in doubt... don't!'

The man had a point and I respected him for it. There were times in life when failure was not permissible. It was a matter of unerring judgement for specific tasks and, if one failed to match up to such accuracy, credibility was at serious risk. 'Tell me about this secret meeting,' I ventured, keeping my mind on the assignment. 'What did you want to tell me about it?'

He walked down the steps of the Cathedral, obviously expecting us to follow him. Carrie took me by the arm and led me down eagerly. We walked a long distance down the road towards Cable Street without speaking and I became irritated by the lack of communication, although I presumed there was a good reason for the silence. Eventually, he stopped at a point where the three of us were alone and turned to face me.

'I've heard of International Three Thousand, otherwise you wouldn't be here,' he began, staring deeply into my eyes, trying to fathom my thoughts. 'There are eight cells covering the whole of Britain. The major one in the south-east is located here in an office across the road.' He pointed a thin finger in the direction of a cafeteria and to the rooms above it. 'The whole area's seedy and depressed, and neither the police nor the authorities take much interest in local activities provided there's no trouble. In any case, few people venture into this part of London at night, and it tends to escape attention.' Berg swung his arm some ninety degrees to point to a decrepit old building which sported a large ill-drawn placard stating: "Assembly Rooms". 'That's where they'll come later,' he told me. 'This meeting will have the distinction of being the first trial held by the organisation in Britain. I'm particularly interested to see how far they will go.'

'Trial?' I echoed. 'A trial is to be held here?'

'A man will be tried for failing in his duty to provide information relating to the forces of NATO, and possibly selling those secrets to another power.'

'NATO?' I echoed with surprise. I was beginning to sound like a parrot at the revelation that an independent political organisation was privy to such sensitive information.

'These people are in business for real. The offices may not look prestigious but it's for real all right. They intend to capture Europe where the Third Reich failed. Only this time they'll do it behind the smokescreen created by the European Community. While every nation in Europe is looking at each other trying to score points, they'll come in from behind and assume control. By then it'll be too late. Tonight is the first trial. In a way it's a test of authority. I'm interested to find out how they handle it.'

'But if it's a secret society,' I asked with concern, 'how did you find out about it... how do we get in to see it?'

He gave me the same smile again. 'Entry is by ticket only, and I happen to have three tickets.'

I didn't pursue the matter. It would have done little good to pry. In any case, he wouldn't reveal anything to me of value. I knew only that three members of the organisation had given up their tickets to allow us to take their places or Berg had forged them. I suddenly recognised this little man was accomplished at achieving results in practically everything he did.

It was an hour later when we entered the Assembly Rooms and handed our tickets to the woman at the door. There were a number of strong-arm men on guard and I recognised one of them as the man who had struck me at the People's Palace the previous evening. Strangely enough, I wasn't concerned too much for myself but I feared he might recognise Carrie and threaten her with physical violence again. However, at the moment we crossed the threshold, he turned to deal with some minor matter and we shuffled inside a little faster than intended to secure our entry.

The hall had been arranged to form a crude courtroom with the judges' table, a dock, a jury, and a witness box. The jury was comprised of five people and they sat on a bench waiting patiently to hear the evidence. It wasn't long before the hall was packed with people. Not only were all the seats taken, with men and women sitting tightly-bunched up to each other on the uncomfortable wooden benches, but they were also standing at the back and the sides of the hall. Carrie sat between Berg and myself and we waited expectantly for the proceedings to commence. At the edge of the stage, two seats had been set aside for the court recorders so that the evidence could be taken down in detail. They took their places and shuffled papers in nervous anticipation.

There was little delay because the triumvirate of judges walked promptly on to the stage. One of them faced the audience briefly to introduce himself. 'My name is Conrad Hayle,' he informed them, 'the Minister of Justice for the south-east of England. Many of you will know my colleagues... Martin Glazer, the Minister of Police, and his brother Terry Glazer, the Minister of State. This evening we are going to hold the trial of Albert Henley who has failed in his duty to the cause. The details will unfold as we continue.'

Berg leaned across Carrie to whisper in my ear. 'Terry Glazer's extremely uncomfortable about this trial,' he told me confidentially. 'If it goes wrong, he's the one they'll blame. A proper trial would take days to resolve because of the weight of evidence required. This lot have only two hours at the most and they can't afford to lose credibility. If they mess it up one hardly needs to guess how the members will take it. So they have to go for the kill. Whenever there's a fight, everyone wants to see blood, and these people here tonight are no different.'

He was silenced by the people pressed close to us and I scanned the figure of the self-appointed Minister of State. If Berg was correct in his assumption, the verdict had been decided on well in advance, regardless of the evidence. Hayle gave the impression he was in total control of the situation, professional and efficient, and I felt he too had decided on the punishment to be meted out to the alleged offender. I also had the feeling the accused would be found guilty whether he was innocent or not. A lamb to be sacrificed for the benefit of the credibility of the organisation.

Hayle took his seat demanding the defendant be presented to the court which was followed by a shuffling movement from some men standing at the side of the hall. A tall stocky young man was brought forward to the dock and I was disturbed at the flippancy of his manner. He acted as though he was participating in a college rag. I knew it to be far more serious. Well over six feet tall, he weighed about eighteen stone and towered above his accusers. I assumed he might be over-confident as a result of his physique. Normally a relatively quiet serious person, he used this occasion to wear a jovial smile expecting the incident to be highly amusing and entertaining.

'Albert Henley,' began Hayle, staring at his quarry with an icy expression. 'Do you swear by all you believe to tell the truth?'

'Isn't the oath supposed to be sworn on the Holy Bible?' questioned the accused.

'There's not much point,' riposted the Minister of Justice. 'If you intend to perjure yourself, swearing on the Bible isn't going to make any difference. We rely on your word of honour, if it's worth anything at all, and our own method of interrogation and judgement.'

'Oh, I'm going to be interrogated am I?' asked Henley cheekily, still wearing the same confident smile. 'Who's going to defend me?'

'Why should you need someone to defend you?' asked Martin Glazer sharply. 'Surely you know whether you're guilty of the allegation or not. Surely you can explain yourself clearly and concisely. You have a tongue in your head! I hope so because no one else will represent you. Third parties not involved only waste the time of the court with pointless arguments.' He turned to Hayle and held out his hand for the sheet of paper containing the indictment. 'Albert Henley, you are charged with offences concerning your failure to pass to us certain information... namely a comprehensive computer print-out, the contents of which were of paramount importance to our cause. The information was vital and it is understood it came into your possession.' He lowered the sheet of paper and looked directly at the man in the dock. 'How do you plead?'

Henley continued to smile as he listened to the charge and shrugged his shoulders. 'Not guilty!' he replied smartly, glancing casually at the faces of the five people constituting the jury.

Hayle was far from satisfied with Henley's plea. 'What do you mean you're not guilty?' he demanded. 'You had the information in your possession, didn't you? And you passed it to someone else, didn't you? But you failed to produce it for the organisation you belong to as you promised on your initiation oath. Is that not the case?'

The accused ran his fingers nervously along the edge of the dock as his smile began to fade. 'Yes, I agree. But I'm not guilty!'

'For heaven's sake!' shouted Martin Glazer irritably. 'You either failed in your duty or you succeeded! You can't have it both ways! I'll ask the question again and perhaps you'll think more clearly this time. Do you plead guilty or not guilty?'

'Not guilty!'

Terry Glazer shifted uneasily in his seat, beginning to imagine the trial was going to be a test of nerves.

'Very well,' cautioned the Minister of Police, 'but if you're wasting our time I'll hold you in contempt of court.' He paused for a moment. 'Would you tell us where the computer print-out is at present and what you've done with it? In addition, would you tell the court whether you can furnish the said computer print-out at the present time. And tell us in your own words why the information was never presented.'

'Well,' began the defendant, 'I planned to steal the information from my employer and I stayed late at the office one evening to do it. I chose a Tuesday because most of the management attend a squash club after work on Tuesday so they're never around after five-thirty. It took me half an hour to set up the procedures... secret information can only be extracted from the computer by means of known codes... and I had to work them out. Then I had to print out the information. I was going to hand it to my rank leader in the organisation but at ten past six, just as the final pages were coming through, one of the senior departmental managers returned to collect some papers and demanded to know what I was doing. I was caught between the Devil and the deep blue sea. My only excuse was to say it was being done for a senior official in France. He made me hand the print-out to him, saying he would send it to France himself. So it passed out of my hands. I can't do it again because I'm under surveillance at the office. There's no chance of getting another print-out.'

'Your value to the cause appears to have diminished rapidly,' commented the Minister of Justice, tiring quickly of the evidence given by the defendant.

Henley bridled at the remark. 'What are you talking about?' he challenged. 'This cause needs people like me! If it reacts every time there's a blip, everyone will be scared of failure. What I'm telling you is the truth. I put my job on the line for this cause. I got you certain secrets on NATO before. Why all the fuss and bother this time?'

'What if we insisted that you obtain the same information again?' asked Hayle. 'What then?'

'I told you, it's impossible! They watching me like hawks. If I made a false move I could end up in jail. Perhaps in six months or a year's time, I might be able to have another go. I'm also trying to recruit someone else in the office. I mentioned the cause and he's very interested.'

Hayle appeared to seethe at the prospect. 'You told a man you hardly know about International Three Thousand! You work in a government establishment filled with secrets and you approach a stranger and tell him about us! Did you never consider he might be employed to check out your activities?'

'Geoff would never do a thing like that!' continued Henley. 'He's not the sort of person they'd employ!'

'You're certain of that, are you?' The Minister of Justice was beginning to apply pressure. 'You'd bet your life on it, would you?'

The man in the dock paused for a moment and shrugged his shoulders. 'Well, I wouldn't go as far as that. But, in my opinion, he's an average employee like myself. We're drinking pals. Last week we went out together and got drunk. We were almost arrested by the police for peeing over the pavement outside the pub.'

A howl went up from the audience that almost rocked the roof. As is often the case when tension prevails, and solemnity is the order of the day, people convulse with laughter at the slightest thing to the contrary. I recalled one of my uncles who couldn't stop laughing at funerals, especially at the scene of the interment. I thought he was stupid and callous until discovering I was the one in error because I didn't understand. It was a reflex action that couldn't be helped. Ultimately, when he died, I found myself laughing as they buried him. The introduction of something amusing in the mock courtroom was spontaneous and had the effect of putting a lighted match to petrol. For a while, it became impossible to control the crowd. Hayle shouted for silence, banging the gavel on the wooden table in front of him, but he was forced to wait until the audience settled down. He glared at Henley afterwards, his eyes narrowing with hate as he considered the defendant was attempting to ridicule the court.

'I'm going to warn you once... and only once!' he cautioned angrily. 'If you waste the time of this court...' he tailed off momentarily. 'Confine your evidence to relevant matters!'

Henley realised he had lost the sympathy of the Minister of Justice...

although he was beginning to doubt whether any had existed in the first place. For his part, he still felt pleased with himself in the belief he was favoured by the jury and the audience. As the hall became silent again, he continued with his story. 'Geoff and I discussed International Three Thousand,' he went on. 'I was determined he should join us. After all, it's everyone's duty to find suitable recruits, and I knew he would be useful. Isn't that what we need... more members?' Henley paused to look at the jury as if to impress his argument upon them.

Martin Glazer's eyes narrowed and a thin smile appeared on his lips. 'You realise you're guilty of the charge brought against you!' he declared. 'You failed to get the computer print-out!'

'No I'm not! There were mitigating circumstances. I've explained it to you!'

A murmur went round the hall and the Minister of Police sat quite still for a few moments fully aware that the eyes of every person rested on him. 'Mitigating circumstances!' he snarled. 'Where do you think you are? This is a court of justice held by International Three Thousand not a case being heard at the Old Bailey. We deal in common law for peace and international government. There's no equity or mitigation when a person is guilty of violating our code of conduct. It's also considered arrogant to ask for leniency when you know damned well you're guilty of the crime. In fact, there's a further charge to add to the indictment of divulging information about this cause to a civil servant who may be one of our enemies. The onus of proof is on you but you can't present it. Therefore, you're clearly guilty!''

The defendant faced reality and he started to become concerned. 'I'll appeal!' he shouted. 'I'll appeal on both charges... on the grounds of injustice!'

The Minister of State entered the fray again to clarify the position. 'You can't appeal unless you have evidence to prove your innocence,' he advised firmly. 'And you don't have it!'

The accused man realised his arguments were wasted, recognising he was up against a system more formidable than he had first imagined. The trial was beginning to assume a sinister trend and Henley began to lose his good humour. He had presumed the evening would offer some harmless fun and entertainment in a mock trial, but now it had turned sour. 'This is a bloody Kangaroo Court!' he yelled. 'That's what it is! A rotten Kangaroo Court! No defence counsel... no mitigating circumstances... no right of appeal! It's a damned Fascist dictatorship!'

'Be silent!' The words of Hayle echoed through the hall as he began to impose his personal authority more tightly. The audience could smell blood and experienced the scent of the hunt. The Minister of Justice knew it would soon be over and that he would be the victor. 'Have you stated your case fully?' he asked finally.

The man in the dock glared at him fiercely.. 'No I bloody-well haven't! And if you think I'm going to stand for this nonsense you've got another think coming. I didn't mind coming here and joining in for a laugh, but you've got to admit a joke's a joke!' He turned to leave and push his way through the crowd, but two men dressed in black uniforms appeared from behind a curtain near the rear doorway and took hold of him. One of them bent Henley's arm behind his back until he howled with pain, and they returned him to the dock to stand guard behind him. A murmur of awe rippled through the hall as Henley's face showed pain and anguish.

The sight of the uniforms took me greatly by surprise. They were jet black and the collars and armbands bore insignias I was unable to recognise. In addition, the men wore jackboots and peaked caps. There was no doubt in my mind they emulated the style of dress worn by the German SS in World War Two in every detail, with the exception of a different insignia on the collars and armbands. I looked across to Jack Berg to check his reaction. His face was tense; his jaw muscles tightly drawn. I could imagine his thoughts playing on the atrocities perpetrated by the regime that sent his parents to their deaths at Dachau, and his resentment of a similar organisation rising like a phoenix in its place some decades later. Why did people always want to emulate the bad elements in life and make the same errors again? They never seemed to learn!

'I thought this was going to be a mock trial,' I whispered but Berg simply shrugged his shoulders.

The accused man was in imminent trouble. He had come along for some sport and realised suddenly the others were playing an entirely different game. 'Look!' he pleaded. 'This has gone far enough. We ought to call it a day!'

Hayle stared at the defendant with a bland expression on his face, glorifying in the fact that everyone was waiting for him to make the next move. 'As you are guilty of the crimes alleged,' he boomed in a stentorian voice, 'there's no necessity to ask the jury for their verdict. However, you still have the right to close your arguments... if you deem it necessary.'

Terry Glazer found himself unable to take his eyes off the men in uniform. The surprise, which showed in his eyes, was sufficient to allow me to believe that one of the leading lights in International Three Thousand was developing the cause in his own way without consultation with his colleagues. The Minister of State had not been informed and the shock made him decide to take the sting out of the trial, regardless of the impact it might have on his personal integrity. 'Albert Henley,' he intervened without warning. 'We know you have the interest of the cause at heart. Bearing that in mind, I suggest you make a profound apology to this court and plead for mercy, promising to make every attempt in the future to obtain the information so vital to the cause. In that way, everyone will be aware of your atonement.'

Conrad Hayle glared at his merciful colleague as though he could cheerfully strangle him, and he turned to the dock angrily in an effort to redress the situation. 'You may well do that!' he growled. 'But I doubt whether it will do you much good! To ask for mercy you must prove you will never commit the same offence again. Unfortunately, you have no proof so this Court cannot accept a promise. I advise you to close your case quickly and let's have an end to it!'

Terry Glazer bit his lower lip to prevent himself from blurting out a tirade in defence of the accused. In his view, Hayle had assumed total control of the trial despite the presence of two other judges acting with him, and the jury.

Henley was upset but he had enough common sense to find a way out of his predicament. His only option was to castigate the leaders, identifying to the audience the danger of lawlessness... of people in authority taking the law into their own hands. 'It's all very well for you to scare me,' he reminded them, staring in particular at the jury, 'but there's one thing you've forgotten. You make the mistake of thinking you're in power. Well... that's not the case! The law of this country prevails. When International Three Thousand eventually comes to power, you can say and do what the law then says. But, until that time arrives, you can do nothing... you're powerless!'

Hayle didn't take the challenge too well, for it was a direct attack on the competence and authority of the organisation. However, Henley had a point and what he said was perfectly true. Yet if the judges conceded, they would be faced with a situation muting their power and preventing any further trials being held. As a result, there would be no control on breaches of policy or subversive activities. 'I cannot concede that point,' he told the blond giant. 'If we fail to enforce law and order now, any small undesirable element could disrupt our programme, hold us to ransom, and stop us from succeeding in our aims. It would be a travesty of justice, acting detrimentally against those members who work so hard for our cause. This cannot be a Court where justice is not allowed to prevail. Is there anyone here who refutes that claim? If so, stand up and make your views known.'

At that moment, another four uniformed men appeared near the stage, and a long silence shrouded the hall. Terry Glazer stared at the audience almost wishing someone had the guts to get to their feet to protest... or at least to question the validity of certain aspects of the trial. When nothing happened, he leaned across to his brother and whispered to him. 'Wouldn't it be a good idea to hold a referendum?' he suggested. His brother remained silent and merely shook his head unhappily. It became patently clear that Henley was on his own... without the support of anyone in the hall.

The defendant became concerned at the silence and tried to whip up some enthusiasm for his welfare. 'Come on, you guys! Can't you see what's going on here? It may be one of you standing here next time!' He paused for a moment and when there was still no answer he made his final appeal. 'I'm one of you. A member of the cause. Do I look like someone who's a traitor?'

His words fell on deaf ears and Hayle was feeling better now the danger of brinkmanship had passed, although he had to admit to himself that the situation had hovered for a while at the cross-roads. 'I presume you've closed your case,' he ventured to Henley. The smile he always displayed when he knew he was about to win showed again on his face. He looked at the audience directly and summarised the case. 'You've heard that Albert Henley pleaded not guilty but then admitted to the Court that he not only failed to provide vital information in his possession but also divulged details of the cause to a person likely to be employed by our enemies. He insists that all his actions are honourable, claiming mitigating circumstances. Let me say that history has exonerated many wrongdoers under that simple claim, but it bears no significance here. It is our ruling that by his own admission Albert Henley is guilty of two crimes for which he must be punished. The verdict of this court must be... guilty!'

As soon as the last word was uttered there was pandemonium in the hall. People waved their arms, scarves, caps, and other articles to show their approval. Although Hayle hammered on the table with his gavel, it was impossible to restore order. The three of us sat silently watching everyone else give vent to their excitement and I became nauseated by the abuse of power where none actually existed. The self-appointed Minister of Justice had totally ignored the decision which should have been made by the jury. I reflected some misgivings in the legal history of Britain in the Middle Ages. At that time, some juries were put on trial themselves because they failed to bring in the verdict directed by the judge. It was clear that in this Court they wouldn't get the chance to offer any opinion at all! Nor did any of the judges confer before the verdict was given! It was as the accused had claimed... a Kangaroo Court! Poor Henley! The rules had been made up as they went along. Whatever arguments he presented had been shot down in flames. Held by the two uniformed men, he waited for sentence to be passed silently as fear welled-up inside him. At one time, a thought went through his mind to attempt an escape, but he decided against it. There was no chance of reaching the front entrance because of the mass of people in the way and the men guarding the main doorway. Then he realised there was the door behind the curtains from where the uniformed men had emerged. It would mean ducking under the two guards, pulling open the door, and running for his life. But which way did the handle turn?

The noise reached a crescendo and Hayle gave up trying to maintain order. He stopped banging the gavel and let the crowd continue to yell and shout until they tired of it. When the last voice had faded, and the attention of the audience reverted back to him, he looked solemnly ahead and pronounced judgement. However, the unhappy man in the dock was still not finished.

'You can't punish me!' forestalled Henley. 'The policy document of the organisation outlines two forms of punishment. Death or deportation to a depressed sector to work for the United States of Europe for as long as the sentence given. You can't do either. The first would be murder and, with all these witnesses here, you won't risk your own skins, that's for sure. And the second one doesn't exist yet so you can't deport me anywhere. So what are you going to do? Beat me up to show you mean business? No... that would make you worse than me, wouldn't it. Beating up a member of the cause. But you can suspend my sentence... or put me on probation. How about that for an idea?'

Hayle was furious at the sudden attack on his authority at a time when he thought the case was over. He nodded to the two uniformed men who took a tighter hold of the man in the dock. 'It's not for you to decide the punishment!' he snarled. 'If it were possible to send you to a depressed sector I would have done so. But, as you so rightly say, it's not yet possible. Therefore, the only alternative is the death penalty.'

The hall fell into a deep silence as the words sank in. They had come to see blood but now that death had been proclaimed they shied away from the reality. Henley was right. If the verdict applied to him, it applied to them all! Terry Glazer leaned across to Hayle. 'No way!' he hissed. 'How the hell can you pass the death penalty? You've gone too far!' The Minister of Justice ignored the caution, superior in his moment of triumph. He intended to exert his power to the full.

Henley didn't share such feelings and he became agitated. 'You're crackers!' he shouted at the top of his voice. 'All crackers!' He tried to move back but he was held too tightly. He looked at the curtains again, visualising the door behind it. Did it open outwards or inwards? If he was going to make a break for it, he had to guess right the first time. There would be no second chance. With a sudden rage, he swung round, shaking himself free of the two men, and tore through the curtains. He turned the handle to the left and pushed hard but it didn't budge. He had guessed wrongly and it cost him his freedom. Before he could try again, they were on him. They placed his hands behind his back, fettering them with handcuffs, pulled the door inwards and marched him out forcibly. There were lots of questions to be asked and many to be answered but no one made the effort. Hayle thanked the audience for their indulgence and the three judges left the stage. It was all over! We left the Assembly Hall with evil gnawing at our minds. The policy document of the organisation clearly segregated Britain into sectors run by people besotted with their new-found power and they were merciless, It was a frightening thought!

We returned to my apartment and sat in the lounge with coffee and sandwiches. 'It's happening all over again!' raged Berg. 'People without authority acting above the law and forming their own army. It happened that way in Germany in the 1930s. It's happening again! Bullying innocent people... holding mock trials... issuing death sentences in private. The same routine!'

At any other time I would have thought he was over-reacting, but not now. I had witnessed a ham-fisted attempt by an immature organisation to impose authority it never had on a poor miserable wretch. The few people in control had acted totally ultra vires with the law of the land. Consequently, until they were brought to book, such men were dangerous. One could define the decisions of a tyrant or despot. However, erratic authority meted out by nonentities who elevated themselves to power brought everyone to the brink of peril because no one knew what would happen next. In addition, the uniforms scared me and brought back many evil memories, but were Hayle and the

Glazers the men to be feared? Or were there others... more sinister... directing them?

The next morning I had an uneasy feeling in the pit of my stomach as I looked at the front page of the morning paper. Exhibited in the centre was a photograph of Albert Henley laying face downwards in the Thames. He had been fished out of St. Katherine's Dock near the Tower of London just before ten o'clock at night... not long after the trial had ended. I thought about his death for a while and recalled some books I had read on modern European history. It had never sunk in before but, suddenly, it dawned on me how World War Two had started. It had happened in 1939, but long before that there were kinds of revolution. In France in 1789 and in Russia in 1917. Thereafter Hitler had begun a cause of a similar nature which was even more devastating. It seemed that mankind would never learn!

CHAPTER FOUR

After reading of Henley's death, I sat in an armchair thinking about the trial. It may not have been an isolated case. It was possible that many such trials were being held by International Three Thousand in other parts of Britain... perhaps all over Europe... .mainly to make the members believe that they were serious! Carrie was still asleep. Sadly, my peace of mind was greatly disturbed for I had been thinking about the trial the whole night through... depriving myself of sleep. I couldn't remember whether I had promised Miss Grayson I would take her to dinner in the evening. Meeting Berg, and going to the secret meeting, had driven it from my mind. No doubt she would be furious with me if I had forgotten. The telephone rang to break through my thoughts. I failed to respond even though it rang many times. The only person so persistent would be my bad-tempered editor. Eventually, I caved in and answered the call against my better judgement.

'What's the matter with you, Savage?' Flanders yelled down the line. I could tell he was angry because he always called me by my first name unless something was wrong. 'I've been pestered twice this morning by some damned smooth-talking woman called Grayson who insists on seeing you. Now I've got you down on my list for a very important assignment. If you want to play around with women that's your affair but don't let it interfere with your work in the 'paper's time! Do you get the drift?' I let the cordless telephone slip to the floor and sat back in the armchair. Ted ranted on until realising there was nobody listening at the other end of the line which didn't improve his temper. 'Are you there, Savage? Hallo... hallo? You get your arse down here right away, you bastard, or you'll be off the payroll before you can say Jack Robinson! Do you hear?'

At that moment, the Lord had mercy on me as the telephone went dead. It was as though someone had strangled Ted Flanders at the other end of the line. There were times in life when one had to weigh up the advantages of opportunity cost.

If there was a choice of spending an extra hour with Carrie or going to work, I preferred the former... even if it jeopardised my job. In any case, with Barnaby out of action, and Jeff Petrie dead, Flanders had little choice in the matter. Later on in the day I might feel somewhat differently about the decision but I would deal with that problem when it arose.

It was nearly three hours later when I went to see Miss Grayson at her office. I took half-a-dozen roses with me as a token of my atonement. She had just gone to lunch but her secretary had been informed I was likely to call, albeit she expected me to communicate by telephone. My request to be allowed to wait for Miss Grayson in her office caused quite a stir. It was in the nature of civil servants to be extremely sensitive where confidentiality was concerned. They were always suspicious of the fact that visitors had roving eyes... especially newspaper reporters. I insisted, however, that I would do the daily crossword sitting quietly in a corner of the room. The secretary was reluctant to accede to my request at first but she yielded under pressure when I started to make a fuss. I placed the roses on top of one of the filing cabinets and sat down facing the chair used by Miss Grayson, opening the newspaper at the back page under the watchful eye of her secretary. After a short while, she tired of the game and left her office to continue with her work, but mindful enough to leave the door ajar. As soon as she had gone, the temptation to snoop was too strong to resist. I dropped the newspaper and moved to the other side of the desk to switch on a small computer. Fervently, I searched the drawers of the desk before coming to a container bearing the word "International". I opened it to find three computer disks inside and placed the first one into the machine. My hunch was correct. It related to International Three Thousand and I began to read the text as fast as possible, pressing the appropriate button on the console to progress quickly through the pages as fast as I could read.

"The policy of the organisation is to create a United States of Europe on a non-violent basis over a period of years starting from the present time. European governments rule their respective countries by means of the majority party, and most changes of elected government tend to reverse the trend of progress or its direction. They keep within the bounds of written or unwritten constitutions, hampered often by ancient laws and precedents, and they apply constraints which cannot be overcome easily. As a result, life in every aspect becomes complicated, difficult, and sometimes unmanageable to benefit mankind. The amount of money wasted in supporting false economies is monumental, as seen by past European butter mountains, wine lakes, and the like, while changes in policy cause lurches in progress bringing disillusionment and lack of co-ordination. Europe is comprised of a group of developed countries tentatively working in principle against each other. They continually weaken themselves by altering policies and fail to underpin progressive economic development. If they were all linked by a single government, with one major policy, Europe might become the greatest major power in the world by dint of its wealth, experience and ability. Unification would allow tighter control of budgets, economies of scale and the on-going benefits of consolidation. Ultimately, the new Europeans would gain advantages in a variety of ways ranging, inter alia, from higher standards of living, greater personal spending power, less unemployment, less inflation, less governmental control... and it would be rewarded by better facilities in hospitals, welfare and education.

In order to establish a unified state, countries in Europe must lose their national identity. For practical purposes, English would become the major language and the Euro would remain the unit of currency. The formation of a European army from the military of existing European countries would be established for the purpose of protection, and all know-how and financial reserves would pooled. The government would be state-controlled with elections held every twelve years. The system of government is detailed on Disk 3. Once established, the United States of Europe would be able to moderate peace by acting as a neutral task force between any warring factions worldwide. See Disk 2. For further details contact Kirk."

I needed to take copies of all three disks to examine the information carefully. It had been good fortune which delayed me in seeking out Miss Grayson, enabling me to reap the advantage of finding this information. I could have been smarter, however, because had I arrived five minutes earlier there would have been time to read all three disks and escape scot free. As luck would have it, Miss Grayson chose that moment to return to her office and I was caught red-handed at her desk computer. Needless to say she was furious.

'Would you mind moving away from the desk please!' she ordered, with relative reproach. 'Immediately! Or I'll call security and have you arrested.'

'Forgive me,' I riposted, amassing all the audacity within me. 'I was under the impression we were supposed to work together on this assignment.'

'No, Mr. Savage,' she returned icily. 'Your role was to communicate information to me. I was to act as the contact between yourself and the government. It was never suggested you should trespass in my office and rifle my desk for information. I was told newspaper reporters have little respect for anyone or anything once they get their teeth into a good story. You've done nothing so far to make me change my mind.'

I put on a sad face pretending to be reprimanded. 'I'm sorry I was unable to take you to dinner. It was unavoidable. Take my word for it.'

She stepped forward, lifted the telephone receiver and pushed it close to my face. 'Do you recognise this instrument, Mr. Savage? It's called a telephone! You merely dial the appropriate number! It saves someone waiting vainly at the other end so that they can also change their plans and get on with their lives! Now... will you kindly leave everything as it is and move to the other side of the desk!'

Miss Grayson was beginning to work herself into a temper and I decided to take the heat out of the situation with some smart talking. 'Tell me, Miss Grayson,' I began. 'How do you come by these three disks? When I was abducted and taken to the House of Commons, the Prime Minister and the rest of your select committee told me they had only just become aware of International Three Thousand. Now I find three disks which hold some very material information. Can you explain that?' I could see by the expression on her face that, momentarily, my challenge had knocked the wind out of her sails.

She rallied well after a brief pause. 'We have information on every organisation known to man here. What the Prime Minister was trying to say related to the danger it might represent to the public interest.'

I stood up and moved to the other side of the desk keeping my eyes on her all the time. 'Is there any other information you have that might be useful? After all, I'm grubbing around in the wilderness for leads and you had the details in your desk all the time. I don't think that's a very clever way of playing the game.'

You're wrong, Mr. Savage,' she returned sharply, regaining her composure again. 'If I gave you this data, you would spend your time following it through. But if you're forced to research from square one, you're likely to uncover much more through alternative avenues. In fact, if I gave you these disks your investigation might be inhibited.'

She had a point but I was unwilling to concede the argument. 'Perhaps it would be best if we met this evening to pool some of our knowledge,' I suggested. 'This time I'll turn up, I promise. How about eight o'clock?' She was about to decline when I moved to the filing cabinet and retrieved the roses. 'I brought these for you. Lovely roses for a lovely lady.'

She wilted faster than a flower in late autumn and looked at me in an old-fashioned way. I knew at that moment she had forgiven me. 'It could be useful to pool our knowledge,' she returned quietly, staring at the roses lovingly. 'But I would like to reinforce the fact that you had the opportunity to meet me and failed to show up.'

'I never carry grudges,' I told her boldly. 'I hope you don't either.' She was right, of course, and I could understand her point of view very clearly. My behaviour was appalling. If the boot was on the other foot, and she had let me down, I would have been furious... and I would have held a grudge.

I left the office and made my way back to the apartment, castigating myself for being stupid. I had been beating my head against a brick wall to find scraps of information and I had overlooked the most obvious person of all. Miss Grayson would have filled in a lot of the gaps, but that was my idiocy in life. Whenever an assignment landed on my desk, I charged like a bull at a red cloth in a manic attempt to gain ground quickly. On this occasion, my actions proved to be erratic and uncoordinated. I wasn't getting to grips with the story at all! The plan outlined on the computer disks was extremely ambitious. Young people, like Hayle and the Glazers, had too little experience to become leading lights in the massive integration of governments and countries. They couldn't even manage the trial of Albert Henley in a professional manner. If revolution came... and it would be a revolution... how would they fare as party members in control? It didn't add up too well!

When I returned home, the door to my apartment was partly open. My first thoughts dwelt on the possibility that Carrie had forgotten to close it. I pushed it open to find myself confronted by a tangled mass of furniture, paper and bric-a-brac which had been rearranged savagely from their natural state. The floor was strewn with glass from broken mirrors still hanging eye-less on the walls and the television set had been smashed to pieces. I trod carefully over the mess dreading the condition of the bedroom. The wardrobes had been stripped and all the clothes flung across the room. The tallboy and its drawers were splintered beyond repair. The television set in that room had been kicked-in, the video tape-recorder destroyed, and everything else in sight was shattered. Material things to me were incidental; but there was far worse to come. To my horror, Carrie lay immobile on the bed. At first I thought she had been beaten up and rendered unconscious, but as I ran to her I could see signs of blood oozing out from a number of stab wounds on her body. The realisation that she was dead stunned me. There had been no reason to murder a young woman who had done no harm to anyone. Questions began to form quickly in my mind as I dwelt on my own survival. The intruders may have been searching for me! If so, how did they track me down? Why did they smash up the apartment? Would they try to kill me a second time? I picked up the cordless telephone to ring the police and then an odd thought struck me. Carrie had been closely involved with Berg. Instinctively, I decided to ring him first with the sad news. I dialled his number and he answered immediately... almost as though he had been waiting for the call!

'Carrie's dead!' I blurted out insensitively. 'Someone ransacked my apartment. She was stabbed to death!'

'Have you telephoned the police yet?' he replied, with a degree of calmness that was uncanny... in view that he had once been her fiance.

'I was just about to do that.'

'Don't!' he advised. 'Don't ring them! Just stay put! I'll be right over!'

The receiver went dead and I looked at the debacle wondering whether I had done the right thing. Why shouldn't I ring the police? It was the law to report a murder without delay. Why was Berg so insistent I should do nothing? What could he do about it? Carrie was dead! No one could bring her back to life again.

I was trying to sort out the wreckage in the lounge when Berg arrived. He looked at the mess and went directly to the bedroom where he stood over Carrie's body for a while, his lips moving in silent prayer. I followed him inside and watched, waiting to find out why he had prevented me from contacting the authorities.

'You haven't rung the police, have you?' he checked astutely. I shook my head. 'Good! We'll get her out of here when it's dark.'

I scanned his face closely. 'What are you talking about? Where are you going to take her?'

He looked straight at me with his cold black eyes. 'I'm sending her body back to her own country.'

'Back to her own country?' The situation was becoming bizarre. 'For heaven's sake! Where's that?'

'Israel. She lived in Tel Aviv.'

The words cut through the air like a knife and I took hold of his shirt collar, pulling him towards me. 'All right, Berg,' I snarled. 'You'd better tell me what this is all about! There's a dead woman in my bed, the place is in a shambles, and I want some answers!'

'Easy! Easy!' he said quietly. 'Give me a chance to explain.' He pulled himself free, took me firmly by the arm, and led me back to the lounge. 'Carrie was an Israeli intelligence agent,' he related candidly. 'It's nothing terrific. There are thousands of agents working everywhere, each one seeking information for reasons of national security. Despite perestroika and the break-up of the Soviet Union, every government has people out in the field trying to find out what's going on in other countries. Some people think that because the Soviet Union has disbanded there's no further need for agents. Don't even consider it for one moment. Believe me, there's lots going on all over the world. No one can afford to sit back and let things happen. The stakes are very high. Carrie was an agent working in Britain for Mossad... Israeli intelligence.'

'I thought she was British,' I intervened in surprise.

'She liaised with me from the start. That's how I knew. I always check the background of the people I'm involved with... including you, Mr. Savage! Carrie's task was not simple. It was always assumed that the Nazi war criminals hastened to South American countries at the end of World War Two. That's only partly true. Some of the best known were seen in Brazil, Paraguay, Argentina and Peru, but many escaped to other parts of Europe. Carrie was told to find those hiding in Britain. It's not easy to find people who have carefully changed their identity. In some cases, they did so many times to avoid being traced and discovered.'

'I understand you're called The Rooter. Why didn't you find them and pass on the information? You've been involved with the Israeli authorities all your working life.'

'My area extends worldwide. There's simply too much work. I can't limit my research when rooting out war criminals. Let me tell you the story of a friend at the time when the commandant of Auschwitz concentration camp was caught. He was present at the interrogation and a question was posed that will never be repeated again in the history of mankind... at least I hope it will never be asked again. The question to the Nazi was: "How many Jews did you kill in the gas-chambers at Auschwitz?" The answer came back curtly: "Half a million!" The interrogator looked at the war criminal for a while before continuing. "That's not true. It was one and a half million." "No," declared the Nazi, "it was half a million. I was absent from the camp for ten months. It's important that the figures are accurate!"

Berg paused for a moment as if choking back some tears. 'Can you imagine the workings of the mind of someone who has to be accurate in the number of innocent people he killed? And who and where was the war criminal who stood in for this monster for the ten months he was away? You see, my work takes me everywhere. I used to envy Carrie. She was responsible for Britain... a relatively small area. But there was a twofold issue which applied. Israel not only wants to capture all the Nazi war criminals and put them on trial for their crimes, but it is also determined to stop the bastards from starting the Fourth Reich. We've had enough of them! There are many young people who keep saying it's time the atrocities of the last war were forgotten. Such people are ripe for recruitment to an evil cause. They have a saying in Israel about the holocaust. It goes: "We must remember never to forget!"

'Who's Kirk?' I asked bluntly, recalling the words at the foot of the first computer disk in Miss Grayson's office.

'I thought you knew,' he returned with an element of surprise in his voice. 'Harry Kirk is the Commander-in-Chief of International Three Thousand in Sector A4.'

'Sector A4?' My attention became riveted to the answer.

'Germany is Sector A1, Holland A2, France A3, Britain A4, and so on. They've carved up the whole of Europe.'

'Where can I get more details?' I asked with ostensible naivety.

He looked at me knowingly and smiled amiably. 'You know the old saying,' he advised sagely. 'If you can't beat them, join them!'

For the next half-hour he helped me clear up the mess in the apartment and then left to make the appropriate arrangements for Carrie. No doubt he would contact the Israeli embassy for transport at London Airport where the body would be shipped to Tel Aviv by El Al Airlines. It made me question whether the world I lived in Is was one of reality. It had gone mad! Half the people lived ordinary humdrum lives: the rest were agents, spies, terrorists, anarchists, criminals and the like. It was no longer possible to be certain of anyone... even if you knew them. For my part, Carrie was a pleasant young woman who ought to have been working in an office or a factory with a view to finding a husband and leading a normal life, ultimately producing two or three children. How could I tell that she was an Israeli agent dedicated to seek out Nazi war criminals? I was far removed from all that. None of my parents, grandparents, uncles, brothers or sisters were slaughtered by insensitive maniacs in charge of concentration camps, who turned the fat of the bodies of their victims into soap cubes, or made lampshades from their skin. When viewed in that light, it wasn't easy to forget even if a person, or their family, hadn't been involved.

Berg returned at seven-thirty that evening. Together we carried the body out of the apartment and laid it onto a wooden board in the hearse he had brought. We climbed into the front seats and he glanced at me as he started the engine. 'We have about a mile to drive,' he told me. 'Someone will meet us and take her off our hands.'

He drove off and I wondered why there was any need for my presence. Perhaps Berg needed someone to give him confidence, or I was still required to do something to assist him. He didn't seem keen to communicate but that was hardly surprising. He was probably deeply wounded by the death of the woman he had once intended to marry. Then I realised my senses were dulled with compassion. What was I doing here? I had risked my life by being in the company of an agent or a spy. Now I was an accessory to disposing of the body of a murdered woman!

'I think we're being followed,' Berg informed me after a while.

I turned to note the bright lights of a car some distance behind us. 'Turn left at the traffic lights!' I commanded. He obeyed the instruction but the car remained with us. 'Turn right here,' I said quickly. Berg acted accordingly but our pursuer still followed at a respectable distance. 'I'm not going to chase all over London with a body in the back!' I complained, with my heart in my mouth. 'We'd better get to our destination as soon as possible!'

Ten minutes later, Berg turned the car into a side road in an area close to the docks. Two men wearing anoraks emerged quickly from the darkness and ran towards us. Berg alighted, motioning me to do the same, and the two men climbed into our seats before driving off at speed. Despite my remorse at Carrie's death, I breathed a sigh of relief at having disposed of her body before the police arrived to ask awkward questions. I had no satisfactory explanation to offer. Suddenly, our pursuers entered the side road and Berg pushed me back against a wall, into the shadows.

The car stopped and one of the doors opened. Two hefty men got out of the car and started walking towards us.

'Run!' shouted Berg, giving me a push in the back to start me off.

Before I knew what was happening, my legs were pounding the rough pavement of the docks area towards an unknown destination. It was obvious our pursuers were not the police. But who were they? I didn't know and I had no intention of staying to find out. They were the hunters; I was the prey! That concept in itself was enough to keep me running! I wasn't sure how long I kept going. Perspiration dripped from my chin, my body was saturated with sweat, and I could scarcely breath any more. I stopped for a moment to hide in the shadows against a strange door and closed my eyes. This was becoming a nightmare! I couldn't afford to rest for long in case they were close behind me. I had to move on. It was ridiculous! Why should I be running for my life? My head began to throb and my lungs felt as though they were about to implode. A sense of urgency passed through my tired body as the sound of footsteps hammered on the rough pavements only a short distance away. It seemed that they were bound to catch me whichever direction I took. I had no idea what had happened to Berg. He might have got away because all the footsteps appeared to be moving towards me. 'Oh, Barnaby,' I thought to myself. 'Why did you have to break your leg? It should be you in my place, running for your life. It should be you!'

The footsteps sounded nearer but it was difficult to determine their precise location. The only advice I could offer myself was to run like the Devil until I fell into a heap. As I was about to drag my weary legs a little further, I heard the faint noise of an approaching motor vehicle. It emerged at the top of the street with its headlights cutting through the darkness. I had to take a chance! Without warning, I stepped off the kerb into the road waving my arms wildly in an effort to force the driver to stop. There was a loud squeal of brakes and it swerved dangerously past me, continuing on its way.

'There's one of them!' The voice sounded very close. The comment indicated they hadn't caught Berg.

They were almost on me when there was the sound of a police siren in the near vicinity. The two men hesitated and stopped. The police car turned into the side road. I believe it may have been chasing the car which nearly ran me down. Whatever the reason, it caused the two men to retrace their steps quickly as I stepped out into the road in front of it. This time, the vehicle stopped and an irate policeman started shouting at me for allowing his prey to get away. By the time he had finished, Berg began calling to me from a doorway and the two men had vanished.

I didn't feel very well at all when I got home. I was clearly out of condition and not used to being hunted down by people who intended to make an example of me. It was nearly nine o'clock when I arrived at Miss Grayson's flat. I think she had given up hope again that I would keep the appointment. She answered the door with an unpleasant expression on her face, but her attitude changed substantially when she saw my dishevelled appearance and the state of my clothes.

'What happened?' she asked, staring at the blood on my hand. I hadn't realised it but I had been struck by the wing mirror of the first car as it raced past me.

'To be honest, I don't know,' I replied unhelpfully. 'I really don't know. It seems that some people have it in mind to play rough.' In the ensuing silence, I thought about my words very carefully. What I had told her was untrue. Berg had advised me to run, but no one had threatened or manhandled either one of us... because we hadn't been caught. I had the strangest feeling in the pit of my stomach. Did Berg stage the whole thing to scare me? After all, he was the only one who knew we were going to dispose of Carrie's body at that time of night! And how did he manage to end up in the same street when the police car arrived? There were lots of unanswered questions which plagued my mind!

'You'd better take a shower,' suggested Miss Grayson, pointing in the direction of the bathroom. 'I'm afraid you'll have to do with a candlewick bathrobe.'

Stripping off my clothes, I stepped into the cubicle, scrubbing myself down with scented soap. After a few minutes, the cabinet door opened and Miss Grayson, who was also naked, stepped calmly in beside me. I almost pinched myself to make sure I wasn't hallucinating. Then desire and lust overcame the weariness and I stared at her lovely face and body close to me in that tiny area.

'To look is not to touch!' she warned, with the water streaming over both our bodies.

'It's okay,' I told her. 'I agree with that but I'm going to have to play the hero and save you from drowning.' I placed my hands on her shoulders pulling her towards me gently. I was delighted to note that she didn't resist.

We stood stock still for a while under the warm torrent of water, but it wasn't long before we were standing so close together that there was no space between us at all. My hands moved gently down the sides of her arms and down her back incessantly. The jets of water from above seemed to stimulate her and before I realised it we were making love with each other in that tiny space. After we emerged and dried ourselves, I laid her face downwards on the bed and massaged her back delicately. Our passion for each other had been strong. Consequently, my love-making had forced her time and time again into the solid tiled wall of the shower cubicle. In hindsight, it was not the ideal place to make love vigorously. For Miss Grayson, the pain and the pleasure seemed to have equal values; she never complained at all!

It wasn't long before I began to feel ashamed of myself. Carrie had only just been murdered in my bed. What kind of a person was I to sleep with her one night and then make love to another woman only a few hours after her death? I recognised that Carrie's wanton attitude might have been the reason for her murder. It was the waste of a good life, whether she was an Israeli agent or not! In any case, what did that matter? She had been a beautiful young woman, and the life of every human-being was most precious. I thought about her without feelings of remorse. Death was the final frontier on earth. For the rest of us, life had to go on... and I now lay in the arms of Miss Grayson who was alluring and exciting, alive and well!

CHAPTER FIVE

I was unable to sleep very much that night. Miss Grayson kept stirring and shifting because of the bruises on her back which kept paining her. I made a note never to make love to her in the shower cubicle again. Eventually, she turned over on to her stomach to lie face downwards, and there was both stillness and silence. I lay with my head on the pillow allowing the incidents of the past few days to run loosely through my mind. It was like trying to solve a crossword puzzle for a desired major prize and I couldn't start it. The clues were too hard and, as time went on, I became more and more frustrated at being so inept, realising I had misguided myself in that I was better at my job than the assignment proved. Perhaps, after all, I was simply a hack writer working for a mundane newspaper... as Barnaby always told me in his own inimitable way... and nothing more!

In time, I dozed off lightly but not for very long. It was early morning when I came to my senses fully. Miss Grayson emitted a loud moan and shifted beside me. I was enthused with an idea to write a number of editorials, if I accomplished my task successfully. The few facts in my possession gnawed at my mind for a while before they marshalled themselves in the right order. No one would believe me if I told them the truth. The sceptics always scoffed at the implausibility of human misdeeds; the do-gooders generally demanded over-tolerance in case the innocent were injured; the realists usually demanded their pound of flesh against the wrong-doers. I had no doubt in my mind, however, that Europe basked in the shadow of a peaceful revolution which would have the effect of transferring, all law, power, sovereignty, control and administration to an entity as yet unknown... at least unknown to the world in its new form. I had no idea how long it would take to materialise, but the sources of evil had already spread like a cancer amongst the children and grandchildren of the Nazis and those people whose life ambitions were intertwined with anarchy and chaos. They would never yield to reason or constraint in pursuit of their cause.

I went into Miss Grayson's study and closed the door behind me. An electric typewriter rested on a reproduction desk which made me feel very much at home. I stuffed a sheet of paper into the machine and let my fingers speak my mind in their own inimitable way, frothing out the words in front of me.

"Revolution is the process of civil disturbance which changes control of the ruling leadership or government. It has the effect of altering all procedures of a state or country according to the new dictates. In most cases, it affects seriously the lives of the people... and only the people. There is a strange premeditated breeze which fans the flame of revolution. It is a feeling in the air; an aroma in the wind. It moves like a virus floating from tongue to tongue. Worst of all, the infection breeds quickly spreading like wildfire, revelling in its own contagion. Yet revolution itself has a vested interest only in change, and there lies the crux of the matter, for it is the people themselves who are sucked into the maelstrom of a new era, breaking the yoke of oppression, and sometimes discovering that the latest regime adopts the line of harsher abuse than the previous rule. Successful revolutions are rarely quick and easy. They often take years to prepare, depending on leadership and resources, in order to bring the forces of anarchy to fomentation. The rupture of society is cause by the tension of political and economic pressures either by military might or as a bloodless coup. However, revolutions of magnitude change the face of modern history, not only for the state or country involved but for the whole world."

I stopped at that point to read through the work. It was punchy and expressed the true nature of the issue. Unfortunately, one of the main flaws in my character was the fact I was in love with my own work which made me a poor critic of anything I wrote. I glanced at my wristwatch to note the hour was still young, and decided to leave Miss Grayson in peace. It was light as I left her apartment. There were no taxis evident so I started the long walk home, allowing the seeds of revolution to fester in my brain.

It was nearly an hour before I got there. A lot of work was required to be done to find more information. On the advice of a friend some years earlier, I had a mortise lock installed as an added protection against burglary. When I turned the key, however, the lock indicated that the door had already been opened. Something was very much amiss for I was a creature of habit and never failed to secure the apartment properly on leaving. It was more likely someone had gained entry. Worst still, the intruder might still be inside waiting to attack me! I eased the door open carefully and peered inside before switching on the light. Everything seemed to be in the same disorder as at the moment I had left. I crept stealthily into the front room and closed the door behind me. Suddenly, the bedroom door opened and a man rushed out at me wielding a large kitchen knife. Instinctively, I reacted with my limited knowledge of the martial arts, disarming him by parrying the stroke and forcing him to the floor with a vicious neck lock which caused him to howl in pain. I kicked the knife into a corner of the room before lifting him by the front of his shirt and throwing him on to the settee to exhibit my physical superiority. 'Who are you, and what's this all about?' I demanded angrily. The perspiration stemming from the shock began to make my skin feel clammy. He refused to answer for a moment and I advanced menacingly towards him as though preparing to inflict more harm.

'No, no!' he pleaded, covering his face with his arms like a boxer under severe attack on the ropes. 'Don't hit me!'

The man seemed to be totally incompetent for whatever role he had in mind. 'What's this all about?' I repeated, drawing myself up to my full height to become even more intimidating.

'You bastard!' he shouted, finding an untapped source of audacity. 'You killed my sister!'

'Your sister?' For a moment I considered the man may have come to the wrong apartment. I recalled several music hall jokes concerning such errors told to me in the past which I had found amusing, but it wasn't so funny finding myself at the butt end of a charade. 'What are you talking about?' I riposted sharply. 'I don't even know your sister!'

'Yes you did! You knew Carrie all right!'

The words came like a bolt from the blue. 'Carrie! Yes, I knew her,' I admitted, mollifying my attitude slightly.

'And you killed her!' He seemed to find a hidden strength from her memory which made him bolder by the minute. So much so that I feared he might attack me again.

'Listen you punk!' I yelled. 'Before you go round trying to kill people with a kitchen knife you'd better be sure of your facts! I saved your sister from being beaten up at a meeting a couple of days ago. I let her live here because she had nowhere else to go! I hardly knew her... and I certainly had nothing to do with her death. You'd better believe it because if you attack me again I'll break both your arms!' My tirade took the heat out of his argument and he sat on the settee trying to gather his thoughts.

'Who killed her then?' he asked eventually.

'It doesn't take a Sherlock Holmes to work out it was the same people who wrecked this apartment, does it? Didn't it ever occur to you that someone broke in here and demolished the place? And that if Carrie was here they would hurt her?'

He rubbed his hand tiredly over his face. 'I don't know what to think any more,' he replied sadly. 'The plain fact is that my sister was murdered and I thought you'd done it.'

'How did you come to that conclusion?'

'Jack Berg told me.'

I poured out two glasses of wine from the only unbroken bottle in the cocktail cabinet as his words sank into my mind. I gave one to him and sat down on the side of the demolished armchair. 'Let me get this straight,' I challenged. 'You say Jack Berg told you she was dead and that I'd killed her. Is that what he said?'

'Not in those exact words, he didn't.'

I bridled at his response. 'Well in what kind of words did he tell you?'

'It was more of an insinuation.' There was a long pause as we both digested the situation, then he decided to reconcile himself and atone his error. 'Look, my name's Hymie. I'm sorry I attacked you,' he apologised. 'Carrie was the only family I had left...'

'One question, Hymie,' I cut in as he tailed off in grief, 'and I insist on a truthful answer. Are you with Israeli intelligence?'

He shook his head as tears welled-up in his eyes. 'I'll tell you one thing,' he replied, with the edge of a sob in his throat. 'I damn-well wish Carrie hadn't been!'

I didn't press the question but merely noted that he never answered it. Well, it mattered little to me whether he was a spy or not. I was only interested in leads. There was always the possibility he had some information of value to me. 'What do you know about International Three Thousand?' It was as though I had waved a magic wand and his sorrow evaporated at speed. Clearly, with Hymie, there were times when personal feelings became paramount... but business was business! 'I know of the organisation and its plans to integrate Europe,' he declared frankly. 'But in my opinion it was likely to happen eventually anyway. I'm trying to find out more about Die Stunde. What information do you have on them?'

I shrugged my shoulders aimlessly. 'Die Stunde? That's the German word for "the hour", isn't it? No... I've never even heard of an organisation with that name. What do they propose to do?'

I sat on the settee next to him, waiting to hear something interesting, but I was to be disappointed on this occasion. Before I realised what was happening, he stood up and moved quickly towards the door. When he reached it, he turned to look at me, in case I tried to apprehend him. 'Is this what you normally do?' I asked with a hint of sarcasm in my voice. 'Break into someone's home, try to kill them for the wrong reason, and then duck out again? Because if you do that again, you're going to end up in a deep part of the Thames with lead weights on your feet!'

He took fright at the question. 'I've got to go!' he said apologetically, almost as though he had paid me a courtesy visit. 'I'm sorry about what happened. Look, Carrie's funeral will be at Cheshunt cemetery today at three o'clock. If you want to go...'

'Her funeral?' My ears pricked up at the information. He stared at me with shame in his eyes. 'Look,' he began, trying to explain his actions. 'I was led to believe you'd killed my sister. What would any other brother have done?'

'Any other brother would have checked out the facts first,' I scolded, taking another sip of my drink. 'You can't go round trying to kill people because you suspect them of a crime. I can tell you one thing for certain. You've never stabbed anyone before... not the way you use a knife. I thought you Israeli agents had sound combat training. Recruitment into the army at the age of eighteen and all that.' He recognised I was taunting him to provide more information but he refused to take the bait.

'I never said I was an Israeli agent,' he replied softly.

'Tell me about Die Stunde.' My question came fast on the heels of his words, I had to find out something about it... anything!

He took fright at the question. 'I've got to go,' he said apologetically. 'I'm sorry about what's happened. As I said, Carrie's funeral will be at Cheshunt cemetery at three o'clock today.'

'I understood she was being flown back to Israel on an El Al aeroplane!' I recalled delivering her body with Berg to two people I had never met before and being chased all over the docklands area until I had run myself ragged.

'There was a change of plan. We have no family so the Israeli government decided she should be buried here.'

The telephone started to ring and I searched for it among the debris. By the time I had found it Hymie had disappeared, closing the door behind him. It was a pity I couldn't earn his confidence to extract further information.

'Well goodness gracious me!' stormed Flanders sarcastically. 'The sleeping beauty has awakened! Where the hell are you, Savage, or have you forgotten about the assignment altogether?'

'Good morning, Ted,' I replied calmly.

'What is it with you?' he continued angrily, intent on taking me apart for my ostensible sluggishness. 'This newspaper's not paying you to take a permanent holiday! May I remind you we have readers out there who want to know what's going on in the world!'

He ranted on for a while in his usual manner even though he knew I wasn't paying any attention. I placed the receiver on the settee and continued sipping my drink until he had finished his tirade. I could see no reason to embroil myself in a pointless argument. Flanders had been a reporter for many years. He knew what it was all about! His problem was one of impatience. When he slowed to a halt, I decided to switch roles and get him working for me. 'All right, Ted,' I told him. 'I want you to move heaven and earth in Research Department to find me information on the following. First, Henry Jacobs of State Security. Second, Harry Kirk... I'll tell you about him later. Third, Die Stunde, a German organisation of some kind.'

There was a pause at the other end of the line before he came at me like a tidal wave. 'I think we ought to get the procedure right, you lazy son-of-a-bitch! If you want information, shift your buttocks over here and tell Research Department what you want yourself! Do you hear me?'

I decided he had used up his share of bad temper on me for one morning so I switched off the telephone. It was an effective means of terminating the conversation. Poor old Ted! One had to have some sympathy for the man. From his point of view, I had been sent on an assignment and had fallen off the edge of the world. Despite his comments, I knew he would contact the newspaper's Research Department and examine every shred of evidence before passing it to me. He had a sharp nose for news and never missed out on anything. Unfortunately, he had a flaw in his character which precluded him from apologising when he was wrong, showering praise on his staff, or giving them credit even if their work was exemplary. The bad temper and bluster was the means by which he tried to hide his weakness. I fixed up a table and placed my lap-top computer on it. The bit was between my teeth and I experienced a tremendous urge to continue writing the editorial on revolution.

"The overthrow of the Russian monarchy in 1917 was a revolution based on a new ideal which could be spread quickly through the poorer nations of the world. In the main, it offered equality to all, involving the conversion of the masses founded not on God-fearing principles but on the doctrine of atheism and total dependence on the State. How a major event of this nature could occur in a world where most people believe in one form of deity or another, where superstition exists regardless of environment, and when ancient practices, customs and legends are paramount, is hard to understand. It serves to prove that revolutions are a disease of the period. The axiom is that no democratic country can afford to sit back smugly without caring to look over its shoulder. The reason is that civilisation can be analogised as a number of balloons filled with air, hanging closely to each other. It takes only one small pin-prick to deflate one of them, leaving the others more vulnerable to attack and collapse."

I stopped at this point wondering how mankind could develop so monstrously, where individuals and groups created fear, despondency and misery to achieve personal power and fulfil their own ambitions. It wasn't as though people lived for five hundred years or more to enjoy the spoils. Working life rarely extended more than fifty years from start to finish. What instincts drove these fanatics so strongly to deceive themselves and others for such a short span of time? If one waded through the centuries, there were so few people who had actually changed the course of history for personal satisfaction. My thoughts dwelt on Napoleon and Hitler. Why did so many others try? It was like a disease where individuals strove to cause change and... as the atrocities of World War Two had proved... it didn't end there either.

The cemetery at Cheshunt was quite hard to find. After driving for an hour, I finally came across Silver Street and parked a little way inside the entrance. There was a small building at the side of the cemetery where prayers were offered over the body of the deceased before interment. I made my way into it and sat waiting for the coffin to be brought. It was always my understanding, and I had seen many films at the cinema in which it had occurred, that various suspects turned up at the funeral of the murdered person. Thereafter, the detective would communicate with one of them, or follow a suspicious character, to continue the case with a new and rewarding lead. On this occasion it didn't happen. Excluding the Rabbi, the only other person who arrived was Carrie's brother.

'Is there not a minion?' the Rabbi asked blandly.

'A minion?' I asked in ignorance.

'No,' replied Hymie sadly. 'She had no family except for me.' He turned to face my inquisitive gaze. 'In the Jewish religion,' he explained, 'any gathering for prayer requires a minimum of ten men over the age of thirteen. That's a minion. If the requirement isn't satisfied, the prayers offered are rather different.'

I nodded although I couldn't fathom the reason why someone couldn't pray to God adequately without the presence of nine other men. An assistant wheeled in the coffin on a vehicle similar to a gun-carriage and the Rabbi began to cant his ritual to despatch Carrie's spirit to a higher elevation. When this ended, the coffin was wheeled out of the other side of the building to the graveyard. Shortly, we stopped at an open grave and the Rabbi invited us to lower the coffin into position by means of two stout ropes. Once this was completed, an assistant pulled the ropes free to leave the mortal remains at rest for eternity. We used a shovel in turn to toss some earth on top of the coffin while the Rabbi completed the appropriate prayer for the ritual. Then we walked slowly back to the building respectfully where Hymie handed some money to the Rabbi and his assistant for their services. We continued outside into the sunlight with sadness in our hearts. There is no pleasure in the interment of a young woman in the flower of her youth and we both grieved in our own particular way. However, we remained in the world of the living and I decided to attack him at his weakest moment. 'You still haven't told me about Die Stunde,' I chided. He shrugged his shoulders aimlessly, preferring not to talk in his hour of sorrow. 'You can't run away from me for the whole of your life, Hymie!'

'This is neither the time nor the place!' he riposted angrily, with a catch in his voice. 'Good God! My sister's still warm in her grave and all you can think about is your newspaper! What kind of a monster are you?'

'Don't you want to find out who killed her?' It was necessary to play on his motive for personal revenge and I rammed the words home, hoping he would rise to the bait.

'Does it matter?' he replied philosophically, finding it hard to breath as emotion overcame him and tears welled-up in his eyes. 'Does it really matter who killed her? If I find the man, what am I suppose to do to him... take an eye for an eye, a tooth for a tooth? Would I be satisfied then?'

His comments surprised me and I became irritated to realise he had been quite prepared to kill me for revenge. 'Of one thing I'm certain,' I told him flatly. 'You don't work for Israeli intelligence or any other intelligence agency! I must be out of my mind even talking to you!'

'Then why don't you leave me alone, damn you!'

He sat down on a seat near the car park and put his head in his hands before sobbing. I waited patiently for him to stop, then he rose and went to his car. I opened the door on the other side and climbed in beside him.

'What the hell do you think you're doing?' he demanded.

'I think we should sit down somewhere away from this place and have a long talk, Hymie,' I suggested calmly. 'Maybe we can pool ideas and help each other.'

He stared directly into my eyes to determine whether I was sincere. 'All right,' he agreed eventually, returning to reason. 'I'll come back to your place. We'll see what we can piece together.'

I climbed out of the car, slammed the door, and walked towards my own vehicle. It was my good fortune he delayed starting his engine for some twenty seconds. There was no reason for either of us to be suspicious; therefore it was unexpected. As soon as he turned his key in the ignition there was a tremendous explosion and his car burst into flame. I could only assume that a bomb had been planted under the bonnet of his vehicle. Hymie never knew what happened. Within seconds, there was a second explosion as the fuel tank ignited. It would have been delightful to report that I became a hero, dragging the victim from the flames at risk to my own life. Unhappily, it wasn't so. There was no opportunity for me to save him; he didn't have the faintest chance of survival. Within ten seconds his body was burned to a cinder. I watched helplessly from a short distance away, shielding my face from the heat with my hands. Someone was determined to eliminate both brother and sister. As I watched the man die, I heard the sound of a rifle shot and a bullet ricocheted from a stone near my feet. I dropped quickly to the ground and crawled to the other side of my car, opening the door slightly before hauling myself inside. Shots were being fired one after another and I could hear them whining as they struck the vehicle. I started the motor and drove like a demon from the cemetery after punching a hole in the shattered windscreen with my fist. When I gathered my senses in an area of comparative safety some distance away, I stopped to examine the damage. There had been six further shots which had hit the bodywork, including the one which shattered the windscreen.

I climbed back into the car and sat there thoughtfully for a while. Someone had planted a bomb in Hymie's car to blow him to kingdom come. Then they fired at me a number of times but never even wounded me. The shot which ricocheted at my feet was the first one. I was out in the open without any means of defending myself, yet not one of the shots hit their target. I could only imagine the marksman was trying to miss me deliberately. I didn't ring the police or Jack Berg this time. Hymie's death had nothing to do with me and I wasn't willing to get involved. I drove around in the car for an hour or so, losing myself in the busy traffic. Then I went to a restaurant for a meal. The assignment was getting out of hand. Two people had been killed and I could honestly say there were three attempts on my life ... the two men in the docklands, Hymie's attack, and the marksman at the cemetery. I hadn't planned to give up my life for the newspaper so early in my career and I considered it was about time Ted Flanders took some flak from me for a change!

After returning to my apartment, I surveyed the wreckage with dismay. Everything belonged to the newspaper... the flat and the furniture. The bill for the damage would have to be sent directly to the administrator of expense accounts at the newspaper, although I knew exactly the tenor of his answer. He would ask many questions about the validity of my claim, comparing it to the level of achievement in relation to the assignment. I recalled the words of Jack Berg when he suggested if you can't beat them, join them. It was good advice and there was every reason to seek membership of the organisation I intended to expose. As I mulled over the situation, the telephone rang. It was Miss Grayson.

'Are we going to see each other this evening,' she cooed, her voice emitting soft golden tones.

I tried to recall whether I had arranged to see her later but I couldn't remember. 'I'll collect you at eight o'clock,' I replied. 'Is that okay?'

'It's okay by me,' she answered. 'By the way, you won't mind massaging my back again, will you? I'm in great pain!'

I felt a degree of embarrassment discussing such personal matters over the telephone. 'I'll collect you at eight,' I repeated to terminate the conversation. I let the receiver fall to the settee and turned my attention to my lap-top computer. I wanted to write more for the editorial although my thoughts were very muddled. I sat facing a blank screen with my fingers hovering over the keys expectantly. Nothing happened for a while, then they began to stroke the keyboard gently. It was almost as though I was holding a seance by myself, trying to capture the words as they passed over from someone on the other side.

"During long periods of peace, governments tend to ignore the fact that revolution can occur at any place... at any time. It is mobile in its nature, consisting of dissent and discontent which fester in the womb of one or more regions of the world to await ultimate birth."

My eyelids began to grow heavy, my arms and legs felt weary, and I fell asleep where I sat. Hours sped by and I remained in the arms of Morpheus... temporarily dead to the world. The sleepless night with Miss Grayson was now having its full effect. It was evening when I awoke... ten o'clock to be precise. I stared at the clock in horror. I had let Miss Grayson down again. It was likely I was the most ill-mannered person she had ever met in her life, but then I didn't think too highly of myself either. I felt a certain sympathy for her and analogised with the story about the bankrupt trader who was about to throw himself off the top of a twenty-storey building when he heard a quiet voice from above say: "Cheer up, my son, things could be worse!" So he moved back off the ledge and cheered up to continue his life and, sure enough, things got worse!"

I went into the bedroom and fell on the bed... the same bed in which Carrie had been murdered. I had no superstitious fears of ghouls and ghosts, or a haunted apartment. Nonetheless, it was a discomforting thought that I had to put out of my mind. In my dreamy state, I kept thinking about Artemus Ward who seemed able to sum up the assignment in a nutshell. He once said: "It 'aint the things we know that cause all the trouble... it's the things we know that 'aint so!" I knew many ways of applying that comment to my own predicament... but they would all have to wait for another day.

CHAPTER SIX

When Jack Berg rang I was in the shower scrubbing myself vigorously. For me, it had always been the most enjoyable sensation at the start of each day, whatever the weather, allowing jets of warm water to gush all over my body. A pundit in a medical magazine once suggested that the instinct for this pleasure stemmed from the time when man was still a reptile. I couldn't vouch for the validity of that gem of information. As far as I was concerned, the shower cubicle commended itself as the only sanctuary in the apartment out of earshot of the telephone when the water was turned on. It offered peace and tranquillity, allowing my trusted servant... the telephone-answering machine... to act capably in my absence. After I had dressed and eaten breakfast, I switched it on, listening to each call until hearing Berg's voice with its quiet tone.

'Mr. Savage,' he began. 'I once told you if you can't beat them, join them! Well now you can do it! How would you like to become a fully-fledged member of International Three Thousand today? It can be arranged. But if you agree, you'd better let me know quickly.'

Why was this reticent shrimp-like person, who figuratively speaking lodged quietly under a stone in the dark for most of the time, suddenly bursting into my life offering me free leads? It wasn't true to form and his actions were suspect. Yet, the option excited me and I warmed swiftly to the prospect. I rang him right away. 'Where and when?' I asked tersely.

'The Assembly Hall at eight o'clock this evening, but you won't be admitted without a signed recommendation by a current member of the organisation.'

I screwed up my face with disappointment, stymied at the first fence. 'How do I get that? Who could possibly recommend me?'

'Conrad Hayle will recommend you personally.'

'Hayle? The Minister of Justice? Don't be ridiculous!'

'I've got his signature on the document.'

I had an uneasy feeling in the pit of my stomach that the evening was going to herald disaster, ending with me being beaten savagely by some of the bully boys employed to keep everyone under control. 'Are you sure it's valid?' I asked apprehensively, knowing that there was no alternative.

'I'll bring it to you shortly,' he offered willingly.

I couldn't allow him to be so gratuitous without a challenge. 'Why are you so keen to get me to join?' I asked point-blank.

'I want to hang on to your coat-tails and get the information I need,' he replied without hesitation.

'Then why don't you become a member yourself?'

'Are you kidding?' he riposted. 'My picture's been plastered in newspapers all round the world for years. I can get away with attending a meeting for one evening but no more than that. If you won't help me, it might take months to get someone on the inside.'

'This wouldn't be some kind of ruse, would it?'

He paused for a moment. 'I don't really want to talk about it over the telephone. I'll see you in an hour.'

He arrived exactly sixty minutes later and I poured him a drink from the lone bottle. He stared at me for a while and then placed his glass on the floor in the absence of the coffee-table which lay shattered on the other side of the room. 'You don't believe anything I say, do you?' he muttered. 'You think I'm leading you up the garden path.'

I went to the window and looked outside. 'Let's just say I'm familiarising myself with my newspaper assignment.' I hoped my face didn't display the feelings of mistrust.

He removed a buff envelope from his pocket and placed it on the settee. 'Here's the recommendation. The only thing I want in return is your promise to keep in touch and tell me what goes on.'

I turned and looked straight into his eyes. 'I hope no one realises this is a forgery. The idea of being thrown to the wolves doesn't move me to ecstasy.'

'Don't worry,' he assured me. 'You won't get beaten up. It's all legit.'

We failed to say anything more and he departed swiftly. Perhaps it was a quid pro quo situation from which we would both benefit. I hadn't asked him why he hadn't attended Carrie's funeral. In view of what had happened he was fortunate not to have been there. But why didn't he attend? It was his intention to marry Carrie at one time, yet when she died he stayed away. Jack Berg was turning into an enigma and I didn't like it... not at all!

I arrived at the hall before the meeting was about to start. I showed my letter of recommendation to the security officer at the door. He examined the document carefully and retained it. At the entrance to the hall, someone handed me a sheet of paper to complete. It was a declaration of commitment to the cause... although it never mentioned the name of International Three Thousand. I was not alone in this practice for every person attending had been invited to do the same. Once the declaration had been signed, each recruit was allowed to enter the hall and sit down. One could only presume that if someone refused to sign it, the bully-boys would toss them out onto the street. I perched myself insignificantly on one of the drab wooden benches with an element of discomfort. The buzz of chatter gradually increased in the hall. There were about eighty people in attendance. A gathering of so few new followers seemed insignificant in itself but, if the number of recruits from all the cells of the organisation in Britain were added together on this particular evening alone, the cumulative total could amount to thousands. When one multiplied the figure by the number of countries in Europe, the final count would be quite considerable. How often did this practice occur? Once a week... each fortnight... every month? My brain began to calculate with astonishment the acceleration by which an organised revolution could be achieved. It worked by geometric progression... the fever which spreads with a popular cause... to recruit millions of supporters over a short period of time. The same thing happened in Germany in the 1930s, sweeping the country like wildfire in the span of five years to encompass the whole German nation. It could easily happen in Europe with the right promotion and a groundswell of discontent with the current European governments which fought each other in committees and assemblies. I turned to the young lady sitting next to me and smiled before focussing my attention on the platform ahead. It was vital to remember to keep a low profile and remain silent unless it was absolutely necessary to speak. If anyone discovered I was a newspaper reporter infiltrating the organisation, I might be torn to pieces by the angry mob or beaten to death by the bully-boys. It was not a thought which comforted me. I would definitely keep a low profile! Shortly, a man appeared on the stage dressed in the black uniform and jackboots now becoming familiar to me. The flashes on the collar and armbands displayed designs of parallel zig-zagged lightning, symbolic of those worn by the SS in World War Two. Conrad Hayle and the Glazers joined him wearing only formal clothing. The new-comer carried a truncheon which he tapped firmly on the table with a slow rhythmic beat to attract the attention of the audience. I had the impression he had surveyed the damp walls of the Assembly Hall, which were pitted with mould, with a element of contempt, despising the thought of offering his brilliant oratory in such grim surroundings. It was hardly the place for one of the leaders of a growing movement to present himself but he was willing to believe that patience and fortitude would reward him in time. Fancifully, he saw himself as the tenant of a place like Berchtesgaden, the town in the Bavarian Alps where Hitler, Goering and other Nazi leaders would go on vacation... but that would be many years hence. He glanced at his notes, waving his arm to the back-stage electrician, and the hall lights began to dim slowly. Clearly, he was determined to make a good impression, especially as the priority that evening was to recruit people from all walks of life to proliferate the cause.

'My name is Kirk,' he began, in a voice which commanded attention. 'I'm the Commander-in-Chief for the south-east area of the organisation you've been invited to join. Now... each of you has signed a declaration of allegiance to our cause, which is one of non-violence, but let me make it quite clear we have no intention of press-ganging anyone into our ranks. Anyone who joins does so of their own volition. We need the support of every individual to achieve our aim. Therefore, if any one of you has doubts or second thoughts, it's recommended you leave this hall now. You're perfectly free to do so. However, if you stay and renege on your commitment at a later date, you may live to regret the infidelity. Your declaration is a solemn promise. The doctrines of any new organisation need to be followed strictly. Unity is the key to survival, while faith is the source by which we multiply. There is no successful organisation in the world able to guarantee the welfare of a traitor. So... if anyone wishes to leave, I urge you to do so immediately to avoid unpleasantness at a later date.'

A long, heavy silence descended on the hall as some of the recruits shuffled their feet and looked gently sideways, forwards and behind them... but nobody moved. After thirty seconds had passed, Kirk nodded with satisfaction and glanced once again at his notes. 'Good!' he continued. 'I'm delighted to see we all pull together in this worthy cause. Let me begin by saying you must not expect rapid results. Our plan is designed to succeed quickly but it won't happen tomorrow. We have grown on an international scale for some time with a current membership approaching two million people in Europe. You did not mishear me. Two million people! The current recruitment drive will inflate that number substantially over the coming year. We hope to achieve major results within the next ten years so don't be discouraged if nothing seems to happen for a while. Indeed, we intend to penetrate the abortive and wasteful government systems of Europe by creating a new party and producing candidates to compete for parliamentary seats to prepare the way for the United States of Europe. Each one of you will realise the importance of a world power of such substance. So let's move on to the strategic plan of our programme. Initially, our objective appears similar to all the governments within the European Community. But they have serious flaws in their plans. For example, no single country wishes to lose control of its sovereignty or its ambitions. Each country nurtures its own interests, to the detriment of the others. It is scarcely the proper way to secure the safety and high standards of living for the people of Europe as a whole. Participants in the European Community make interesting noises with regard to unity and stability, but they are so protective of their own interests their allegiance to Europe is false. Most of them are incapable of running their own countries properly. As such, why should we allow them to meddle in our affairs, creating high taxation, greater unemployment, more hardship, and less freedom to do as we wish? I don't think so! Our cause will disband all the governments of Europe and erase the borders of every European country. It's the only means of uniting Europe to create a single powerful entity. Just think of it! No separate countries. They would all lose their identities. We would emulate the United States of America... one government, one nation! Naturally, it will take time to establish a single language but, as generations pass, we shall replace the old with the new to the benefit of all those who live within the United States of Europe!'

He strutted to the back of the stage and unrolled a large map of Europe hanging from the wall, using his truncheon to guide the eyes of every recruit in the hall. 'When Europe is unified, countries will relinquish their present names to be known by Sector numbers. For example, Germany will be known as Sector one. Holland, Sector two. France, Sector three, Britain, Sector four. The national language throughout will be English. All European countries are included in the programme with the exception of Russia. The government elected will be totalitarian at the outset. There's good reason for this. You see, change will be sudden and it will sweep through Europe with monumental force. At first, there will be confusion... even chaos. In order to avoid serious disruption, it will be necessary to establish tight controls and to provide direction to ensure stability and justice. As soon as positive order is maintained, the aim will be to set up a series of temporary ministries... one for each Sector. In due course, these would be disbanded, according to the exigencies of the system. The objective is a bloodless revolution, planned to be swift and effective. The policy will reduce all kinds of wasteful effort to encourage a two-fold effect. Firstly, a stable economy followed by remarkable productivity and growth. It will allow the United States of Europe to compete effectively and successfully against other nations. Secondly, more manpower can be released for useful working purposes and transferred between Sectors swiftly, reducing unemployment. A Minister of Peace will be appointed to ensure safety and security. The European military will consist of a million service personnel with all military equipment required for its needs. The pooling of the military will secure a massive reduction in, what is currently known, as defence expenditure. At the same time, the United States of Europe will become a major world power. The law will not continue under its present structure. In matters of criminal justice, each court will consist of three judges. Juries will be abolished. They are served by people who know little of the law and even less about criminal nature and psychology. In the criminal court, punishment of those guilty of homicide and violence against human-beings, including sexual assault, will be the death penalty. For other offences, those guilty will be sent to prisons to be built near the Arctic Circle. If a person is found guilty of crime on three separate occasions, he or she will be considered anti-social and face the death penalty. Additionally, any person found carrying a deadly weapon will be deemed to be prepared to use it for the purpose of violence. There's no room for criminals in the new society. In the civil courts, the process will continue as at present. Social welfare will continue to provide services to promote improvement in health and for prevention, diagnosis and treatment of illness. The cost will be met by the State. Can you imagine the advantages of the concentration of research into the many diseases which ravage mankind? All knowledge would be pooled and large research centres will be built containing the best equipment in the world. Within social welfare is the matter of population control, the mentally sick and handicapped, and the elderly. Under population control, no family will be allowed to have more than two children. After the second child, both parents will submit themselves for sterilisation to avoid breaking the law. It's necessary for both parents to be involved as divorce may occur at a later date. If a third child is born to a family, the working parents will pay fifty per cent of both his and her earnings as a penalty. If neither parent is working, the third child will be offered for adoption to a family with less than two children. Single parent families will be limited to one child only. With regard to the mentally sick and handicapped, the natural family will be required to look after them. Alternatively, the State will deal with the afflicted in its own way. Elderly people with terminal illness, permanent illness or severe disabilities will be mercifully treated by euthanasia in specified hospitals. The policy is to create an efficient society, fit and healthy in both mind and body. In the field of education, children will continue at school and college until they reach the age of twenty, becoming more involved in new methods of training which offer practical experience in industry and commerce rather than ploughing blindly with academic subjects. The Minister of Education will be responsible for teaching English in all schools so the use of national languages will become less and less in the effluxion of time. In housing, the State intends to build widely in areas hitherto untouched enabling the needs of many homeless to be met. Private enterprise will exist in its present form except that our organisation will pool technological know-how to ensure that essential economies will come into force at all levels. One measure to achieve this aim will be to merge some of Europe's largest industrial companies to achieve economies of scale... which also means less waste. I do not intend to go into details on finance and taxation, but I assure you the wages and salaries of employees within the United States of Europe will be sufficient to maintain a higher standard of living from the moment we gain power.'

'But how do you meet the costs of defence, hospitals, housing and the like?' intervened one inquisitive man some distance to my left.

Kirk did not hesitate in his reply. 'By a certain level of taxation and the proper use of minerals and other natural resources. Do you realise how much wealth is available from energy products alone. It's staring you in the face! Large reserves of North Sea oil, tremendous pockets of natural gas, massive stocks of available coal, and various other minerals. There is also wind power and energy from the sun with solar panels, The people of Kuwait don't pay taxes because of the revenue from oil. If we use our resources properly... for the benefit of the people... the United States of Europe will be well on its way to successfully funding itself.' He continued to outline various aspects of the revolutionary idealism while his captive audience listened with great interest. The elements of the programme were unfolded with a measure of realism. The enthusiasm of the people around me emulated the concept I had written in my editorial. Revolution... it was like a disease... floating in the wind! As for myself, I had to sit patiently through the whole charade. It bored me stiff! On many occasions, I had been present when issues of European disharmony had been debated in the past. I was much in favour of a united Europe, but that view had been taken on the grounds that individual countries would secure closer relationships with their neighbours and seek to liaise and assist each other at all levels. In the case of International Three Thousand, a single authority was being formed to eradicate every government in Europe. Soon afterwards, the peoples of those nations would be forced to accept new measures without having the opportunity or the right to protest. Although I had grave doubts on the efficacy of democratic rule, the new United States of Europe would be totalitarian... the State would reign supreme under a Fascist dictatorship! It was the equivalent of unleashing a whirlwind! In my opinion, ninety-nine per cent of the people never knew what they wanted anyway! There was another issue which triggered warning signals in my mind. Who were these people assuming such high appointments in the new regime? No one had ever seen or heard of them before! They were tin-pot characters electing themselves into positions of power and I, for one, didn't trust any of them... especially when they were supported by a herd of bully-boys who stood in the background as a direct threat to all of us. If ever in doubt, I could always rely on the memory of the photograph of Albert Henley laying face downwards in the Thames to prove my point. These men were murderers... and possibly fools into the bargain. I sat perfectly still and quietly, closing my ears to the rhetoric until Kirk began to wind up his speech.

'In order to ensure our plans become effective,' he concluded, 'it's necessary to appoint men and women to various official posts. Never forget the way ahead is through commitment. Some of you here tonight who have that commitment may stand to merit promotion within the organisation. I sincerely hope this to be so. Finally, now that you have a general understanding of our plans and ideals, let me stress we're not drifting with a utopian ideal. It is a programme designed for immediate use, but a great deal of patience is required. I welcome all of you to International Three Thousand! Thank you for being so attentive!'

He sat down and a few people began to applaud until everyone in the hall joined in to show their appreciation. When the noise died down, Kirk stood up again.

'May I take this opportunity to introduce Conrad Hayle, the Minister of Justice for the south-east region.' He sat down, stretching out his legs, extending his jackboots under the table.

As Hayle rose, one of the bully-boys handed him a sheet of paper and he glanced at it briefly. 'I have here a letter of recommendation for a recruit attending this evening to which I put my own signature.' He stared at the sea of faces and my heart missed a beat before it began to thump quickly in my chest and loudly in my ears. They had discovered the forged document and I was in deep trouble! I recalled the premonition I had earlier that the evening would fall apart at the seams. This was the moment to face the truth. The exits all seemed so far away, while the gangways were well served with ex-boxers and wrestlers to keep the peace. There was no means by which I could escape. For a moment I felt the same terror experienced by Albert Henley at the end of the trial. Coincidentally, it would be the same Minister of Justice so it was likely he would mete out identical punishment. In my mind's eye, I envisaged Ted Flanders staring at my photograph on the front page in the next edition of the newspaper, face down in the water somewhere in the vicinity of the Surrey Commercial Docks.

'Mr. Savage!' he called out authoritatively. 'Would you raise your hand to identify where you are?'

I lifted my arm slowly, waiting to be surrounded by men with broken noses and cauliflower ears menacing me with their fists. Instead, Hayle looked at me and smiled.

'I'm glad you could make it, Mr. Savage.' A gleam of recognition appeared in his eyes. 'Yes. You were at the meeting here yesterday, weren't you? Well, as a new-comer, why don't you come up on the stage and give us your views of the intentions and aims of our cause? We like to hear opinions from the grass roots.'

I wasn't sure whether to feel relieved or not. It became abundantly clear that within the span of twenty seconds that I had made an astounding leap from the proverbial frying pan into the fire. For some reason unknown to me, Hayle didn't reveal that the letter of recommendation was a forgery. I got to my feet and climbed the steps to the stage wondering what on earth I was going to say to the audience. I knew no more than the rest. Perhaps that was the answer! Hayle was going to play with me like a cat toying with a mouse and then disclose the fact I was an infiltrator, bringing the house down about my ears.

'Good evening,' I began hesitantly, feeling extremely nervous and uncomfortable. 'I thank the Minister of Justice for allowing me to speak to you although, like yourselves, I have only just been initiated.' I paused for what seemed to be an eternity, then an idea formed in my mind and I followed it through. 'Apart from all the advantages offered by a United States of Europe, the idea of accountability by human-beings is a very important factor. For example, most of us work very hard and we have to support large numbers of idlers who have no intention of making any kind of contribution to society. That's unfair! Equally, there are many families who decide to emigrate from poor countries to those most prosperous in order to feed off their success. They've never contributed to their new place of residence in the past but are only too eager to accept money, housing, benefits and the like, which their own native nation wouldn't give them. And they don't even have to work here. Why should they under the present system? They don't have to! But we have to! Because we're the workers who pay for their welfare... yet they are strangers, foreigners! That too is unfair! I would like to see a united nation where everyone is accountable... where people can take out only what they put in. And if we all have to carry identity cards to counter illegal immigration or reduce crime, well so be it! I'll be the first one in line to get one. Anyone who doesn't work for the new society shouldn't be granted any benefits. Why should they? The administration of criminal justice was outlined earlier but I would go further on the issue of drugs. I believe the new administration should deal harshly with both drug addicts and drug traffickers. Society would do well to be rid of both elements once and for all. Do you agree?' There was a vacuum of silence so I repeated the question more vehemently. 'Do you agree?' About thirty per cent of the audience assented, some fairly enthusiastically. 'Come now, my fellow recruits!' I urged persistently. 'You can do much better than that! I ask you for the last time. Do you agree!'

There was a resounding chorus which echoed all round the hall, ending with applause as I moved to descend from the stage. My performance was sound but I still felt as if I walked a tight-rope with a long distance to cover before reaching safety.

'Thank you, Mr. Savage. Well done!' commended Hayle, as I resumed my seat. 'Well done!'

He bumbled on about law and justice in the new society but I didn't hear a word. My hands were still shaking in the fear of being unmasked as an infiltrator. I took a deep breath as my heart beat even more loudly, drumming away in my ears. This assignment was getting completely out of hand. I was now appearing as a model recruit for the organisation I intended to expose. I noticed the young woman beside me smiling sweetly, and I tried to put on a pleasant face under duress. It was a difficult task, however, because my fate was in the lap of the Gods!

The meeting ended forty minutes later and I turned to smile at her having, by then, secured full control of my fears and nerves.

'What's your first name?' she asked amiably.

'James, but most people call me Jimmy,' I replied. 'Why do you ask?'

'One day you may become famous in International Three Thousand. I want to be able to say I sat next to you and listened to your first speech.'

I shrugged my shoulders, looking at her with a wry expression on my face. 'I don't think I'm destined to become famous,' I told her candidly.

'You're too modest!' she countered. 'By the way, I'm Tania.'

At that moment I noticed Hayle walking swiftly in my direction. This was the moment the axe would fall. Instead, he took my hand and pumped it vigorously. 'That was a fine contribution, Mr. Savage,' he commended. 'A fine contribution.'

I prayed to heaven he didn't ask me where we had met before or how I came to be in possession of the letter of recommendation. To my astonishment, nothing was further from his mind.

'Tell me,' he went on. 'What sort of work do you do?'

'I was in the armed forces for a while and returned to take up an appointment in a bank,' I lied.

'I see. What rank did you obtain in the forces?' He seemed relaxed and amiably inquisitive.

'I was only a corporal.'

He smiled knowingly. 'Hm,' he mused. 'A corporal. It seems to be a popular rank for those who wish to achieve power in movements such as our own.'

I laughed by way of reflex action. He was clearly referring to Adolf Hitler who had been a corporal in the World War One, and I recalled that Mussolini, another fascist, held the same rank at one time. I also remembered seeing a photograph in the files of the newspaper of an angry mob dragging the corpse of Il Duce through the streets of an Italian city at the end of the war with hatred.

'We'll be holding another meeting shortly... more of a party, with food, drink and entertainment. It's designed for key people in our movement. I'd like you to come along.' He stared briefly at Tania. 'Why don't you bring your friend as well.' He produced a business-card from his pocket. 'Ring me in a few days' time and I'll let you have further details.'

I took the card but before I had a chance to reply he turned and charged towards one of the exits. I glanced at it and turned to Tania with a brief smile touching the corners of my mouth. 'Well,' I laughed, 'it appears to me we've been tagged together. How do you feel about that?'

Her eyes seemed to dance with humour. 'If you treat me as a friend over the next seven days,' she replied sagely. 'I'll tell you in a week!'

I stared at the heart-shaped locket which hung around her neck. 'May I see that?' I asked. She obliged me by opening it to allow me to gaze at a tiny photograph of a man and a woman. 'Your parents?'

She nodded. 'Yes, they were a handsome couple.' Her eyes took on a dreamy look and, as she spoke of them in the past tense, I resisted the temptation to enquire further.

We left the Assembly Hall to walk towards the Tower of London and I hailed a passing taxi. Ten minutes later we were installed in one of my favourite restaurants. It was a relationship forced on both of us although, if the truth were known, we were both happy with our fate. We enjoyed the meal but it became noticeable that, having spent the best part of the evening listening to plans which planted the seeds of revolution, neither of us mentioned the movement or any of the people involved. It was as though neither of us had attended the meeting... . it had never happened. And that fact really troubled me because I was unable to understand the reason for its total exclusion from our discussion the whole evening. From experience, I knew instinctively, as Shakespeare had put it in Hamlet, there was something rotten in the State of Denmark!

CHAPTER SEVEN

I could have cheerfully strangled Ted Flanders when I returned to my office the following day. Admittedly I was often absent from the building because my enquiries took me to a distant part of the country or to some remote spot at the far end of the world. On this occasion, I came to collect the information. I had requested. As I passed the window of the editor's office, he emerged swiftly like a boxer coming out of his corner at the start of the bell in the first round of a contest. He had removed his jacket, both his shirt-sleeves were rolled up, his tie hung like an inverted noose around his neck, while the butt end of an old Havana cigar rested uneasily on his lips.

'My humble apologies,' he called out, bursting with sarcasm. 'Had I know that the Prodigal Son was going to return today I'd have rolled out the thick red carpet!'

He could be a real pain in the thigh but, as an employee of a national newspaper, it was important to display some element of tolerance and a certain amount of deafness to sarcasm and innuendo. 'Good morning, Ted!' I greeted cheerfully. 'You look as though you slept the night on the couch in your office.'

'How can I sleep with incompetent staff and a newspaper to run, when they don't communicate on major assignments?' He rubbed a hand over his face. 'I can't understand why I haven't suffered a heart attack. Come inside, I want to talk to you!.

I followed him into his office closing the door behind me. Whenever Ted became quiet it was time for concern. I sat down watching him closely.

'Okay,' he began. 'What have you got to tell me?'

It was the first time I had seen him so pressed for news in the early stages of an assignment. 'Hell, Ted!' I riposted. 'What's it been? Two day? Is the paper that short of news?'

'I can feel that we're on to something big,' he ventured, with an odd expression on his face. 'Alternatively it could be a bummer.'

'It's big all right,' I divulged, wondering whether I ought to reveal any information at this juncture. If I let the story slip, Barnaby might recover in the next few weeks and the assignment could be transferred to him. If it turned out to be a scoop, I wanted to be the man awarded the shield from the Press Association as the Reporter of the Year. 'My apartment's been wrecked and there have been attempts on my life,' I told him. His eyes opened wide as he absorbed the information. 'When you see my report, it won't need a Sherlock Holmes to realise that something big in happening. What did the Research Section find out for me?'

He looked genuinely sad and troubled. He looked at the folder in front of him. 'Who's Henry Jacobs?' he asked.

'Some kind of big-wig in State Security.' I checked that the door was close before continuing. 'Between you, me, and these four walls, I don't want you to repeat this to a living soul. I met Jacobs at the House of Commons with a small select committee n the presence of the Prime Minister.'

There was a long silence and he sat quite still as though frozen to the chair. 'Are you kidding me? Is what you're saying true?'

'Look Ted,' I sighed impatiently. 'A lot of water's passing under the bridge. It's complicated. Why do you think I'm not telling the truth?'

He opened a desk drawer and took out an old cigar which had seen better days and he lit it puffing smoke to the ceiling. 'I checked up on State Security and on Henry Jacobs. Neither of them exist.'

'Well you know what they're like in MI5 and MI6. All cloaked in secrecy.'

'So there's no agency called State Security and you saw the Prime Minister!' He said it in the form of a challenge.

'Come on, Ted!' I remonstrated. 'I wasn't duped. No one's going to impersonate someone as high up as him.' I drew in a deep breath. It was possible that the man was a ringer. They did that in the last war with both Churchill's and Montgomery's doubles. It opened up much wider issues involving treason, conspiracy, breaches of security and lots more. No…it was too much to accept!

'You'd better tell me all about it,' he demanded.

'I think I've already told you enough,' I returned, regretting that I'd said anything at all.

He puffed at his cigar thoughtfully, the dry leaves curling up at the edges. 'You don't understand,' he snarled. I'm not asking you, I'm ordering you!'

His outburst was more like the old Ted Flanders which made me feel completely at home. I realised that there was a time for reticence or silence and this should have been it. I'd been a fool not to keep my mouth shut! 'I was abducted by a man called Gates who took me to the House of Commons,' I blurted. 'I met a group of people there, including Henry Jacobs, Then the Prime Minister came and asked me to carry out an assignment. I suggest that Research Department look deeper into the subject. There must be a State Security Department somewhere!'

Flanders ignored my request and stared down at the folder again. 'What's Die Stunde?'

'It means 'the hour' in German. Has Research dug anything up about it?'

He shrugged his shoulders aimlessly. 'Nothing, he uttered. 'They couldn't find anything.'

I rolled my eyes to the ceiling as if asking for help from a higher authority. 'I think you need to recruit better staff for the Research Department. There must be something!'

'They're qualified all right,' he snapped. 'I want to know your sources.'

I groaned inwardly because I knew that he wouldn't believe me. 'It was the brother of the Israeli agent who was killed in my apartment. He was killed later after someone had rigged his car with a bomb in the cemetery.'

I couldn't blame him thinking that either I had lost my mind or that I had entered the realm of fiction. He chewed on his cigar before continuing. 'I think you might need a holiday, Savage. You're overworking. I can see that now.'

'Look, Ted,' I went on. It's best I keep it all under wraps for the moment. You'll learn all about it in due course. I don't suppose anyone's heard of a Harry Kirk.'

He stared at me looking down again at the folder. 'His first name's really Heinrich. He happens to be the grandson of Heinrich Himmler. No doubt you've heard of him and his exploits during World War Two. A man who attained one of the most prominent positions in the Nazi regime. Born in Munich, he followed Hitler even before the unsuccessful attempts to gain power in 1932. Chief of Police in all Germany in 1936 at the age of thirty-six. Minister of the Interior in 1943, Minister of Home Defence in 1944. Committed suicide a year later when captured by Allied troops. As Head of the German police, including the Gestapo, he ordered the deaths of millions of people beginning in 1934 ending with systematic killings in the concentration camps.'

The news sent my mind reeling and I was forced back on the defensive. 'Well how about that?' I managed to utter.

'Do you need help with this assignment?' he said, mollifying his attitude.

It was probably the first and last time I would ever hear him make such an offer. He clearly realised the importance of the assignment. 'No thanks,' I replied, 'but I do need more information.' I picked up his dictating machine and turned it on. 'I'd like to know about Lieutenant-Colonel Topham involved in Defence, Sir Peter Cavenham, Home Office, Miss Grayson, a Technical Adviser on defence matters, and a man called Maitland who's the Personal Assistant to the Prime Minister. I also need information on Conrad Hayle, Martin Glazer and his brother Terry Glazer.' I switched off the machine. 'You'd better get someone working on that right away.'

Flanders face adopted a very serious expression. 'Just a word of advice, Jimmy. Don't get yourself killed.' He stubbed the cigar out in an ash-tray before it burst into flames. 'This assignment is far too impermanent. I don't want to have to appoint someone else to it if you died.'

'Thanks, Ted,' I returned sarcastically placing my hand over my heart. 'Your concern for my welfare gets me right here!'

I stormed out of his office slamming the door behind me. The man had a heart of stone. He was interested only in selling newspapers, making sure we held our market share. The rest of us was merely cannon fodder at his disposal. I had no intention of throwing my life away to please him and the readers. As I left the building, I thought about our conversation at length. Who the hell was Henry Jacobs and what was State Security? What was going on in Whitehall under the nose of the Prime Minister? Worst still, I had no leads. Miss Grayson appeared to be the only key to unlock the mystery. I had to go and see her. As I emerged from the elevator, her secretary looked up at me, recognising me from the previous visit.

'Mr. Savage,' she greeted with an icy tone in her voice. I presumed that she had been ordered to prevent me from entering Miss Grayson's office.

'I've an appointment with your boss,' I told her.

'Not possible!' she countered sharply. 'She's on leave. She won't be back until tomorrow.'

'That's not true, is it?' I challenged. 'She's in her office but you won't let me see her.'

She appeared genuinely upset by my accusation. 'Mr. Savage,' she uttered coldly. 'I'm not in the habit of telling lies. She's not in today!'

'Well there's only one way to find out,' I persisted, moving swiftly towards the office door and opening it. Needless to say, it was empty and I turned to face an irate secretary guarding the office jealously.

'Sorry,' I apologised with embarrassment. 'I must have confused the appointments in my diary.'

'I think you'd better leave this building before I call security,' she warned tensely.

'I want to use the telephone to ring Miss Grayson at home.'

'Mr. Savage!' she exclaimed unrelentingly.

I raised my hands in a form of surrender, making an attempt to mend my appalling behaviour with an amusing remark. 'All right, I'll leave, but don't think your attitude towards me will get you in my good books!'

She took the trouble to escort me off the premises and I hailed a taxi to take me to Miss Grayson's apartment.

'Hey, Guv!' called out the cabbie after we had gone a short distance. 'Didja know you're bein' followed? There's a red Austin be'ind that's tailin' us!'

I looked out of the rear window to stare at the pursuing vehicle. 'Are you sure?'

'No doubt about it, Guv,' he went on. 'Same route, Same streets. You're bein' tailed.'

I alighted outside Miss Grayson's apartment, paid off the cabbie, ignoring the red car which stopped a short distance away. It took me two minutes to discover that Miss Grayson was not at home so I removed my plastic card to gain entry. Everything was in apple-pie order. I sat on the bed thoughtfully and then my eyes fell on a locket similar to that worn by Tania which rested on the dressing-table. I opened it to reveal a photograph of herself as a young girl. Suddenly a red warning light flashed in my mind. There was something about it that troubled me. I felt that it contained a valuable answer... if only I could find the question!

As I left the apartment, a man wearing a dark raincoat and a broad-rimmed hat approached me with a request for a match to light his cigarette. I was about to reply when I felt an object sticking in my ribs which I presumed was a lethal weapon.

'Keep your mouth shut and get in the car!' he growled menacingly.

In that moment, the frustration of being abducted for a second time bent every fibre of my tolerance. He pushed me in the back seat of the red Austin, continuing to point the revolver at my head.

The driver started the engine and drove towards St. Katherine's Dock where I was blindfolded before leaving the vehicle. In a short while, I was led aboard a vessel which left the marina for an unknown destination. I stiffened with fright believing that they would put lead weights on my feet and toss me overboard into deep water. It needed to be only six feet deep! My heart began to beat faster as the motor stopped This was the moment of truth! I was pushed forward roughly and felt my feet touch terra firma. They were not going to drown me! I was led to a building that seemed like an aircraft hanger, due to the echoes that reverberated when the doors were closed. My hands were secured by ropes to a metal bracket secured in the wall and the blindfold was ripped from my face. My first impression was that I had been taken to a rifle range in the Surrey Commercial Docks. There were shooting targets set at positions either side of my head and I could see two men a short distance away loading pistols.

'Who are you?' asked one of the men, his voice echoing throughout the building.

I thought the question to be stupid. I mean why did they abduct me if they didn't know my identity? It didn't make sense!

'Who wants to know?' I demanded firmly although I didn't feel confident at the time. 'Why have you abducted me?'

The man placed a pair of ear-muffs over his head to deaden the noise before pointing his pistol at me. He released on shot which ricocheted off the wall causing me to wince.

'Who are you?' I repeated, bearing in mind that he couldn't hear me with the ear-muffs on. 'Why are you threatening me?'

He pointed the pistol at me again and fired three times at speed. The action was sufficient to terrify me.

'There are thousands of people joining International Three Thousand every month!' I shouted defensively. 'Why pick on me?'

'Why do you pursue Miss Grayson?'

These people were not using blank cartridges. It was necessary to think fast to offer responses to satisfy them. 'I met Miss Grayson only a few days ago at a meeting and... I fell in love with her...at first sight!' It was a very lame excuse but it was all I could think of under such pressure.

A shot rang out and blood spurted from a flesh wound just above my left elbow. They were beginning to get rough and I was the lamb to the slaughter.

'I fell in love with her!' I shouted in desperation as fear welled-up inside me. 'Is that a crime? I'm besotted with the woman!'

'Wer ist die Bankvorsteher?'

'I don't speak German,' I replied weakly. 'What are you saying?'

'Who is the bank controller?'

'Which bank controller are you talking about?' I rued the fact that I had told anyone that I worked in a bank.

'Not the bank you work for, you idiot!' returned one of the men. 'Die Bankvorsteher relating to Die Stunde.'

'I don't know what you're talking about,' I riposted, bearing in mind that I was tied to a wall with a gun pointing at my head. 'What's Die Stunde?'

'I'll give you five seconds to answer before I blow your head off,' returned one of the men, leaving me with no doubt with regard to my situation.

'Let me tell you, my friend,' I told him frankly. 'I have no intention of giving up my life for any person or organisation in this world. I know nothing of Stunde whatever it is. Nor do I know anything about a German bank controller. I can't tell you what I don't know and, if you don't believe that, then go ahead and shoot me!'

The two men gave each other a brief glance and one of them pointed his gun directly at me with deliberation. I stared at the muzzle prepared to meet my maker., closing my eyes as the shot rang out. I once read that a person who was shot would never hear the sound of it. I always wondered how they could come to that conclusion. They explained that it was the speed of sound against the rate at which the bullet travels to its target However I had heard the shot, therefore I was still alive!

The last bullet had cut through the ropes holding me and I managed to free myself. The men were gone and I could hear the sound of an engine fading away quickly in the distance. They must have believed me that I was unable to answer their questions. I had no idea why they should have put me through all that agony with regard to Miss Grayson. She clearly had a connecting link in the mystery.

I found a leaky old barge tied to a painter and slowly ferried myself to the northern shore of the Thames. Who were my abductors? They certainly didn't kill for the pleasure of the hunt or I would have been terminated. I examined my left arm, touching the injury most tenderly. It wasn't serious... the bullet had only nicked the skin and outer tissue before passing on.

It took me the best part of an hour to reach my apartment. I sat on the settee with relief after pouring myself a stiff drink. My hands were still shaking and there was a sharp pain in my head which I put down to shock. After a while, I fell asleep to be awoken by the ringing of the telephone. I reached out for the receiver believing that Miss Grayson had decided to make contact.

'I understand you wanted to see me,' she began in a smooth voice.

'There was something I wanted to ask you,' I returned trying to clear the cobwebs from my mind.

Her tone suddenly became waspish. 'Well…what do you want to ask me?'

'Not over the telephone. I think we should meet.'

'Can I trust you to keep an appointment?' she reproached strongly.

'Let's say eight o'clock this evening,' I suggested.

'I'm sorry,' she retorted. 'I've already made arrangements.'

'How about at your office then?'

'I'd appreciate it if you didn't go to my office again. You'll not be welcome there. Let's say eight o'clock tomorrow evening at my apartment!'

The line went dead as she hung up and I smiled to myself. Here was a woman who still bore the bruises from sexual activity with me in a shower cubicle and the best she could do was to start a sentence with the words: 'I'd appreciate it,' How did one cope with such a woman? I thought about her insistence to stop me from going to her office. However I decided that a closer look at the evidence in her desk was necessary, A plan of that nature was not only illegal but dangerous. If I was caught, I could hardly claim immunity as an industrial spy to attract a lesser degree of penalty in the Courts. They would throw the book at me yet it was a task which had to be carried out!

I took the opportunity to ring Conrad Hayle. A female voice answered to tell me that he was not available. I mentioned the recent invitation at the Assembly Hall and listened to the hoarse crackle of pages being turned over in a diary. Then the woman advised me of the date, the time, and the address of the party, informing me that she would add my name to the invitation list. I looked forward to the venue hoping that it would take me further down the road I was travelling... .not up the garden path! There were already enough indiscriminate red-herrings littering the way. It was time to be decisive and sort out the wheat from the chaff!

CHAPTER EIGHT

Many people consider burglars to be criminals who plunder the properties of victims at random... sometimes quite clumsily. It occurred to me that breaking into a building is a form of art not generally appreciated. Invading a public building which contained confidential files of the government, however, was another matter entirely. The penalties suffered on arrest and sentence by a Court in a situation of this kind were horrendous. An intruder needed to be endowed with nerve, courage, the ability to think quickly, sufficient reaction to move swiftly, and the capability of achievement in a short space of time. I couldn't match up to any one of those standards. If anything, I was a coward, fearful, deliberate in thought and slow in action... a person who tentatively blundered through life at his own preferred speed. Immodestly, I was smart in deduction, but that was like being able to complete a difficult crossword at leisure, which proved nothing!

I stood outside the building where Miss Grayson's office was located and familiarised myself with the movements of the reception staff. Some people had been issued with identification passes which they showed to the security guards at the reception desk as they entered, and they ventured forward to the lifts to go to respective parts of the building. Unfortunately, I didn't have a pass. The regular procedure would involve my name and address being entered in the visitor's book after which, for security purposes, someone would contact the person in the building I intended to visit. That was no good to me. I needed to obtain a pass so that I could enter without anyone taking further interest in my activities.

It was late in the afternoon when I decided to proceed with my plan. Many employees were beginning to leave the building. The security guards always faced a difficult period at this time because of the volume of people moving to the exits. However, this suited my purpose perfectly. I spurred myself into action as a number of people converged at the reception desk to make enquiries at the same time. Moving forward, trying not to draw attention to myself, I entered through the swing doors and walked past the desk without glancing at anyone. I deceived them beautifully by holding up one of my credit cards at a reasonable angle as though it were an authorised pass. In the flurry, I found myself standing at the lift doors without being apprehended and I wondered whether anyone had noticed me at all. I took the lift to a floor higher than Miss Grayson's office and hid in a small stationery store-room without a window. There was nothing for me to do than to sit on a stool in the far corner of the room and wait until all the staff and the cleaners had gone home. It was the only way to eliminate all risk of being detected. There was still the caretaker, whose job entailed that all windows and doors were closed and the lights were turned off and, of course, the night security officer An hour later, the caretaker arrived to carry out his duties. He opened the door of the store-room gently to peer inside before pulling it shut and locking it with a key on the chain he carried. Finally, he turned the handle to make certain it was secure and walked slowly away to his next port of call. It was all I could do to prevent myself from alerting him to the fact he had locked me inside the room. After he had gone, I slapped my leg with the flat of my hand in anger, trying to think a way out of my dilemma. My credit card wouldn't release the lock from the inside and the measures I took became more desperate as time elapsed, ranging from using letter-openers to prise open the door, which bent too readily, to twisting large paper-clips into unusual shapes in an effort to open the lock. In due course, I passed my hands across the top of the tall cabinets, searching for a large inflexible object to use as a lever, when something fell off and rolled at my feet. It was a wood-chisel left by a carpenter. I could only presume it had been sent to me by an angel. I began to chip away at the door until I had removed sufficient wood to allow it to open without the necessity of turning the handle. I was extremely annoyed with myself. Being trapped in a stationery store-room bore all the hallmarks of an exceptionally inept amateur!

I worked my way down the stairs quietly and proceeded along the lower corridor until arriving at the room of Miss Grayson's secretary. This time my credit card worked like a dream and I began to appreciate its true value... not only as a substitute security pass but also for the purpose of opening doors. I went to the inner room... Miss Grayson's office... and locked the door behind me before sitting at her desk and turning on a small table-lamp. The drawers were locked but I carried a simple set of skeleton keys which coped adequately and I rummaged through the drawers searching feverishly for something meaningful to advance the assignment. Shortly, I came across the computer disks I had seen before and turned on the computer. But there were other disks bearing code names... one with the letters DS. I became even more excited as I realised the import of the two letters. They were the initials of Die Stunde!

They had to be! My hands trembled as I pressed the keys on the console to reveal the information I needed so badly. My eyes followed the text eagerly to focus on the names of no less than fifty alleged Nazi war criminals and my eyes followed the text readily.

"The Weisenthal Centre in Los Angeles has identified those Nazi criminals who have settled in Britain. A dossier containing another forty names, provided mainly by Eastern bloc governments, have been compiled and is to be forwarded to the Director of Public Prosecutions. The Government has commented that, in order to prosecute alleged war criminals of the Second World War, it will be necessary to advocate legal changes in criminal law. At present there is no scope for anyone accused of war crimes to be tried in British courts. The Home Secretary is under pressure from Members of Parliament to bring justice or to expel any person suspected of having committed war crimes. There is a lobby which suggests that such a long time has passed it is only reasonable to forgive and forget, or that the criminals are so old by now the threat of imprisonment or death holds little fear. There is also the suggestion that it is not the war criminals themselves who are the danger to a democratic world but their children and grandchildren. Such offspring have been raised with the concept of a Master Race in mind. Some people may recall the effect of those teachings on the Hitler Youth movement. Such ideals still live on today in the offspring of those who caused the deaths of millions of innocent people, mostly by inhumane methods. The secret to the emergence of a movement likely to surface within the next decade lies in the financial base established during the Second World War. At that time, the Third Reach plundered art treasures, gold, silver and other valuable, from every country they occupied. In the past three decades, most of those treasures have been sold and the money invested worldwide. It is estimated that the funds available when Die Stunde arrives will amount to over fifty billion United States dollars."

The frustration began to build up inside me again. The information was stunning but it didn't tell me anything about Die Stunde... except for the odd term "when Die Stunde arrives"! I had assumed it was an organisation of some description. The data now led me to believe it was a stated time. But when, where, what, why? As my feelings began to subside, I thought about the fifty billion United States dollars in the kitty and wondered who controlled it. There had to be a treasurer somewhere who managed the funds. My blood froze as I reflected the words of my abductors that day. 'Wer ist der Bankvorsteher?

Who is the banker?' So that's what they meant! They were looking for him too! At least it gave me the opportunity to recognise who were the good guys and the bad ones. I had an inherent wish to join forces with the two men who used me as a target... although they might be criminals eager to get their hands on some of that money. But who was the banker? And from where did he operate? There were many questions flooding my mind. One of them in particular demanded an answer which could not be found. For what purpose were the funds going to be used?

I began to rummage through the drawers frantically, trying to find something substantial, but my time had run out. Unknown to me, the night security officer undertaking his routine inspection had noticed the reflection of light from the lamp as he traversed the hallway. He walked into the outer office, approached the door of Miss Grayson's office and turned the handle in vain before calling out to me.

'You can stay locked in there as long as you like, feller,' he shouted casually. 'I've already contacted the police.'

I weighed up the situation rapidly, assessing it as a canny poker player... a talent I had learned as a young cub reporter during the less busy periods of the newspaper business in my early days. His statement was unlikely to be true. When he saw the light, he would have investigated immediately to discover the door was locked. After all, the light may have been left on accidentally. He would never have called the police before checking out the situation. Of one thing I was certain. Had he telephoned the police, he would have waited for them to arrive before challenging me. He would never have risked his life in the process if they were on their way. It was time to fold my cards before losing out on the deal. I darted to the door, unlocked it quietly, pulled it open swiftly and rushed out at speed, knocking the security officer to the floor by the sheer impetus of the charge. I ran down the corridor to find the lift doors open. I hurried inside and released the switch to close them, sending the elevator to the ground floor. My heart thumped firmly in my ears as I reached the front door. It was only then I realised the major flaw in my plan. The door was locked! I had ignored the means by which I would make my escape from the building. However, I was fortunate because the key rested sweetly in the lock on the inside. Clearly, the rules for the security staff guarded against an onslaught from without. There were no proper measures taken to resist an enemy from within!

I locked the main door from the outside as I left and tossed the key far into the darkness before walking away from the building. At that moment, the wail of a police siren could be heard to cut through the night air. In a minute or so, police officers would reach the spot trying to gain entry to the building. They would be firmly denied. In the confusion, I would elude capture to pursue my enquiries. I hailed a passing taxi which took me back to the newspaper office where I found Ted Flanders scanning the proofs of the next day's edition. I walked in and he glanced up at me with an ugly scowl on his face, resenting the interruption.

'Don't you ever go home?' I asked him seriously.

'What for?' he snapped. 'There's no one to go home to!'

'Don't you ever relax or watch television? There's life after work, you know. Didn't anyone ever tell you?'

'When you read the news day after day, Jimmy, you realise what a horrible world exists out there. I'm much better off in here... even if it does get lonely at times!'

'Well,' I responded sadly, taking Miss Grayson's locket from my pocket, 'there's no fool like an old fool!' He shrugged showing his dislike of the cliche but it failed to arouse any other emotion within him. 'Can you get the boys to enlarge this photograph?' I continued. 'I want them to concentrate on the necklace around this woman's neck... in the picture. It may be nothing but I have a gut feeling.'

He took the locket and stared at it. 'Good looking woman. Who is she?'

'Miss Grayson. A technical adviser on defence matters.'

He stared at me for a moment and tossed it indelicately on his desk before picking up a folder. 'Research Department has been busy on your behalf,' he informed me. 'Is that what you've come back for?'

I sat down on one of the armchairs in his office and draped myself across it as he stood up and poured out two drinks from a bottle hidden in the bottom drawer of his desk. He passed one to me and we sipped them for a while until he opened the folder. 'What do you want first?' he joked. 'The bad news or the very bad news?' I shrugged aimlessly allowing him to continue at random. 'Sir Peter Cavenham is a highly-respected civil servant with an eminent appointment at the Home Office. There no need to go into details. You can look him up in Who's Who at your leisure. Henry Maitland is the Personal Assistant to the Prime Minister. He seems clean enough. Miss Linda Grayson is a civil servant with ten years of service who started off at the Ministry of Education before attaining promotion to the Ministry of Defence. We're having trouble with Lieutenant-Colonel Topham. He doesn't seem to hold office either in the civil service or in the official military lists. In effect, like Henry Jacobs and State Security, he doesn't exist.'

'Well I wasn't witness to a mirage, Ted, that's for sure. They were all at that meeting as large as life!'

He ignored my comment. 'There was nothing on Conrad Hayle, although they're still working on it. But the Glazers were tracked down to the name of Glazermann, a name of German extraction. They're working on that as well.'

The office fell silent for a while as he stared at me. I took another sip at my drink and thought about the information. There had been two people at the meeting in the House of Commons whom, I was informed, did not exist... and that was in the presence of the Prime Minister! What was going on?

'Can you get me a full run-down on the gold and treasures plundered by the Nazis between 1940 and 1945 from all the countries they occupied in Europe?'

'What for?' he asked without showing any emotion or surprise.

'Because it's important to the assignment, that's why! I want to know everything... especially the name of any person who might have been appointed to take charge of the loot.'

'Come on, Jimmy,' he cautioned. 'Do you know what you're asking? How can Research Department find out something that's remained a mystery for so many years? You're asking too much.'

'Why don't you let them try to find out? They might just turn over the right stones to discover something evil lurking underneath. That alone would be a scoop for the paper!'

Flanders appeared irritated by my persistence. 'Do you realise the cost of switching people in Research Department on to this kind of work?' he accused, as though I was wasting money recklessly. 'You're lucky you've got such a good-natured and understanding editor like me. I've got to answer to some very hard-nosed superiors when it comes to cost. A lot of others wouldn't let you do it.' He screwed up his eyes to look at me closely. 'Are you sure it's absolutely necessary?'

I allowed him to fall silent until deciding to try a new tack. 'Fifty billion United States dollars, Ted. How does that grab you? That's the kind of figure we're talking about. Nazi war treasures liquidated into cash and invested in various money markets, securities, bonds and currencies throughout the world.'

He took a large fresh cigar from the top drawer of his desk and slowly removed the tip with the blade of a pen-knife. I felt a tiny twinge of conscience as the person responsible for driving him back to the habit of smoking cigars again.

'Fifty billion dollars,' he muttered dryly. 'And I suppose you're trying to find the man who's in charge of all that money. The banker!'

I remained perfectly still but my eyelids flickered before I stared at his face. 'What do you say that?' I asked calmly, as my heart beat faster at his choice of words.

He puffed furiously at his cigar to make certain the end was burning brightly. 'Say what?'

'Der Bankvorsteher!' I returned quickly to test his reaction.

Der Bank... what?' he challenged in a puzzled tone. 'What the hell are you talking about?'

I reproached myself for believing that he was involved with the conspiracy, warning myself at the same time to calm my nerves and fears. The effect of the incidents of the past few days was beginning to make me paranoid. I was becoming suspicious of everyone. I needed to restore some semblance of order to my mind. Poor old Ted! He really didn't know what I was talking about. He always tried to keep one step ahead of his reporters but this time the water was way over his head and we both knew it. I left the office shortly afterwards to muse on my own problems. I took the view it was important to visit the Dog and Duck again to talk to Calvin. This time the newspaper would have to pay handsomely for his services but I reckoned it would be worth every penny... if he could deliver the goods!

I took a taxi to the old tavern in Backchurch Lane before it closed and bought a drink at the bar. Calvin sat on his usual stool pretending not to have noticed me. After a while, I edged across to him to start the process. 'Two things, Calvin,' I ventured hopefully. 'Die Stunde and Der Bankvorsteher. I need some answers fast. What can you tell me about them?'

He stayed poised on his stool for nearly half a minute without moving a muscle. The wheels of his mind, however, were grinding at a rate of knots as he swung his right arm automatically to guzzle a mouthful of beer. 'The information you want is going to cost you a bomb, Mr. Reporter,' he muttered softly. 'An absolute bomb. I hope you understand that.'

'Name your price,' I offered eagerly. The administrator of expense accounts at the newspaper would have had a fit if he could hear me now.

'Two thousand to start with. That's my price. And no bargaining!' He sounded very adamant but I knew Calvin better than most other people. He was a money-making machine in the field of information and no reasonable offer was ever turned down.

'Halve it and begin!' I negotiated in terms that he knew.

He looked at me with a dull expression on his face. 'Don't trade on brotherly love with me!' he insisted, taking a firm stance. 'I'm not bargaining on this one!' There was a long silence and then he decided to yield. 'Fifteen hundred but no less. That's my final offer!'

Another long silence prevailed as I feigned anguish at the price. 'Twelve hundred and that's cash in the bank, Calvin. What more do you want? Cash in the bank!'

The choice of words seemed to turn the tide for he nodded his assent. 'Okay,' he agreed quickly, ready to be that much richer in the space of a few minutes with no tax to deduct from the payment. Calvin offered information to everyone who was prepared to pay for it. The only institution with which he maintained total silence was the Inland Revenue.

'What's Die Stunde?' I asked, waiting impatiently for the answer, intending to get value for money.

'Comes to mind,' he began, with the same twang and intonation as W.C. Fields, 'that you've got it all wrong, my friend. It's not what, but when!' He paused for a while. 'Comes to mind, the hour is midnight on the first day of June.' He stopped for a moment to pass wind noisily, like the sound of an agitated seal, and I turned my head away at the foul stench emerging from the horrid man. 'Sorry about that,' he apologised, with complete absence of sincerity. 'I've got to pay a visit. Look after my stool, will you. I'll be back in five minutes.'

He slid off his seat and I watched him stagger under his great weight to the gentlemen's toilet at the far end of the bar. I concentrated on my aperitif thinking about the information he had given me. Die Stunde... midnight on the first of June! Why had that date been chosen? And what was going to happen then? How did Calvin manage to get the information? Unfortunately, destiny decided to play its own hand at that moment although I was unaware of the consequences. I waited for nearly ten minutes with frustration building up inside me. I wanted to know more... much more... and Calvin was willing to reveal it to me. I have no idea what motivated me to search for him but in my impatience I decided to go and find him. It wasn't very difficult because he lay dead on the floor in the toilet drenched in a pool of his own blood. There was a large metal stake protruding stoutly from his abdomen like a giant kebab skewer. All twenty-two stone of quivering flesh lay still and silent. I stared at the inert body with a sense of deep sadness, rueful that all the knowledge stored in that brain now lay fallow. Everything I wanted to hear was locked forever in his large head, or had been carried with his spirit to the next world. If he had rested on that stool for a little longer... just a few minutes more... I would have been that much wiser. Alternatively, if the call of nature had occurred later, Calvin might still be alive. My mind reverted back to the trial of Albert Henley. If his simple misdemeanours were considered grave... sinful enough to cause his death... what punishment would be inflicted on the person who offered information? After all, Calvin seemed to know some of the most innermost secrets of International Three Thousand and used them for capital gain? The big fat man knew all about the movement; there was no doubt in my mind about that! He didn't realise how dangerous it was, or that the information was too sensitive to handle. I returned to the bar to stare at his stool for the very last time. For a moment I could swear I could still see him sitting there, his right arm holding a glass of beer which he swung automatically towards his mouth. I could picture him saying: "Comes to mind, my friend... comes to mind..." and I made a hasty retreat before someone else found the body and called the police. There was no reason for my implication in the enquiries following his death. I was not a witness to the crime and I wouldn't be able to help them in any tangible way.

When I arrived home, I poured myself a stiff drink and sat on the settee blaming myself for not going earlier to see Calvin at the Dog and Duck. Had I gone with him to the toilet there, my own demise might have set the seal on a very imperfect day. It was better to count one's blessings and think nothing more of it. I swallowed some highly-proofed gin I had bought at an off-licence on my way home and felt a sudden urge to ring Tania. I had no idea why the call should be imperative but she had a right to learn of the arrangements concerning the party to which we had been invited by Conrad Hayle. Her voice sounded strange and halting which set me back a little. She had been so sweet and charming when we left the recruitment meeting, I felt there was an affinity between us... similar to the one shared with Carrie. After a brief one-sided conversation, I threw the receiver to the far side of the settee in disgust. Women were impossible at the best of times! Tania had given me the impression of being a very pleasant person. Now all the warmth and emotion was gone. Why should she react in that way towards me? I sipped my drink miserably, nursing an injured feeling, mainly because I had always praised my ability as a good judge of character. I had assessed her as a tranquil person with a depth of gentleness and passion. It was uncharacteristic for her to display coldness and indifference. There had to be a reason. I had to get round to her place to find out what was happening... hoping I wouldn't be too late!

There was another problem which concerned me greatly. Every detective or reporter knows that no person ever realises they're being followed... unless they suspect someone is tailing them in the first place. As I drove out of the car part underneath my apartment block, I noticed a dark car behind me. It was as I suspected. However, there was no time to shake off my pursuers in view of the exigency of my purpose, and I reached my destination shortly, parking outside the block of flats where Tania lived. As I climbed out of the car, the dark vehicle sped towards me without braking. I dived over the bonnet of my car to avoid being crushed and started to run towards the doors leading to the stairs which led to the apartments. The dark car turned swiftly, almost like a charging bull, and spurted towards me again. I rolled over on the ground scrambling behind another vehicle, wincing as my sharp elbows came into contact with the concrete. As I made further headway towards my planned escape route, there was the harsh sound of tyres screaming and the car turned swiftly, heading back towards me. This time, I lost my nerve to experience paralysis in all my limbs less than ten yards from the stairway. Fear overcame me and I was unable to move a muscle. Reporters are trained to assemble facts and write them into a form satisfactory to their editors and the public. They're not used to being hunted by predatory vehicles. My life didn't flash before my eyes partly because there was insufficient time for it to happen. In any case, my brain had seized up, anticipating the agonising pain at the point of impact. At the back of my mind, I heard a single, short, sharp report which sounded like a shot from a rifle and the dark car swerved before careering past me, missing my body by a whisker. It crashed into the concrete fence at tremendous speed, pushing its way through it to hurtle twenty feet downwards on to a broad strip of concrete which sported a large well-arranged rockery. I pulled myself together and hurried on to Tania's apartment. From outside the door I could hear the faint voice of a man inside. Then came the voice of another man, only this time it was far more menacing. Stepping back a few paces, I charged forward, lifting one leg to waist level which acted like a battering ram, and smashed open the door. As I entered, I took a martial arts stance and surveyed the scene. Tania was tied to a chair and the two men were showing her little chivalry in their quest for information. One of them lunged at me and I side-stepped before using his weight to carry out a simple throw. It was most unfortunate for him because the impetus carried him to the window ledge and he fell backwards, sailing out with the glass framework which smashed to smithereens on the concrete below. The other man, witnessing the fate of his colleague, decided not to press his luck and he raced past me to lose himself in the night.

'What happened?' I asked as I untied her.

She remained silent until I released her arms and she began to rub the soreness away. 'The doorbell rang and one of the men told me he was the new landlord wanting to talk to me about an increase in the rent. As I opened the door they charged in and tied me to the chair.'

'What did they want?' By this time, I had undone the ropes on her legs.

'Information about you.'

I rubbed her ankles and looked up into her eyes. 'About me?'

'They had a notion we worked together and that I knew all about you. When I didn't answer their questions they became very angry. Then, mercifully, you rang. I couldn't say anything to you for fear they would hurt me, but you realised something was wrong. How very clever of you!' She took my hands and pulled me towards her, kissing me fully on the mouth with the softest lips I had ever tasted. 'Should we notify the police?'

I tried to concentrate but the effect of the kiss made it difficult for me to focus my mind. 'The facts are that you've suffered a smashed door,' I began practically, 'which means that anyone can gain access. You have no security. Equally, there's a vacant window, which doesn't help matters at all. It looks like I'll have to stay the night to protect you... in case of further trouble.'

She laughed at my intentions. 'I must be honest with you,' she said sweetly. 'I've only one bed here and the couch isn't fit for a dog.

I shrugged my shoulders casually and kissed her on the lips. 'I'm sure we'll make out somehow,' I told her. 'We'll just have to rough it for tonight.'

The evening could have ended in sheer disaster for both of us. If things had been slightly different, the police would have questioned me on the death of Calvin and perhaps have charged me with manslaughter concerning the man who fell through Tania's window. They would have asked a multitude of questions for which I had very feeble answers. As it transpired, the man who fell through the window had not been badly injured. He was seen being helped into a car by the second man, albeit he was limping badly and appeared to have a broken arm. Tania was fortunate my suspicions were enough for me to rescue her. Who knows what might have happened to her at the hands of the two men! As luck would have it, I had the company of a charming, grateful and delightful female companion for one rewarding night. Beyond the bedroom, the absence of a front door and a missing window caused the apartment to become excessively draughty. But then, I mused to myself, it's an ill wind that blows nobody any good!

CHAPTER NINE

At first light on the following morning, I left Tania sleeping in bed, dressing quickly in the draught and dampness of the windowless lounge. I left the apartment without delay. She would be disappointed at my flight. However, there were a number of matters skimming through my mind and I had to get them out of my system. The first related to the car which tried to mow me down. It was almost like a nightmare and I had to pinch myself to check it had really happened. I proceeded to the rockery and gazed at the vehicle which was poised indelicately on top of a number of jagged granite rocks like the form of a giant sculpture. The vehicle was empty and I presumed that, apart from a sound shaking, those inside the car had escaped without serious injury. I scaled the rockery to examine the interior of the vehicle. There were stains of dried blood on the dashboard which led me to believe the driver's nose came into contact with the steering wheel at the moment of impact, as the vehicle careered over the edge of the car park. I was not a vindictive person, but the fact that the driver had suffered pain and discomfort in his attempt to murder me offered some kind of vengeful satisfaction. Even better, as far as I was concerned, he had failed in his task to kill me. As I recalled the moment when all my limbs became paralysed through fear and I faced instant death, I realised I couldn't find it in myself to turn the other cheek. I was left only with the impression of moments that should have been the final seconds of my life. The recall of the shot from a rifle echoed at the back of my mind, and I examined the tyres carefully. I discovered a neat round hole in the front off-side tyre which had been made by a bullet. It had penetrated the tyre, causing it to burst, so that the vehicle veered away from me at the most critical moment. I was grateful it had happened but there was even greater comfort to know that someone out there was taking care of my welfare. I had no idea who that person might be, but I didn't mind in the least if my fairy Godmother, or Godfather, carried a rifle instead of a magic wand. After all, survival was the name of the game!

A buff envelope rested on the mat in my apartment when I opened my front door. The mandarins at Whitehall had been working like gnomes in the night for the letter was delivered some time between the hours of midnight and dawn. A small thought pervaded my mind that the messenger may have known I was occupied elsewhere. This gave ground to the possibility I was under surveillance all the time. I shrugged off the idea, ridiculing the notion that a mere newspaper reporter should be accorded such elevated importance which could never be justified. I was simply a tiny cog in an exceptionally large wheel, uninvolved with the charade of spies, undercover agents and the like. Why should anyone be remotely interested in my work except for my editor and the owners of the newspaper?

Inside the envelope nestled a note from Maitland set out on plain paper, scribbled in ball-point pen. He didn't define his capacity as Personal Assistant to the Prime Minister, but merely requested my presence at the House of Commons at ten o'clock that morning. I wondered what would have happened had I stayed with Tania. Presumably, someone would have contacted me at nine o'clock on her telephone to pass on the summons personally. No doubt, I was being watched all the time! What could Maitland want to say to me at this early stage of the game? Perhaps the Prime Minister had changed his mind about my involvement and wanted me to drop the investigation. An order of that magnitude would hardly go down well with Ted Flanders who was already champing at the bit for a major scoop. I realised I could drive myself insane trying to fathom out the reason for the summons. My best course of action would be to make myself a hearty breakfast and meet the man at the House of Commons with an open mind.

I caught a taxi there, leaving my car in the garage to avoid being caught up in the massive flow of traffic towards the centre of London, and asked for Maitland when I arrived there. A uniformed attendant led me though a maze of corridors to a small well-furnished wainscoted room, rich in the smell of wood varnish. I sat in a comfortable armchair reading the newspaper I had brought with me, admiring the work of some of my colleagues in the latest edition while a large clock on the mantelshelf of an ornate hearth ticked away with monotonous regularity. It was almost ten-thirty before the door opened and Maitland appeared. By that time, I had read the newspaper twice and almost finished the crossword.

'I apologise profusely!' he declared, feigning the expression of a young boy caught stealing apples. 'The exigencies of the day have been such that our agenda is stretched to the full. Please forgive the delay.'

'What do you want to see me about?' I asked impatiently, cutting to the chase.

'The Prime Minister would like a brief word with you,' he replied flatly. 'He'll be here in a moment.'

In a flash, he left the room, leaving me on my own. It had to be important summoned here... for the Prime Minister to speak to me... something more grand than to be told to drop the assignment. I didn't mind if they wanted to end it. It would be a relief to be given another task by Ted Flanders... something within the normal confines of human nature... something where people would resist the temptation of trying to kill me. I stood up waiting for the great man to arrive. If only my father could see me now, I thought, he might have respected my insistence to become a newspaper reporter. It was his wish, before he died, for me to become professional in law or finance. He strongly resented, in his own words, "my desire to waste my life as a hack for some damned daily rag!" Little did he realise my calling would bring me into contact with such eminent people... practically the highest in the land. Shortly, Maitland opened the door again to allow the Prime Minister to enter.

'Sit down, Mr. Savage,' invited the senior politician, taking another chair as his Personal Assistant left the room. 'I regret having to bring you here at such short notice but information on the matter we discussed earlier is urgently required. Are you able to offer anything of value?'

I sat down opposite him, trying to gather my thoughts cogently. 'I've become a member of International Three Thousand,' I revealed confidentially, 'and I hope to be able to report something useful in a few day's time. There are some side issues in which you may be interested.' I paused for a moment nursing a horrific notion that the person to whom I was about to offer information might not be the Prime Minister at all. No... it was too absurd that an imposter would invite me to the House of Commons. Yet it had happened in relation to Henry Jacobs and Lieutenant-Colonel Topham. Ostensibly, they didn't exist! 'A number of people have been killed over the past few days in connection with this assignment. Indeed, there have been four attempts on my own life. It transpires that a date known as Die Stunde has been set for the first of June although I'm not certain yet of its inference. Secondly, I'm desperately seeking Der Bankvorsteher... the banker... a person handling funds amounting to fifty billion United States dollars accumulated from the sale of Nazi war treasures. I understand the funds have been invested in markets and currencies all over the world.'

The Prime Minister listened intently without showing surprise or emotion. 'Do you have any further details?' he asked quietly.

'Not at present. There's a lot of mystery, but I'll find out in due course.'

He glanced at the clock on the mantelshelf as though pressed for another appointment. 'Do you have anything else to tell me?'

I paused once more and then decided to express my concern about his welfare. 'Yes, there is,' I went on, as my heart beat loudly in my ears. 'I think you may be in great danger yourself. My research indicates that the person you know as Henry Jacobs doesn't exist... nor does the agency known as State Security. The same applies to Lieutenant-Colonel Topham. I presume you're aware of their infiltration because you've chosen to talk with me directly rather than communicate through Miss Grayson.'

He stood up and walked to the door. 'Thank you for your helpful comments, Mr. Savage,' he said, with a brief smile touching his lips. 'I regret you found yourself in danger, but the excellent work you're doing for your country is much appreciated. I hope you will continue with your efforts. If you wait here I'll arrange for Maitland to see you out.'

He opened the door and departed. The man seemed genuinely sympathetic towards me, but that may have been the reason why he was elected to his eminent position... he was sympathetic and grateful to everyone. Maitland appeared almost instantly. 'The P.M. is very pleased with you,' he told me politely, although I came to the conclusion that he made the same comment to practically everyone.

'I attended the meeting here the other day,' I began, digging for information. 'Did you convene it?' He nodded, giving me the impression he was in a particular haste to be elsewhere. 'I've been trying to get in touch with Henry Jacobs. He offered to lend me support with his man... Mr. Gates. Do you know where I can find him?'

'I'll see what I can do,' he replied diplomatically, showing no sign of hesitation or emotion at the request. 'Now, if you'll follow me, I'll take you to the exit.'

To his irritation, I decided to thwart his attempt to oust me from the building. 'Before I go, there's a favour I want to ask you,' I pressed. A small twitch of annoyance appeared on his face as I placed him under pressure again. 'May I look at the books in your main library? As a newspaper reporter I have few opportunities to attend the House of Commons. I would take it as payment in lieu of my services.'

He thought about it for a moment and then conceded. 'Very well,' he replied tiredly. 'I'll get someone to take you there.'

He left the room and I waited until a uniformed attendant arrived to lead me to the library. He left me there when I told him I would see myself out of the building. After he had gone, I travelled along the corridors until reaching the room where the initial meeting had been held. Inside, I sat down on a chair and looked round the room slowly. It was real, and all the people there had been real. I recalled the words of Carrie when she was boasting about the excellent work of Jack Berg. He had fooled a Nazi war criminal by taking him to an ordinary room adjoining the Crown Court which had been set up to represent an authentic Court-room. The judge, jury and the public had been actors employed to carry out the charade to obtain the information required. I questioned whether something similar had happened in this room on the day I was abducted. Members of the public were not normally carried off to the House of Commons to be given dangerous assignments for their country. Or were they? Had I been introduced to a world of make believe far beyond the run of the normal citizen? And why were people in attendance who didn't exist in the annals of the Civil Service or the Military List? Even more intriguing was the fact that they focussed their attention on a newspaper reporter. What did they really want with me? And why should the Prime Minister seek a private interview with me when Miss Grayson was the person responsible for passing information directly to him and the other members of the committee. It didn't make sense... and it left me in no man's land!

I made a mental note that if I managed to survive long enough to write my memoirs I would record that the life of a reporter was often the loneliest in the world. Secrecy had to be maintained at all time, not only to preserve the assignment but also to screen it from competitor reporters. In addition, one was bullied, harassed and hounded by editors and interviewees into the bargain. At that moment, a shaft of inspiration seared through my brain and I thought of a new tack which would set the newspaper alight. The main problem was to present it in such a manner that Ted Flanders believed he had formulated the idea himself. It was the only way to get the story into print! I returned to the office and sat waiting for Flanders to finish a telephone call. After replacing the receiver, he picked up a half-smoked cigar and started puffing on it, choking on the smoke in the process.

'What are you doing here?' he growled, wiping his mouth as dribble eked out of the end of the cigar. 'I put you out on assignment and you end up spending most of your time here. This isn't a holiday camp, you know. Go out and get some news!'

'I need some more research, Ted,' I told him bluntly. 'It relates directly to the assignment.'

'Not more research!' he complained bitterly. 'What's it this time? Looking for the man in the moon or trying to find Noah's ark?'

I shrugged off the sarcasm calmly. 'What do you know about the children and grandchildren of dedicated Nazi leaders and senior officers... starting with people like Goering, Himmler, Borman, Goebbels, and so on?'

He stared at me for a while without speaking and I wondered whether he had fallen asleep with his eyes open. Eventually, he shifted in his seat, puffed his cigar, waved the clouds of smoke away from his watering eyes and coughed a few times. 'What are you after?' he muttered.. 'A lot of gaps exist in the records. Too many. But Research might come up with something interesting. They might at that.' A serious expression crossed his face as he began to develop his thoughts. He was taking the bait. I could have blurted out the means by which he could achieve a fantastic scoop if Research Department managed to produce the essential data, but I had to allow it to ferment gradually in his mind.

'Hey, I've had a terrific idea!' he exclaimed excitedly, applauding himself for the effort. 'If we track down the sons and grandsons of the Nazis and beard the bastards in their dens...' He tailed off as his eyes lit up from the vision of millions of newspapers being sold containing the scoop. 'I can see it now! Where are they... the sons and grandsons of that awful regime? What are they doing? Are they affected? Are they following in their fathers/grandfathers footsteps? It would make a great series, Jimmy. You follow my lead and you'll do all right, boy!' He puffed furiously on the cigar, lost in his own imagination. 'We can run it over a period of two weeks in the daily editions... and as a five-part serial in the Sundays. It could have a tremendous impact.' He bobbed up and down in his chair with excitement. 'Better still! The other newspapers will lose their lead time. We'll be a month ahead of them with the research at least. I knew this assignment would bear fruit the moment I gave it to you!'

I was less than enthusiastic at his euphoria, and the prospect of the assignment being revealed to the public at large. Admittedly, in normal circumstances, I would have been just as excited, but these were not normal times. It was the only way I could get Flanders to allocate more staff to undertake research on my behalf. And it worked! As far as the story was concerned, the government would issue 'D' notices to prevent it being published, but Ted didn't think of that. I had some strong views about International Three Thousand, and my instincts led me to visualise its type of power source and control. But there were many details which baffled me, as well as a number of people whose roles were still enigmatic. If Ted Flanders could flush out people like Harry Kirk, who had the debatable honour of being Himmler's grandson, and established their whereabouts, I was on my way to cracking the assignment with flying colours. It was important to recognise, however, that the investigation into a revolutionary cause of a handful of anarchists seeking absolute power in Europe was not a red-herring. It threatened European governments and masked a different motive. Germany had gone to war against the world on two separate occasions in the twentieth century and had lost on both counts. Its teeth had been drawn the second time when it was divided into the Federal German Republic and East Germany to prevent it re-enacting its nationalistic ideals again or perpetrating crimes against other countries, races or creeds. Now Germany had reunited... the giant was about to awake. The ideal of national socialism... Nazi fascism... did not die at the end of World War Two... it was merely laid to rest temporarily. The ancestors of many leading Nazis now had the means to regroup in modern style, using International Three Thousand as its spearhead to gain control of Europe. That was its initial aim... domination of Europe. In due course, it would aim to dominate the world. Germany had lost in two world wars; it would win successfully without casualties in the peace. Supporting it, were the funds stemming from the sale of Nazi war treasures. If the facts were known, they would not make comforting thoughts for those who fought to establish democracy against fascism, or those people who lost loved ones in the conflict. I knew there and then it was my role to root out these fanatics to prevent misery, bloodshed and tyranny. Because one thing was certain... once they achieve domination they would rule Europe more fiercely than any known dictator or tyrant known to the world since time immemorial!

'By the way,' advised Ted, bringing me back to reality. 'The Science Lab have done the job you wanted. The photograph you gave me. The one in the locket.' He opened a drawer in his desk and handed the enlargement to me before placing the locket on the desk.

I stared at the lovely face of Miss Grayson in her earlier years and focussed my attention on her necklace. Something in the photograph attracted my attention and it soon became apparent it was an emblem I recognised... the Star of David!

'What's so significant about that?' commented Flanders. 'Thousands of people of the Jewish faith wear them in this country. You can buy them in most jewellery shops.'

'Indeed!' I returned as a matter of form. 'But this one might have further implications. I need to investigate.'

'Well, if it's personal, I'd be grateful if you did it in your own time. Remember the newspaper pays good money for business not personal situations!' He puffed on his cigar again, obviously pleased with himself in the expectation of a scoop.

I stood up and went to the door of the office leaving the photograph but taking the locket which I placed in my pocket. I had a strong urge to be spiteful to Flanders in retaliation for all the flak he fired at me, but I thought better of it and preserved my dignity. Why should I let him feel I had slipped to his level! On reaching the street, I filled my lungs with fresh air to expunge the ugly stench of cigar smoke, concentrating my thoughts on the delectable Linda Grayson. It was possible that she too was an Israeli agent who had managed to infiltrate the Civil Service and establish herself in a senior position. She was a technical adviser on defence to Lieutenant-Colonel Topham who didn't exist. Maybe he was an agent of some foreign power as well. And Henry Jacobs. That sounded a Jewish name too. What about him? The Prime Minister could be living in a snake-pit surrounded by enemies of the State, or people who nurtured interests counter to the welfare of the United Kingdom. Each time I considered the matter, I felt more like a minor pawn in the game. After all, the nation employed its own intelligence agency. How come such unwarranted situations were in evidence?

At eight o'clock that evening I called on Miss Grayson and rang the doorbell. She seemed surprised to see me, having firmly believed I would let her down again.

'I would have made dinner for both of us,' she informed me, 'but your past record in failing to keep appointments didn't stimulate me to do so.'

'That's understandable,' I agreed tersely.

She invited me inside and poured out two sherries before springing open the conversation. 'I believe there are things we have to say to each other.' She handed me a glass, with an unfriendly expression on her face before sitting in an armchair.

'Really,' I returned quietly. 'Well you start first.'

'My office was broken into last evening. Do you have any ideas on that score?' She used her tone as a form of accusation. There was no doubt in her mind that I was the culprit.

'Someone broke into your office?' I returned, feigning innocence. 'How would I know anything about that?'

'Because you're the only person who seems to be interested in the computer files in my desk.' It was clear her tolerance was fusing at low point.

'Then, with respect, I'm the most unlikely suspect,' I told her, playing a cat-and-mouse game. 'Who would do such a fool thing if they were under suspicion? In any case, how do you know I'm the only person interested in your files? How do you know the intruder wasn't after something else... or perhaps in the wrong office?'

'Do you deny it?' she persisted, driving home the question at point-blank range.

'Of course I deny it!' I lied. 'You know as well as I do there could be a dozen people interested in what you might have. Why does it have to be me?'

Her face indicated displeasure at my response and she was obviously less than satisfied with my answer. I wondered about her reaction had I admitted the felony. It would have been interesting to find out but I couldn't afford the luxury of being honest for fear of arrest and imprisonment.

'I believe you gained access to the building and rifled my desk!' she accused, tiring of the silly game.

I stared at her lovely face, trying to make up my mind what to say. 'If you're wrong... and I can prove you're wrong ... I demand a forfeit. What kind of forfeit would be worth a false accusation of trespass and burglary?'

'As well as damaging property and assaulting a security officer!'

My hands were free from marks or blemishes and I held them out towards her. 'Do these look like the hands which assaulted a security officer or did damage to property? In any case, I can prove I was with my editor all last evening.'

She dispensed with the break-in and returned to mundane matters. 'I presume you came here to provide information for the committee. What have you to tell me?'

I was grateful she let the burglary drop. She would still have her doubts but without proof there was little point in continuing to press her claim. 'I'm not sure what's going on,' I told her frankly. 'This morning I was summoned to the House of Commons by the Prime Minister who asked me for the latest details. Doesn't that strike you as strange?'

'Not necessarily. The P.M. often requires information urgently.'

'You're a technical adviser on defence. What do you know about Lieutenant-Colonel Topham?'

'He's head of Special Services at the Department of Defence.'

'That's interesting,' I continued. 'He doesn't seem to exist. Nor does Special Services!'

'Don't think you're the cat that got the cream. Many agencies exist in the Civil Service and the military which are not listed for security reasons.'

My eyes scanned her face. 'Do you mean to tell me there are military sources in this country no one knows about?'

'And a few civil ones. Don't get frenetic about it,' she laughed. 'Every country has them!'

'Well you could have fooled me,' I countered, appalled at the measures taken at the highest level of politics. 'Do we really have to adopt such methods to remain civilised?'

'I don't know why you fuss,' she replied coolly. 'Human-beings are quite prepared to annihilate each other with arsenals of horrific weapons. All the major powers admit to storing nuclear missiles... for the purpose of retaliation only, of course! I think you ought to learn to live in the real world, Mr. Savage!'

'I'm beginning to wish I didn't,' I commented, deciding to change the subject. 'How about dinner at a decent restaurant near the Tower of London?'

To my surprise, she assented readily and we left for The Samuel Pepys which had always been one of my favourite haunts. The meal was sumptuous and we talked of art and literature, avoiding being drawn into any discussion relating to her work or mine. After we arrived back at her apartment, she turned into a well-rehearsed hostess, plying me with drinks and then suggested we watch a programme on television in her bedroom. We removed our clothes and settled down full-length on top of the bedclothes. She leaned across and kissed me gently on the lips and I returned the favour, taking her into my arms. Suddenly, I felt her nails tear deeply into the flesh of my upper arm causing a substantial amount of pain.

'Hey!' I called out in alarm. 'What are you doing?'

'You broke into this apartment, didn't you!' Her nails went deeper and the suffering made me open my mouth in agony.

' Yes, yes!' I admitted in haste. 'But how did you know it was me?'

'Your after-shave, you dope! It lingered. What did you steal from me?'

'Only your locket. The one with the photograph inside. It's in my jacket pocket.'

She withdrew her nails, showing no empathy at the blood oozing from the wounds. 'Why did you steal the locket?'

'Not steal... borrowed. There was something about the photograph which drew my attention.'

'Such as what?'

'Such as the Star of David you wore round your neck when it was taken.'

She seemed to freeze where she lay on the bed. 'What's so strange about that,' she continued, with a strange hollow sound in her voice.

'I'm assuming you're an Israeli agent who infiltrated the Department of Defence. Why do you people do it?'

She burst into laughter and shook her head in amusement. 'You're precious!' she grinned. 'I come from Jewish stock. There's nothing wrong with that. Many people in the Civil Service are of the same faith.'

'The last Israeli agent I knew died earlier this week. I'd only known her for a couple of days.'

'Will you stop inferring I'm an Israeli spy!' She was beginning to get angry and I could see no margin in seeking to force her into submission.

'How about my forfeit?' I asked amiably, changing the subject.

'After you've cleaned off the blood,' she said, cooling off quickly. 'I suggest you take a shower.'

I recalled the last occasion I had taken a shower at the apartment, remembering the experience was delightful. If I made a mental note that Miss Grayson sometimes showed her claws, our relationship could still develop into one of pleasure. I entered the cubicle and turned on the water until it reached the correct temperature, harbouring the hope I wouldn't be in there alone for very long... and I wasn't disappointed.

CHAPTER TEN

I worked solidly in the Research Department of the newspaper for nearly two hours trying to absorb as much information as my brain would allow. It was the first time I had laboured in that area for years. The newspaper's researchers didn't consider it unusual for reporters to become involved personally, however, they didn't expect them to do it so fiercely or intensely. The main task concerning any story surrounded certain basic facts which had to be written in a fashion suited to the newspaper's policy and its effort to inform the public. By custom it needed to relate true facts as well as to adopt bias or prejudice according to the Chief Editor's political principles. For that reason, research was a dedication which couldn't be ignored. A reporter could easily write surface news which happened day by day... most of which came over the 'teleprinter' anyway. But assignments of an esoteric nature necessitated digging deeply beforehand. The staff in Research Department generally undertook the delving; on this occasion the exception proved the rule. If I failed to research properly there was a distinct possibility my life would be in danger again. Either that or my progress would be inhibited. If my plan was to succeed, when I attended the party thrown by Conrad Hayle and his cronies, my understanding of their motives and the way I conducted myself had to be perfect in every detail. It was going to be the only opportunity to cut the Gordian Knot to ensure my induction as one of the pack. I had no idea how I was going to achieve that aim. I would have to act on instinct and impulse, keep a low profile, and speak only when spoken to. In order to do that effectively, it was vital for me to learn every detail about the Nazi regime from alpha to omega. Once the information was lodged in my mind, the next step involved my performance in the company of wolves later that day. The strategy was firmly fixed in my mind: unfortunately, it was the tactical plan which proved to be the problem. I was one of those lucky souls with the ability to let an enigma run wild in my head and draw a satisfactory conclusion in due course without a great deal of effort. In the past, most problems were resolved overnight in my head, and I would wake the following morning cognisant of a clear-cut solution... having worked it all out in my sleep. I couldn't afford the luxury this time because too much was happening so quickly. It was no use blaming myself because the research had been left far too late.

At this point, I was feeling very tired, especially as Miss Grayson and myself had been unable to get to sleep until the very early hours of the morning. She was a tigress in bed! Additionally, two hours of research and study in preparation for the party that evening did even less to raise my spirits or inspire me to feel on top of the world. Without sufficient sleep I was wearing myself down, like a battery losing its power. I went for a short walk and had a quick meal at a fast-food restaurant, returning home to splice the mainbrace with the rest of the gin. After that, I fell asleep on the settee leaving all the cares of the world far behind me.

It was three hours later when the telephone rang. Berg was at the other end of the line.

'I've got a lead for you,' he told me gratuitously. 'A great lead!'

I tried to focus my mind and muttered something incoherently into the mouthpiece.

'But you'll have to come with me to Germany,' he continued. 'I hope you can convince your newspaper to pay for both our fares and expenses.'

I screwed up my eyes to look at my wristwatch. 'Germany?' I repeated hoarsely. 'What are you talking about? Why do we have to go there?'

'I'll tell you all about it when I see you. How soon can you be ready?'

'Hold your horses!' I shouted down the line, with a dull feeling that told me I was returning to the real world. 'Whenever you ring me we end up with some disaster. Are you one of those accident-prone people? I mean, does it happen to you all the time?'

'I don't understand,' he countered, sounding puzzled.

'You don't understand! My God! First there was Carrie's death... then the chase in the docks... then Hymie's death and someone shooting at me with a rifle at the cemetery! Since then I've been abducted and shot at! What next, Mr. Berg? What next?'

He didn't seem to be put out by my bleating, shrugging it off without effort. 'If you want to accumulate, Mr. Savage, you have to speculate,' he replied philosophically. 'We're in a very volatile business, clearing up the dregs of a society which slaughtered millions of helpless innocent people without being consciously affected themselves. If that's too hot for you, you ought to get out of the kitchen!'

I began to realise I could least afford to turn him down if he did have a further lead. It meant placing my head in a noose again... a thought I didn't relish... but that was routine procedure as far as Jack Berg was concerned. It had become part of the rich tapestry of my life. 'All right, I'll go to Germany with you, providing you can give me sound reason for doing so, but I can't make it today. I need more space.'

He made an odd noise at the other end of the line in a token of annoyance, almost as though he had just bought airline tickets to leave immediately, and paused to adjust his plan. 'Very well,' he said shortly. 'But only a few days. I can't leave it too long or I'll lose the thread of it. Give me a ring when you're ready.'

The line went dead without warning. There was little doubt he regarded the matter as urgent... whatever it was. I shook the rest of the sleep from my head as I flung the telephone to the far end of the settee before starting to question his motives. Why did he want me to travel with him to Germany? Berg always worked on his own. Suddenly he needed my companionship. Why should he want me to go with him? And how hot was the lead? Did it warrant chasing half-way across Europe? It was amazing how the man always managed to aggravate me even when he was trying to be helpful... or was he? I couldn't forget how he had helped me dispose of Carrie's body that night for shipment to Israel, only for me to learn she was being buried in Britain. In his particular case, very few parts of the jig-saw seemed to fit at all.

I collected Tania at eight o'clock that evening from her apartment. She was looking radiant in a stunning outfit, having embellished her natural beauty with a delicate application of expensive make-up, a modicum of alluring perfume, and an excellent hair-do which proved to be a masterful exhibition of tonsorial artistry. The ugly scene in her apartment was forgotten for the moment, even though she sported some nasty bruises about her body which I noticed during our intimacy in the draughty apartment that night. They didn't seem to trouble her at all.

'Where did you get this morning?' she asked, with an amused expression in her eyes. 'I looked all over the bed but I couldn't find you.'

'This early bird catches the worm,' I related enigmatically. 'Some of us have work to do, you know.'

'In that case,' she chided sweetly, 'you shouldn't spend so much time at play.'

We continued to banter conversation until I hailed a taxi which took us to the appointed place. This time it wasn't the Assembly Hall in the East End of

London but a large private house in Islington. In the past, the property had been owned by a wealthy doctor who had maintained servants and domestic help. Later, I learned that when he sold it, a nominee had been entered in the deeds of the property for the purpose of anonymity.

We walked through the portals, which comprised a number of Corinthian columns supporting a balcony, to arrive at a large open door guarded by three bully-boys. Hesitantly, I mentioned that we were guests of Conrad Hayle and a scrutineer examined a guest list carefully before marking crosses against our names. Then the path cleared and we walked the length of the massive hallway before being ushered into a large crowded room furnished with tables laden with victuals. A number of people were wearing the black uniforms I had seen before, with fulgurously-designed armbands, and jackboots. The rest wore formal or informal clothing. They tended to congregate in groups of six to eight people, talking to each other seriously, and drinking well in an attempt to capture some kind of fraternal spirit. Tania and I hovered in the background where we were handed cocktails, and we stared at the groups in isolation feeling totally out of touch with the situation. Neither of us knew anyone in the room and there was the likelihood we would spend the time by ourselves without making any contact whatsoever. It would be just my luck to end the evening exactly where I had started... without a lead... without making any progress at all! My conclusion was reinforced by the fact that Tania and I were total strangers. We stood uncomfortably at the back like two lepers in society, sipping our cocktails slowly without a hope of penetrating any one of the groups in the room. We smiled at each other weakly, aware of our predicament, and continued to regard our prospects as dim for some time. Then Conrad Hayle espied us from a distance and left one of the groups. He approached with a broad smile on his face.

'I'm so glad you could come, Mr. Savage,' he greeted amiably. 'Let me introduce you to some of our colleagues!'

He took my arm and led me to a group which included Harry Kirk. Tania followed and we listened to a flawed discourse on national socialism expounded by an extremely young man in a black uniform. Suddenly, I realised this was the moment I'd been waiting for... my chance had come even though I was totally unprepared to take advantage of it. I felt like an actor who hadn't learned his lines, finding himself thrust on to the stage as the curtains opened for the first act, to face a large hostile audience.

'I don't agree with you!' I blurted out, to the astonishment of the other members of the group... and also to myself! 'You seem to bear the false impression that national socialism has developed to a degree far beyond its original concepts.' I hesitated to gain everyone's full attention. 'Never forget that the basis of our ideals don't emerge from a corruption of the doctrines fundamental to our national background, because change is not necessarily infinite. If you gnaw at the edges of specific tenets without question, one or more different trends will occur to alter the earlier patterns beyond recognition, until you create a monster totally unfit for any purpose. It's essential to revert to the original ideas through Fichte, Hegel, Nietzsche and Spengler. Otherwise, you're talking through your hat and, in addition, destroying the natural development of our cause.'

They were all staring intently at me by now, including some members of other groups who started to join us. I was uncertain whether my outburst made me look a fool or a rebel, but the research I had conducted that very morning was beginning to focus in my brain, enabling me to churn out tracts of texts, none of which really interested me. The important thing was for myself to believe what I was saying... even if it was only for the moment!

'This is Mr. Savage, a banker,' announced Hayle, introducing me to the enlarging circle. 'He's one of our latest recruits who delivered a short speech on his initiation which impressed us all. I had no idea he knew anything about national socialism.'

I decided it was time to play one of my highest trumps, particularly because Kirk was listening. 'My real name is Erdbeer,' I declared.

'Erdbeer?' laughed a man in a plain tweed suit, before the others followed with mirth. Perhaps I shouldn't have been surprised that they all spoke German.

'Yes, Erdbeer,' I repeated. 'It means strawberry. I'm not quite sure of the derivation. Some people consider it may have come from a strawberry fool, but no one knows. I certainly don't feel a fool... or a strawberry.'

There was laughter all round at my amusing comment after which Kirk eyed me from head to toe. 'A banker... of German stock, eh?' he began. 'Why don't you tell us more about your views on national socialism?'

This was the big chance I had been waiting for. It was important for me to focus all the attention within my power on an oration of some magnitude. If I failed, Ted Flanders would flay me alive for missing the opportunity. I thought of him at that moment as an irritable chimpanzee waving his arms wildly and leaping about, babbling foul language if I came to a halt in this assignment. It was sufficient to goad me into doing my very best and I stepped into the limelight. 'Well, as everyone knows, national socialism became a profoundly revolutionary movement, although it happened mostly in a negative sense. It's now a matter of historical record to define it rejected rationalism, the rule of law, and human rights. In effect, the replacement of such elementary features of weak government included the encouragement of instinct, arbitrary authority, and subordination of the individual to the State. Most people who define themselves as democrats are appalled at these facets of rule mainly because they themselves develop traits of self-indulgence which detracts from a cohesion of effort within the State. Democracy creates egoistic casual attitudes, laziness, waste and anti-State aggression!' I stopped for effect... and breath... and began to remonstrate strongly with my arms to give my words more emphasis. It was also the way their Fuehrer acted in the 1930s and 1940s. 'National socialism seeks to purge competing political, religious and social institutions which drive a stake through the heart of a nation. It's often also necessary to suppress them. The singular purpose of the common man is spread in a variety of directions causing division and segregation by random person choice. Such actions erode the will of mankind in general as we have seen so often in the past. Which one of you hasn't been pressed by several political organisations, each of which has developed its own brand or style to inflict on an unsuspecting and trusting public? The usual harassment at General Elections! A few years later, other parties become elected to change those policies to the detriment of the State, and this chaos continues indefinitely. Which of you hasn't been sought out by specific religious bodies, each one claiming a new dawn or a different path to heaven? In all truth, what value are such people or religious organisations to our society at large? No my friends, the doctrine of national socialism rejected Christian and humanitarian ethics quite rightly because they were regarded as inhibitive to State rule. In their place, an ethic of reality was advanced, to show meaning to our existence in a world deteriorating all around us. It destroyed distinctions between social class, drawing in people from all social classes. And why not? National socialism has a true value in offering every person a chance to establish themselves within our midst. Certainly it's revolutionary in its methods of coercion and mass manipulation. Every army is governed by its leader... not from its ranks. And why shouldn't it use propaganda through all cultural and information media?'

The young man in the black uniform clearly felt aggrieved at my challenge, and he made a brave attempt to save his face, intending to do so to the point of self-destruction. 'I disagree,' he countered, embittered that his thunder had been stolen by a stranger in formal clothing. 'The underside of propaganda was its apparatus in terror, administered by secret police...'

I allowed my temper to flare quickly and interrupted him, raising my voice for all to hear. 'How dare you challenge the wonderful regime supported not only by my grandfather, by the German nation as a whole, and by the glorious Third Reich! Have you not seen the record of our people on film, and the way they were dedicated to our dearly-beloved Fuehrer? Are you the kind of person who disregards the lessons taught to us by our masters, or is your ambition so high you consider you are better?' I was taking a big chance throwing all my weight behind the idea that these people intended to emulate their predecessors... the hierarchy and the officers of the Third Reich. If I was wrong, the house would fall in on me and my fate would hang in the balance. In the meantime, I rested on the horns of a dilemma. I had thoroughly enjoyed the role of demolishing the argument of the young man, much to his displeasure, noting that the crowd about me now comprised every person in the room. They all wanted to hear what I had to say. I turned to Hayle in disgust. 'Who is this man?' I demanded angrily. 'Why is he allowed to preach subversion contrary to our cause? If he took the time to understand the essence of national socialism, then all of us would be that much richer!'

'Who was your grandfather?' asked Harry Kirk, trying to dampen enthusiasm at my rousing diatribe.

'Heinz Erdbeer, a proud member of the Schutzstaffel... the SS. The elite corps of the Nazi party with immense police and military powers.'

'Yes, yes, I know all about the SS,' replied Kirk softly. 'What rank did he hold?' He lifted a bottle from the table behind him and filled my glass from the contents, although his eyes never seemed to leave mine.

The room fell silent as I paused to reflect an answer. 'Colonel Heinz Erdbeer,' I repeated proudly, clicking my heels together in true Prussian style.

Kirk returned the bottle to the table and turned back to me filled with suspicion. 'A Colonel, eh?' he said, almost in a whisper. 'An eminent rank indeed. No wonder you're so proud. You know of course that the SS were schooled in racial hatred and admonished to harden their hearts to human suffering. Do you have any idea of their chief virtue and their motto?'

His question was directed to find me out. If I failed to answer correctly my reputation would turn to dust. At the very best, the others would tend to regard me as a promotion hunter... someone with a silver tongue and little else to offer. Inwardly, I prayed my research that morning had been accurate. During the next ten seconds I would live or die by the information I had gleaned. 'The chief virtue of the SS was their absolute obedience and loyalty to the Fuehrer who gave them their motto: "Thy Honour Is Loyalty!"'

'Which Section of the SS did your grandfather command?' Kirk did not intend to give up easily.

By this time I realised I had dug a pit for myself and I was sinking deeper and deeper into it each moment. There was no end of questions he could ask me to challenge my validity. I was walking the tight-rope because my knowledge of the SS was relatively shallow. It was essential to draw on memory as hard as possible. 'At first, he was in the Allgemeine SS dealing with foreign intelligence and espionage. Then he was transferred to the Waffen SS to command a division in the Verfugunstruppe... the Disposition Troops... serving alongside the regular army. They had a reputation of being fanatical fighters.'

'Did he survive the war?'

I knew it was impossible to answer affirmatively, for that would lead to a whole series of new questions which would finally sink me. 'Sadly, he was killed defending Berlin from the enemies of the Third Reich.' That answer would have to suffice. I wasn't going to be drawn any further into the game and paused to take a sip from my glass. 'But surely we're here to discuss the campaign. I've been guilty of boring you with my idle talk for far too long!'

'Not at all,' replied Kirk, seeking the attention of all the guests. 'Damen und Herren! I think we owe a debt of gratitude to our new colleague, Mr. Savage... Herr Erdbeer... who has shown us, in just a few words, how our thoughts should be aligned. Too often we forget the true nature of the old ideals which could easily have encompassed Europe in a relatively short space of time... and then the world. But it's of no consequence, because we have learned much from previous errors to establish our own plan of campaign. We are practically guaranteed success over a period of time to win Europe by peace instead of war, and I'm personally grateful to Herr Erdbeer for imprinting on our minds the need to conduct our lives by instinct and subordination of the individual to the State. We have to bring good order to society and some of you will be aware of the formation once again of the Geheime Staatspolizei... the Gestapo!'

I froze where I stood, recalling the text I had read that morning about the

Gestapo. It was a section of the SS which ruthlessly eliminated all opposition to the Nazis in Germany and its occupied territories. The agency operated without civil restraint, with the authority of preventative arrest, and its actions were never subject to judicial appeal... similar to the case of Albert Henley. Thousands of leftists, intellectuals, Jews, trade unionists, political clergy and homosexuals simply disappeared from society, most of them turning up in concentration camps. But most horrific of all... the Gestapo had mobile killing squads, and they laid claim to their victims without conscience! I began to cringe inside. To any outsider I was as evil as the men and women I intended to expose. Instead, this quirk of circumstance had turned me into a hero and, before I knew what was happening, everyone had raised their glasses in a toast to my good health. Everyone, that is, except the young man in the uniform whom I had defeated. He stared at me with half-closed eyes as though he could cheerfully strangle the life from my body. I had made a true enemy within!

After Kirk's simple speech, the gathering broke up into smaller groups again. I looked at Tania and shrugged, wishing I could tell her the truth about me, but I couldn't take a risk of that magnitude.

'So your grandfather was German,' she said, allowing me to notice an icy tone in her voice. 'Colonel Heinz Erdbeer.'

'A person can choose his friends but not his relatives,' I responded. 'The trouble is that the legend follows. I could never live up to his reputation.'

She let the matter drop and I sought a reason for her quietness from that moment on. Perhaps she felt inadequate in the presence of all the people at the party, or she had reason to dislike me knowing I was of German descent... which I wasn't! I had no idea what she was thinking and alerted myself to the fact that she had willingly allowed herself to be recruited to International Three Thousand. She either supported the cause or had joined it for some other purpose.

It was nearly two hours later when the party began to fold. Many guests started to leave and the number of people in the room reduced substantially. I looked at Tania as if to ask whether she wanted to go and she took my arm readily. We offered our farewell and walked to the door to find ourselves confronted by Hayle and Kirk. They wore serious expressions on their faces.

'You never fail to surprise me, Herr Erdbeer,' began Hayle.

His words sent terror through my heart for I believed he was now going to uncover me as an infiltrator. 'I had no intention of causing you embarrassment, Herr Hayle,' I replied, waiting for the axe to fall.

'On the contrary,' he smiled. 'I meant surprise... not embarrassment. I'm proud to have recommended you personally.'

'Tell me, Erdbeer,' intervened Kirk. 'Which bank are you with... and what's your position there?'

Hayle was a tough character but Himmler's grandson was much harsher, and far more direct in his attitude. The game was to be played with full effect now! 'I'm the senior executive in Demby Banking Corporation. It's a private bank with a branch in Switzerland.' Fortunately, the newspaper always had a back-up company for reporters who wished to conceal their identity, Demby Banking Corporation was one such company. It was quoted at Companies House but it didn't trade.

Kirk examined my business card carefully. 'You may be assured we shall check out all the facts,' he told me, almost reading my thoughts. 'You see, we search very hard for people like yourself... those able to command respect, who dedicate their thoughts to the movement, and who show an aptitude for leadership. If everything's in order, we may be able to find a well-appointed position for you in our new society. Would that be in accordance with your own wishes?'

I pretended it was a thought which had never cross my mind and paused for a few moments wearing a doubtful expression on my face. 'This is all rather sudden,' I replied. 'But I'm sure I'll be able to reconcile with it in due course.'

'I'm sure you will,' returned Kirk, starting to take his leave. 'I'd like you to come to a meeting at my house in three days' time. Would you do that?'

'I can be there. Where... and at what time?'

'I live near Epping Forest. It'll be for lunch, say, at one o'clock. Conrad will give you the address. Good night!' With that, he turned on his heel and left.

Hayle produced a pen and a piece of paper from his pocket to jot down the details. I thanked him for his help and left the building. Outside, stood the uniformed young man whose ego I had dented so badly. He glared at me with hatred showing in his eyes. I mused I needed an enemy in the organisation like I needed a hole in the head. But that was the way it stood!

I took Tania back to her apartment. She still seemed a little depressed and I couldn't fathom the reason. 'What's the matter?' I asked sympathetically. 'Do you have a headache? Or did I upset you by grabbing the limelight?' She shook her head and gave me a half-smile without speaking. 'I didn't mean to sound off like that. Really I didn't. But that young prig was a bit too full of his own importance. I felt I had to knock him off his perch. Come on, what's troubling you?'

We stood in the kitchen and she turned on the kettle to make some coffee. 'I'm all in favour of a united Europe,' she said dolefully. 'In fact I joined the movement because I strongly believe it might be the salvation of mankind to create a United States of Europe, establishing it as a major world power. But tonight was something different. First of all, I came to the party hanging on your coat-tails. I shouldn't have been there at all really. Secondly, I had the feeling something sinister was happening. Suddenly, there are men in uniforms. Why were they wearing them? How come everyone was talking about national socialism... the concept followed by the Nazis? And how many people there had relatives who held senior positions in the old German hierarchy?

'How can you say that?' I asked, wondering how she could devise such a high-grade list of questions so quickly. A suspicious thought entered my mind and I stared at her face closely. 'What do you work at, Tania?'

'Mail-order,' she replied instantly. 'I work for a mail-order firm.'

I didn't believe her for one moment and stalked into her bedroom, pulling open the drawers of her dressing-table indiscriminately. She start to protest but I ignored her. If I was wrong she would throw me out on my ear and I would deserve such harsh treatment. But, if I was right, I was going to discover her true identity and find out why she had become a recruit of the movement. As I suspected, there was a plastic card in a handbag in one of the drawers and I glanced at it angrily, knowing exactly what it represented.

'You bitch!' I exclaimed unfairly, going back into the kitchen. 'You're a bloody reporter from another newspaper! I knew it when you started to ask those questions!'

She looked equally angry, furious that I had discovered her identity. 'We all have to earn a living, you know!' she defended boldly. 'I worked hard to get initiated into International Three Thousand but now it's all over. You'll be delighted to tell them about me. It'll gain you a few more bonus points!'

I sat in the lounge for a while in silence as she made us some coffee. The woman had done well to get that far. She had shown a lot of zeal. In truth, we were probably the two most advanced reporters on this particular assignment. It made sense to join forces, especially where contacts were concerned. She returned from the kitchen and set two cups of coffee down on the coffee-table.

'You said... "You're a bloody reporter from another newspaper". What do you mean... from another newspaper?'

I started to laugh and stood up, taking her into my arms. I had no alternative but to come clean.

'I'm no grandson of a German,' I admitted. 'My ancestors were all Scottish. The antics of this evening were a charade. You see, I'm also a newspaper reporter.'

She drew in a deep breath and displayed mock anger towards me. 'You rat!' she snapped, staring into my eyes. 'And there was I all miserable because you were one of them! I was going to hang on to you to help me get my story. Fat lot of use that is now!'

There was a short silence and then we both saw the funny side of it. Peals of laughter echoed through the apartment and out of the open window which had not yet been repaired.

'Why don't we join forces,' I suggested seriously. 'Together we can get to the bottom of this awful business. You realise what's going on, don't you?'

'Tonight was an eye-opener. They even wear uniforms like the old Nazis.'

'Do we join forces then?' I asked, holding her close in my arms.

'I don't know,' she said doubtfully. 'Have you any idea what my editor would say if he found out? There would be hell to pay!'

'Why does he have to find out? I'm not going to tell mine!'

We both laughed at the thought and kissed each other gently on the lips. No doubt her editor was very similar to Ted Flanders in all he said and did!

'I've got a great idea,' she continued quietly. 'Why don't we continue this conversation in bed?'

The idea of a partnership with a competitor reporter had never surfaced before. There were many newspaper people who would have considered it undesirable and obnoxious. Somehow, with a woman like Tania, it held certain attractions, and I was more than flattered to recognise she had been miserable because she thought I was one of the bad guys. We went into the bedroom and closed the door behind us to shut out the draught. It was going to be a successful alliance. I could feel it in my bones! As I sat on the bed, I visualised Ted Flanders wincing with pain, like the victim of a voodoo expert who had just pierced his likeness with a sharp pin. It would keep him puffing away at those cheap cigars for a long time to come!

CHAPTER ELEVEN

I recall waking very early on the following morning although consciousness merely existed in a state of awareness, My mind was full of complex thoughts and I twisted and turned uneasily. Despite my malaise, it was one of those days when one is never sure whether restful sleep in present or restless awareness prevails. I was delighted at the preparatory work I had made in advance of Hayle's party. I had set the bait. It was a day off for Murphy's law... where the rule is that if anything can go wrong, it will go wrong! I breathed a sigh of relief at being offered a further invitation to Kirk's residence near Epping Forest. At last I was approaching the gates of Hades without having to fight off the three-headed Cerberus, Although I was being drawn into the situation, to the point of no return, it was counterbalanced by the promise of results.

Tania awoke much later having slept quite well. I made breakfast and we began to share information on progress as we had agreed the night before. She was like a moth flying across a naked flame without getting singed. The incident in which she had been tied to a chair was the first of its kind. There had been no other attempts on her life which led me to consider that I was the one who was expendable. Yet only those in the committee at the House of Commons knew of my assignment. At best, my position seemed to be extremely vulnerable. However none of them knew that Tania worked for a newspaper. She had developed her researches independently, basing her work on Nazi records held by various agencies.

'Before we start,' I asked, 'how did you manage to get invited to the recruitment meeting?'

She hesitated for a moment before forcing herself to trust me. 'From one of my contacts,' she replied, sitting on the fence.

'Look,' I growled. 'If we're going to be honest with each other, we can't hold back. It's up to you!'

There was a long pause and then she caved in. 'It's a man called Calvin at the Dock and Duck in the East End of London. He's one of my informers. My newspaper pays him well. He's the best in the business.'

'Was!' I returned flatly. 'He was the best. He was my contact as well.' It was clear that Calvin worked for anyone who paid him, moving the goal posts to his own advantage.

'Why the past tense?'

'I found him dead in the inn.'

'Dead!' she echoed, patently unaware of the man's demise. 'This assignment's beginning to give me the creeps! People are getting killed simply for information.'

'Or the suppression of it,' I returned. 'What about your researches?'

She aligned her thoughts for a moment. 'The United Nations War Crimes Commission was set up in 1943 by the Allies in London. The Commission lists all war criminals which, believe it or not, amounts to more than twenty-five thousand. Can you imagine the chaos after the war before the trials at Nurenburg? The Nazi war criminals and officers of the Third Reich looked for ways to escape capture. History records that some of them were caught but thousands managed to get away. Most who escaped emigrated to other countries, such as South America, changing their identities to avoid discovery. They brought up their families in those countries waiting for the day when the Fourth Reign would be formed to take up where Hitler left off. When that time arrives, if it ever does, they have substantial wealth obtained from the treasures they acquired from their occupation of other countries during World War Two. Regardless of that, their aim is to establish the United States of Europe with them in control and they call it International Three Thousand. Instead of war, they intend to control the situation throughout peace, And this time there'll be no neutral countries'

'In truth, I think it's a very tall order but things change very quickly in the political climate. I mean if you add up the number of new recruits to the organisation, it could reach many millions over the next ten or twenty years. It could act like a chain reaction as it did in the 1930s in Germany.'

Tania nodded seriously. 'The key character in the business is a man called Simon Weisenthal. Born in Russia, he emerged as an Austrian Jew who helped to bring more than eleven hundred Nazi war criminals to justice. Although his centre is in Los Angeles, he was the founder of the Jewish Documentation Centre in Vienna. It gathered information on the present location of Nazis who avoided capture. The biggest fish they ever caught was Adolf Eichmann, the former German officer responsible for deporting Jews to Nazi concentration camps. Israel agents rooted him out in the Argentine. He was sentenced to death and hanged. But now it's the children and grandchildren of the Nazis that they're looking for. The Israelis are hopping mad that the United Nations claimed that the War Crimes Commission was defunct and that each country was responsible for its own files. Australia's the only country giving blanket access to its records.'

'It really looks very bleak,' I muttered sadly.

'Not quite,' she returned quickly. 'There's always some people willing to betray their country for money. How valid such information is open to question.' I know of one contact in Munich who's willing to put us on the right track. His name's Kaspar Levenson. He stays at the Vier Jahreszeiten Hotel in Maximillianstrasse in Munich.'

'That's odd!' I said, looking at her strangely. 'One of my contacts, Jack Berg, has asked me to go to Germany with him. He might only want a free ride on the back of my expenses.'

'Be careful of your timing,' she warned. 'You've agreed to visit Kirk at Epping Forest.'

'Yes…Harry Kirk...the Commander-in-Chief.'

'I presume I'm not invited.'

I shrugged my shoulders innocently. 'He didn't include you but you can come along with me if you wish. The problem is that if my cover's blown, you go down with me. I think you ought to put some distance between yourself and the organisation. I'll let you know what's going on.'

She stared at me suspiciously for a moment as though I was trying to cheat her. 'It wouldn't have anything to do with pulling off a scoop on your own account, would it? I don't fancy being left high and dry.'

'You have my word on it,' I told her sincerely. 'Devious I may be, but dishonest, never! My main interest is to protect you.' I kissed her gently on the nose and looked directly into her eyes. 'And that leads me to another thing. I want you to move into my apartment while I'm away.'

'What for?'

'Those men who tied you to a chair might come back again. I won't be here to protect you. My apartment's in a terrible state but they won't look for you there. Promise me you'll do that!'

She thought about the idea for a moment and then nodded. 'But don't think it's a permanent arrangement. I'm still not sure about you, James Savage... .or Herr Erdbeer!'

I laughed realising how much I enjoyed her company. She brought freshness and a new dimension to my life. 'Good,' I responded happily. 'I'll visit Kirk and then go to Germany. What are you going to do in the meantime?'

'I'm making an all-out effort to open the files of the War Crimes Commission. My appointment at Whitehall is with a Mr. Jacobs of State Security.'

I froze in my tracks, shaking my head slightly as though my hearing was impaired. I felt a strong urge to tell her of my meeting at the House of Commons until the words of the Prime Minister echoed in my brain. 'In effect Mr. Savage, this meeting never took place and none of us have ever seen you. Equally you have never seen us and no one is to be told anything.' It was time for silence and I allowed the matter to fade into my mind. 'An agency called State Security,' I managed to say. 'I think you ought to check it out.'

'I've already set the wheels in motion,' she returned boastfully.

I chuckled inwardly in anticipation of the results of her research. 'Let's get your stuff over to my place.'

'By the way,' she went on as if not hearing me. 'Have you ever come across someone called Strogoff?

'Strogoff?' My voice almost sounded in a gasp.

'He's a Russian who escaped from one of their Siberian camps. He seems to be creeping up all over the place.'

'What do you mean?' I asked her with interest.

'I saw him speak at a rally in the East End of London.

We'll talk about it on our way to your apartment, Let me just tell you that he's after all the Nazi treasures, gold and shares. He's found some Nazi criminals and is blackmailing them. They have no option but to pay up. There's plenty of fish in the sea! But he regards that as only bread-and-butter stuff. He's after the whole caboodle.'

'I was at that rally and he seemed to be on their side,' I said without surprise.

'He's on any side that suits him,' she countered swiftly.

I dwelt on what she had told me as we collected her clothes and essential items. At least she was safe and sound, as far as I was concerned.

It was past noon when I arrived at Miss Grayson's office. She hadn't left for lunch but my appearance did not improve her disposition towards me. Despite our previous intimacy, she still viewed me with suspicion, firmly believing that I had broken into her office to steal her computer disks from her desk drawer. Nothing would ever change her mind even though she was unable to prove it.

'Would you like me to take you to lunch,' I invited pleasantly, trying to win myself back to popularity.

'I already have a luncheon date!' she returned acidly. Don't you think our contact is somewhat of a paradox, Mr. Savage,' she went on. 'Whenever we make an appointment for dinner your presence becomes noticeable by its absence, yet when I've arranged something you turn up like the proverbial bad penny!'

'It seems like fate, Miss Grayson,' I told her calmly. 'The Gods deem that the path of true love will not run smoothly between us.'

'Don't patronise me!' she scolded.

'You have to realise I'm doing battle above and beyond the call of duty. The Prime Minister asked me to do so. Perhaps…as an Israeli agent…that doesn't count with you.'

She showed no sign of emotion except for a slight dilation of her nostrils which flared fractionally at the comment. Whether she was an Israeli agent or not failed to enter into the reckoning.

'Do you have any information at all?' she demanded icily. 'If not, there's no point in continuing this conversation. ' She glanced briefly at her wristwatch and looked up again. 'I'm already late for my appointment!'

I sat down in the chair opposite her, resting my feet on the desk, determined to take her down a peg. It was no surprise that my action annoyed her.

'Please!' she protested, stunned that I could be so crude. 'Let's be civilised!'

'Why should we?' I laughed. 'Is it because we're in the Civil Service... with the emphasis on 'civil'?'

She found the remark singularly unamusing and glared at me with her beautiful eyes. Was she sincere in everything that she did? The woman had an excellent brain and probably many academic qualifications and she had achieved a high-ranking appointment as a technical adviser on defence matters I now considered everyone of the Jewish faith to be an Israeli spy.

'All right,' I conceded, removing my feet from her desk. 'You go for your luncheon date but there's just one thing I want to ask you.'

'It'll have to wait,' she told me point-blank, standing up after closing her desk drawer.

'If you leave this office now,' I savaged. 'I'll have no option but to tell the Prime Minister that you put your personal life before your duty. If you think I'm bluffing, go ahead and leave.'

'How dare you!' she remonstrated angrily, staring at me as though I was something slimy that had just crawled out from under a rock. 'You bastard! Do you think I gave myself to you for sheer duty? What a pity you know so little about women! Well perhaps I can enlighten you with a few words of wisdom. When you walked into that room in the House of Commons, I saw you as a real man. For the first time in my life I felt I'd met a good honest person, warm in spirit and understanding. How wrong I was! You're shallow and insensitive! You have no empathy or manners!' She paused having succeeded in making me feel like a rat which had invaded her office by gnawing through the floorboards. 'My judgement was impaired when it came to you and I'll have to live with it.' She sat down in her chair and picked up the telephone receiver. 'Jenny... cancel my luncheon appointment, will you. Give my usual apologies.' She replaced the receiver and returned her attention to me. 'Right, Mr. Savage, what do you want from me?'

I had to agree with her that the way I had treated her was absolutely shallow. I blamed my breeding in the newspaper although it was no excuse. It was impossible to rely on the trust of politicians, solicitors, doctors, priests and even judges. However with regard to my relationship with Linda Grayson I had gone too far. I needed to find it within myself to make peace with her if nothing else.

'I want to apologise to you most sincerely,' I told her with a very apologetic expression on my face. 'I was way out of line. I didn't mean what I said about reporting you to the Prime Minister. It was in bad taste. Can you forgive me, Linda... please!' Her eyelids flickered at my comments. 'If you want to go to your luncheon date, I'll see you later on.'

'It's already cancelled, Mr. Savage!' she snapped, as her anger began to subside. 'Do not even consider that we have a personal relationship. That's over!' she ranted. 'What did you want to ask me?'

I knew at that moment I had made an enemy for life. 'I need to examine the files held by the British Government relating to the United Nations War Crimes Committee. I believe that several thousand names are on the register.'

'Why do you want to see the files? Why this line of investigation?''

'The war criminals are of no interest to me. Most of them are dead anyway. I need to track down the children and grandchildren of the people on those files. I think I have proof that they intend to start the Fourth Reich.'

She thought about the request and then typed out some words on the keyboard of her computer. She read the text as it came up and then turned to me. 'Those particular files are lodged with the appropriate United Nations agency in the UN Assembly building in New York.'

'Hold on a second,' I cut in sharply. 'The United Nations disclaim all knowledge and state that each individual member country of the War Crimes Commission holds its own files in secret. Who's the person controlling that information in this country?'

'How should I knew?' she countered curtly. 'I'm a technical adviser on defence matters. It's not in my field.'

'Come on, Linda!' I persisted. 'You weren't elected to that committee in the House of Commons for no reason! If the British Government faces the possibility of being ousted, like all the other European countries, by the offspring of the Nazis, you must be in possession of a number of useful facts. You've got to help me out!'

'You presume too much!' she retorted angrily. It was clear that she intended to dig her heels in as hard as possible.

'You must realise the measures being taken by International Three Thousand are a danger to our national defence,' I went on trying to find a chink in her armour. 'When I read the first disk you have in your desk drawer, you had the whole thing set out. Die Stunde, Harry Kirk, the lot. Mind you, I didn't see anything about Der Bankvorsteher.' I watched her very closely but she didn't take the bait.

'You had no right to rifle my desk!'

I was sad that my comment failed to produce any reaction so I ploughed on doggedly. 'I wonder why the Prime Minister had me brought to the meeting when you had the information all the time.'

She toyed with a pencil between her fingers showing her nervousness. 'I thought you understood that. An independent evaluation of the situation was likely to expose different avenues of approach.'

'Was it? Then let me have those files on the war criminals who found safe haven in Britain. Point me in the right direction, Linda.'

'The issue's beyond my control. You'll have to contact the Prime Minister.'

'Or Henry Jacobs of State Security,' I forwarded.

She stopped playing with the pencil and stared at me with a puzzled expression on her face. 'Henry Jacobs?'

'Someone I know has made an appointment with him to look at those files.'

'I thought you told me that Henry Jacobs doesn't exist.' I recognised that she was playing a cat-and-mouse game with me.

'He exists all right. I've seen him and so does State Security.'

She pursed her lips tightly. 'Then you'd better make an appointment with him as well, Mr. Savage. I'm not my brother's keeper!'

It was obvious that I would make no headway with her. She was too upset from my earlier behaviour to be willing to help. 'Okay,' I continued unabated. 'Let's talk about Lieutenant-Colonel Topham.'

'What about him?'

'He's in defence and that's in your field. Where can I find him?'

'He's on a course at present. Somewhere near Epping Forest in Essex. But he doesn't exist in the Department of Defence! If you want to see him that badly go and find him yourself!' she snarled, her attitude becoming quite intolerant. She picked up the telephone receiver. 'Jenny,' she spoke into it. 'Would you mind telling my luncheon date that I'm now free.' She replaced the receiver and stared at me coldly. 'I think we've finished our conversation, Mr. Savage. I must ask you to leave these premises immediately. If you feel like rifling my desk please do so. You'll find nothing there of any interest!' She stood up and went to the door opening it for me to leave.

There was nothing more to say so I left the building. So Topham was in the vicinity of Epping Forest. It was too much of a coincidence that he was in the vicinity. On reflection, I had shattered my image in front of Linda Grayson's eyes. Clearly she was disappointed but, as far as I was concerned, despite how beautiful she looked, I much preferred the company of Tania.

CHAPTER TWELVE

The drive to Epping Forest was a delightful journey, mainly because most of the traffic was moving in the other direction. Even thought the morning began well with Tania by my side, and the sun shone brilliantly, I started out in an indifferent mood. First of all, I had no idea why Kirk had invited me to his home. I had got involved with these people far too quickly He was Heinrich Himmler's grandson which didn't endear him to me. Under normal conditions, I would never blame any grandson for the indiscretions of his ancestors. However this bad seed had been passed on. Harry Kirk wanted to follow in his grandfather's footsteps and he could possibly turn out to be an even greater monster!

The residence was a large Victorian building surrounded by many acres of land. The façade still bore signs of the excessive craft and artistry of the nineteenth century masons even though it had been repaired and renovated on a number of occasions during the past century. The great portico with its graceful iconic columns and the large metal front door bearing the grotesque head of a savage lion, had admitted gentry by their hundreds for many centuries, I doubted whether Kirk had any legacy with which to buy such a prestigious property... except through Nazi funding.

I was welcomed by an old butler who led me into the enormous hallway. Everywhere there was exhibited affluence and luxury. I was shown into the library and selected a book from the shelves. As I became involved in the text, the door opened and Kirk entered. He was wearing a black uniform, with the new insignias on his collar and sleeves, and the familiar jackboots. Under his arm he carried a baton as though it was his authority.

'Guten morgen, Herr Erdbeer,' he greeted cheerfully as he crossed the room. 'I've been thinking about you. Come...there are some things I want to show you!'

He hustled me out into the corridor and led me out of the building to a parade ground. A number of men stood to attention as he appeared, giving a German style salute. The men began to sing the strains of 'Deutschland Uber Alles' before running a flag up the flagpole I had never seen before... a red circle against a black background, pierced by two lightning flashes streaking through the centre. It was practically the same insignia worn on the uniforms.

'Great, eh!' muttered the Commander-in-Chief, showing his admiration for the flag by offering a similar salute to the men.

'Why am I here, Herr Kirk?' I asked politely.

He smiled at me in a strange fashion which scared me rigid. What was going on in that Devilish mind? Himmler died at the age of forty-five so his grandson never knew him. The Nazi had been a racist and a fanatic... .it was all in the blood!

'That was an excellent and rousing argument you presented the other evening. I was very impressed!'

'All I did was to expound some fundamental principles of national socialism. There was nothing new in what I said.'

'That's where you're wrong, my friend,' he countered. 'You see, as generations pass, we forget certain basic tenets, Modern society brings change and it causes us to adjust our thoughts and ideas to new trends. Apart from the quality of your speech, you brought our attention to the original doctrine. It was most refreshing. Come, let me show you some of our work here!'

Kirk snapped his fingers to direct the men into action. They began to exhibit a grand martial arts display, performing many set-pieces to show their prowess. In due course, he led me back into the house, laughing gently as we strolled along the hallway to another room.

'Don't be troubled, Herr Erdbeer,' he commented. 'Our men are crack fighters. We have similar units all over Europe in advance of our campaign.'

'You mean you're developing an army,' I observed fearfully.

'We cannot afford to look weak and vulnerable. Even though our plan is currently passive, we need to develop an army for purposes of protection. We have to be strong to establish a United States of Europe. A strong army will ensure that it happens.'

We stopped outside another ornately-carved door as I pondered his words carefully. This time Germany did not intend to fail by sheer dint of error... as it had done in the last two World Wars. It was designed to ensure that the sons and grandsons of the Fatherland controlled the whole of Europe. I had to admit that, if it was allowed to continue, no one would be able to defend themselves against such a carefully prepared plan.

'I congratulate you on the way you're developing the Fourth Reich,' I told him, biting my tongue as the words left my mouth.

He laughed loudly. 'Not only the Fourth Reich, my friend, but the Fifth and

Sixth. The Fourth will take us through the twenty-first century. The Fifth will establish national socialism on a far wider scale than has ever been seen before. The Sixth is expected to complete the programme to its fullest extent right up to the third millennium. What do you think of that?'

My mind was at sixes and sevens. The Sixth Reich would be totalitarian in every respect having absorbed every country in Europe into a Reichland. What would they try to do after that...conquer the rest of the world? It would be within their grasp in time if they were allowed to continue!

'I nurse only one private regret,' he went on. 'I wasn't able to be a member of the Hitler Youth Movement. I hadn't been born at the time. We're planning to introduce a similar system in due course.'

I smiled weakly as though I was in favour of the idea although deep down I dreaded everything he had told me. The enemy stood at the gates and it was no longer possible to close one's eyes to the danger.

'Come!' he repeated, opening the door to usher me into the room.

There were approximately thirty people inside sitting in a hemisphere as they listened to a lecturer who spoke to them in front of a blackboard. He droned on for a while explaining the law of diminishing returns before launching himself into food production in the United States of Europe. Kirk withdrew me from the room by taking hold of my arm and closing the door behind us.

'All very boring stuff to the creative mind,' he complained, pulling a long face to accentuate his feelings. 'If they placed all the economists in the world end to end, they wouldn't reach a conclusion.' He stopped to laugh at his own joke. 'No doubt you can see how important it is to train people in order to integrate Europe both economically and financially for the future. Herr Graube, the tutor, is absolutely correct in his theories. There is so much waste in Europe which is absolute nonsense!'

He led me to another door and entered, allowing me to follow him inside. There were about the same number of people in this room listening to a different lecturer. He was in full flow when I arrived to a very obedient audience.

'The reform of the legislature in Britain can only be accomplished by the dissolution of the House of Commons and the House of Lords.,' he ranted vociferously, 'There will be no Members of Parliament, only five Law Committees in various parts of Britain. Ultimately there will be no General Elections. A Central Committee will be appointed to ensure the rules of the new order are always in place. The laws with be made within the United States of Europe to encompass all the countries therein. They will be simple in their entirety with imprisonment for all crimes. Prisons will be very stark with no facilities of any kind for the inmates. The idea is to eliminate crime very quickly and the laws of indictment are swift and will include the death penalty for serious offences. Court cases will be kept to one single day, allowing Plaintiffs and Defendants half of one day each. There will be no very rich barristers and lawyers in our new society. Any changes will be unified and carried out by the Central Committee. We shall brook no delays or folly.'

Kirk took me out of the room nodding his head in agreement, 'You see, Herr Erdbeer, we shall not require different governments to waste time and cause chaos. Our legislation will be simple and effective.'

He was right in a way but I deplored the concept of totalitarian control where people had no democratic rights. Clearly Kirk had been brought up to think that way. He led me to yet another door and then turned away. 'No... this lecturer is very boring,' he confessed. 'You won't mind if we give this one a miss but I think you'll find this one interesting.'

We entered another room to find an entirely different set-up. A number of people were working independently on charts of different countries, checking information on population, as though operating an election campaign. On the wall hung a large flag with a circle on a black background. Inside the circle, the face of a lion, and the letter ITT were boldly displayed.

'We call this the Election Room,' boasted Kirk. 'As our recruitment drive continues, we intend to prepare ourselves for future elections. I saw you looking at the flag. Our marketing and public relations staff assure me that the face of a lion is not only attractive to the eye but meaningful. And, of course, ITT stands for International Three Thousand. The lion will roar when we achieve success.' He walked up to a man working on a chart of Italy. 'What are you doing?' he enquired.

The man looked up and got to his feet quickly before pointing to the chart with his index finger. 'The continuous red line indicates the electorate of Italy at the present time, excluding children, criminals, gypsies and the like,' he informed us. 'The dotted red line is the estimate in ten years' time. The black line indicates the number of ITT members in ten years' time. The green one represent ITT numbers in twenty-five years' time. It all identifies the timing of our electoral development within Italy in time to come.'

'Forgive me for saying this,' I cut in foolishly. 'Elections normally take place every five years at which times the electorate make their own views, often changing sides.'

The man looked at me with a surprised expression on his face. 'There's an easy way of removing opposition,' he said flatly. 'Reduce their survival rate. Anyone who stands in our way will be eliminated. That will ensure our success.'

My host began to laugh loudly as he led me out of the room. 'Don't look shocked,' he told me. 'Once the programme gets under way, we cannot allow obstacles to stand in our path. Opponents will meet with unfortunate accidents. We've given it the title of 'Planned Progress'.'

I considered such acts to be unsolicited murder but it would have been exceedingly foolish for me to express my views. Now I understood why Die Stunde was set for the first of June. That was the kicking off time to start the new programme on a softly, softly, catchee monkey plan. They would, no doubt, start to integrate themselves as a new election party. The thought chilled my bones and I felt an urge to tell the Prime Minister what was going on at the earliest opportunity. I went to the window to see the men still performing martial arts and I could see an observer standing to watch them. I recognised him instantly as Lieutenant-Colonel Topham! There was confusion in my mind as I looked again to make certain that my eyes were not playing tricks. I was losing control of the assignment. No one seemed to be what they appeared to be, and they tended to turn up in all the wrong places.

We went back to the library where Kirk closed the door and sat in a comfortable chair behind the desk.

'We've checked your credentials which proved to be satisfactory,' he related, pausing to choose his words carefully. 'There's a vacancy for a qualified person in the banking field in our organisation. As you know, we recruit at all levels but it's difficult to find people in the Category A of the socio-economic scale. It's even harder to find someone who's fanatical about International Three Thousand. And then, suddenly, you appear on the scene...a senior banker... who appreciates the purist doctrines of national socialism. We are doubly blessed!'

'Are you asking me to join ITT on a permanent basis?' I asked, expecting him to stuff me into a room with other bankers. If so, my fate would be swiftly sealed for I knew little about the intricacies of the banking profession and would soon be found out.

He stared at me closely before replying. 'There's a man... Der Bankvorsteher... who's in New York but he will visit us in a few days' time. He controls many billions of dollars in money markets, currencies and investments and we need someone to assist him. You're of German descent, with an obvious pride in our ancestry. Your grandfather was in the SS, and I believe that you are the man we need. You're unmarried which is a bonus as the job requires a great deal of travelling. What do you say?'

I held my breath for a moment at the breakthrough. If I could meet Der Bankvorsteher and learned more about the Nazi funds, I could possibly set the organisation back a lifetime. Without sufficient funds, the ITT would be brought to its knees.

'Your offer sounds most attractive,' I responded. 'Would it not be possible for me to retain my present employment and help out Der Banvorsteher in between?'

He laughed easily and shook his head. 'There's no time for complacency, Herr Erbeer,' he countered, moving on to the attack. 'Not for a man like you with national pride. You wouldn't be able to cope with both appointments at the same time. Would you care to sleep on it and give me an answer as soon as possible. As I said, he will be here in two days time. It would give you a new meaning in life.'

I allowed some moments to pass, pretending that I was toying with the idea in my mind. 'You have a point there, Herr Kirk,' I told him. 'It would give my life meaning.' I could have cursed Jack Berg for telling me, if you can't beat them, join them. It had got me into a real mess. I wanted to meet Der Bankvorsteher urgently and the opportunity would arise in two day's time but what could I tell Kirk in the meantime as he was going to press me for an answer?

'Perhaps it's best if we take it a little slowly until we really get under way. You can meet Der Bankvorsteher when he arrives. Come again here for luncheon and meet him.'

'It'll be my pleasure,' I returned, nodding as a gesture of his good hospitality and clicking the backs of my heels.

'Good!' he uttered, rising from his seat and picking up the baton. 'Come, I want you to meet the man who is helping us to build our army, I'm sure he'll impress you!'

We left the room together and I began to experience an uncomfortable feeling in the pit of my stomach. I knew in advance what was about to happen.

Outside the building, the warriors were still in action as Kirk led me to the man I least wanted to meet. I had come so far in such a short time, now all my efforts were going to be dashed. I would do well to consider any avenue of escape. I felt like a listing ship drifting helplessly on to jagged rocks with my life in serious jeopardy. I thought about Barnaby laying in a hospital bed with a broken leg and curse him for his good luck in staying out of this dilemma. If my life was to end here, I swore that I would haunt him forever!

'I'd like you to meet our mentor and strategist,' announced Kirk proudly as the man I had met in the House of Commons walked slowly towards me. He stopped a few feet away and my heart sank into my boots as he stared directly into my eyes with a grim expression on his face. Kirk looked at us both for a moment before he made the introduction. 'Herr Obersturmfuehrer Mueller meet Herr Erbeer.'

Topham stuck out his hand quickly and I grasped it trying not to show my surprise. 'Haven't we met somewhere before?' he asked sternly, diverting my thoughts by directing the conversation into a routine channel.

'I don't think so, Herr Obersturmfuehrer,' I replied, sighing inwardly with relief, keeping my voice on an even keel. 'Not unless you need finance from a private bank.'

'Well,' continued Kirk, 'you'll have a lot of time to talk over the meal. In the meantime, please excuse me. I have much work to complete.' He turned to me courteously with an awkward smile. 'If you wish to visit any of the lecture rooms, feel free to do so. But don't forget what I told you. The legal lecture is boring.'

He left the two of us together and marched back into the house. Topham turned to me with a brief smile touching his lips. 'You must tell me all about your work in banking, Herr Erdbeer,' he suggested, showing no emotion whatsoever. 'It's a field in which I'm particularly weak. We military men have to concentrate our minds on other matters.'

I assumed that he was keeping up the charade in case the place was bugged and someone could overhear us talking. We strolled to the point where he had been watching the men in combat and stopped to view them for a while. I found myself still shaking at the interface with him in this place but he appeared to be as cool as a cucumber. My mind then started to ask questions about him. What was he doing training the army of ITT? Who was he actually working for or was he a double agent? However there was one question of paramount importance. Why hadn't he exposed my identity to Kirk? I was unable to supply reasonable answers to those questions. But one fact was obvious to me... I had aged ten years in the past few minutes!

The affairs of the morning acted as a two-edged sword. On the one hand, I would have the opportunity of meeting Der Bankvorsteher which afforded me the opportunity to develop the assignment positively. I was still in danger that Topham or Herr Obersturmfuehrer Mueller would reveal my true identity. The thought passed through my mind that I ought to ask Ted Flanders for a desk job doing obituaries or the like, or maybe even retire to write a book and slowly starve to death in a wealth of rejection notes. Either one was better than suffering a heart attack as a front-line reporter.

After an excellent lunch, mingling with members and tutors, I decided to go home. I was about to climb into my car when I looked towards the house with an uncomfortable feeling that someone was watching me. Beside the front door stood a man dressed in black uniform, leaning against the door frame with his arms folded. It was the same man I had disgraced at Hayle's party and his expression hadn't changed. He still sought vengeance for the way I had treated him and he was prepared to wait patiently until his moment arrived. I drove off quickly with my heart pounding fiercely in my chest. There had never been any doubt in my mind that the visit would be charged with tension but I had moved at least another rung up the ladder in my research. I wondered if Linda Grayson knew that Topham was working on the side of the bad guys. The man was obviously a double agent. He had no intention of revealing my identity for fear of ruining his own cover.

I felt a little better an hour later after pouring myself a large glass of brandy. Tania wasn't there but I intended to tell her all about the visit when she returned. My main task was to pack a holdall for the trip to Germany and confirm the arrangements with Jack Berg. The pace of life was beginning to accelerate and I thought more about my future with the newspaper... as a sports writer or a society columnist... anything but a dangerous assignment like this one! It would not upset me to leave all the exciting stuff to other reporters... .not in the least!

CHAPTER THIRTEEN

After touching down at Munich Airport, Berg and I passed through immigration and hired a taxi to take us to our destination. Berg was anything but a bright spark, with a face as long as a fiddle throughout the whole journey, leaving me with the impression he wasn't too enchanted with the flight.

I asked him on a number of occasions to explain the reason for the trip but he avoided the issue, defending his silence bravely, persistently requesting me to be patient. Each time I became even more angry at his reticence, however I had little alternative but to wait until the moment suited him. Eventually I came to the conclusion that he was unable to tell me anything because he was unaware of the facts himself. If that was the case, there was no harm in tagging along with him for a couple of days hoping something useful might turn up. I also made a mental note to look up Kasper Levenson at the Vier Jahreszeiten Hotel in Maximilianstrasse as Tania had mentioned, if indeed he was still there!

The taxi ride allowed me to take me first view of Germany. Munich was the capital of Bavaria. In 1923, national socialism was founded here but Adolf Hitler failed in his attempted Munich "beer-hall putsch"... a coup aimed at the Bavarian government. During World War Two, three-quarters of the old city was destroyed; one-third of the inhabitants lost their homes. Munich had the distinction of being the beer capital of the world, sporting also the Oktoberfest... a country fair in the city... and Fasching... the carnival leading to the Mardi Gras. The city exhibited numerous museums and art galleries, beer halls, castles and other attractions.

'Where are we going?' asked the taxi-driver, speaking in gutteral English. 'Luisenstrasse,' Berg told him. Ein hundert und zwansig Luisenstrasse.'

'One hundred and twenty,' translated the cabbie. 'I learn good English, eh? We have many tourists to Munich. Your first time here?' He turned the vehicle sharply to move in the right direction. 'Well you've come to the right place for fun. Lots of beer. Lots of sights to see. So many in fact you shouldn't search too hard for them or you'll get a headache. And lots of other sights too. I can take you to the Bavarian Alps. They're not that far away.'

'What's the river below this bridge we're coming to?' I asked, looking through the windscreen at the way ahead.

'The green Isar,' he replied. 'It flows under many bridges connecting the centre of Munich with its eastern districts. There's an island in the middle called Museum Island because it houses the Deutsches Museum. This is Maximilianstrasse. A little further down is Maximilianeum, built for King Maximilian the Second. It's now the Bavarian Parliament building. The advantage of living in Luisenstrasse is that you're not far away from the train terminus. It's at the end of the street. Here we are... .a hundred and twenty Luisenstrasse!'

He stopped outside a block of apartments and I paid him off. We went up to the second floor where Berg produced a key and entered, leaving me to bring in the luggage. The accommodation was complete with a tiny kitchen, bathroom, a small living-room and a bedroom. The architect had been quite ingenious, using every millimetre of available space. The walls were coloured chalky white and carried the odour of new plaster, while the furniture was extremely scant. It needed to be if one intended to move within the apartment. The place was cheap and uncheerful, reminding me of the niggardly-minded administrator of expenses at the newspaper. I realised instantly there were others exactly like him in the world.

Berg opened the shuttered windows to let some air into the room which flooded immediately with sunlight. He stared at the traffic outside, concerned that it would keep him awake all night. 'I managed to get the accommodation from a friend of mine for nothing, but it's just our luck to be on the road leading to the railway terminus,' he complained, throwing his suitcase on to the bed. 'Still, I suppose it could be worse.'

'When are you going to fill me in with the details?' I asked again.

'All will be revealed soon,' he replied evasively. 'I have to get in touch with my contact first.' He lay on the bed next to his case and yawned loudly. 'Close the shutters, will you? The noise of the traffic might keep me awake but at least the sunshine can be controlled.' He closed his eyes and yawned again.

I did as he asked, plunging the room into darkness once more before moving to the door. I opened it to let in the bright sunlight again. 'I'm going for a walk,' I told him. 'It helps me to unwind after a flight.' Although the journey caused me to feel tired, it was the first time in a week I hadn't been under pressure. Leaving London for a while was good for my health and I was determined to make the most of it.

Munich was a fascinating city in the southernmost part of Germany, and the apartment was right in the heart of the action. Although it was an industrial city, everyone seemed to be employed in making beer, but it had many other roles as well... in printing and publishing, in the fashion industry, in manufacturing optical and precision instruments, and even in the motion-picture industry.

Wandering along the streets in the centre of the city, I discovered many museums, theatres and night-clubs. After strolling for an hour, I retraced my steps to return to the flat. Berg was awake, sitting up on the bed as he perused a sheaf of notes.

'Couldn't sleep, eh?' I commented. 'You're probably suffering from jet-lag.'

'I had my sleep,' he returned calmly. 'Thirty minutes is sufficient for me to catch up during the daytime. By the way, I got in touch with our contact. He's a man called Kaspar Levenson staying at the Vier Jahreszeiten Hotel in Maximilianstrasse, just a short distance from here. We're to join him for tea, which doesn't leave us much time.'

I stared at him in disbelief. It was the same person... the same hotel... as mentioned to me by Tania. It was too much of a coincidence to ring true. Yet it was the same man!

The Vier Jahreszeiten Hotel was known as a super-de-luxe hotel. It was exquisite in every sense of the word. Not surprisingly, the prices for meals and drinks were set to balance the quality of the hotel and the service. For most people, spending a day at the hotel with their family would cost almost as much as a month at home in Britain, but no one ever complained it wasn't worth the expense. There were head-waiters and flunkeys willing to do one's bidding at a moment's notice, a menu that could hardly be challenged, luxury beyond the belief of most travellers in the food, furniture and furnishings, and a priceless atmosphere which only money could buy. In addition, one could use the heated indoor swimming-pool, the jacuzzi, and the well-stocked gymnasium. A flunkey took us to the restaurant where Kaspar Levenson sat at a table. He was leaning back with his eyes half-closed. There was no reaction as we stood before him.

'I'm Jack Berg,' introduced my colleague meekly. 'Carrie told me I should come to you if I ever needed help.' There was still no movement from the man. 'Do you know she's dead?' he went on.

The words appeared to be the key which opened the lock. Levenson allowed the shields to fall from his eyes to scan us both in one long glance. 'Welcome to my table,' he greeted with a total lack of sincerity. 'Sit down!'

We settled into the comfortable chairs and I became sensitive about the state of my crumpled clothes which had creased badly during the flight. Levenson, on the other hand, was immaculate, wearing a tweed jacket, a spotlessly-white shirt, and a neat red bow-tie. I presumed he was about forty-five years' old but it was difficult to tell because he was very fat. His shiny bald head reflected the light and his eyes seemed to be too close together. In a way, he reminded me of Calvin, my informant at the Dog and Duck, but there the image ended. He snapped his fingers to order tea and it was set out on the table shortly afterwards.

'Let me make two things clear,' he began dispassionately. 'One. There's no way I would even talk to you if it hadn't been for Carrie. She was a distant relative on my sister's side. I don't deal with small-fry! If I did, I wouldn't be able to afford to stay at this hotel. I'd be sweating it out in a small apartment in Luisenstrasse.'

The poor humour of the philosophy, or the irony of the truth, failed to inspire me. It did tell me, however, that Kaspar Levenson was well-informed. Apart from other things, he knew exactly where the small-fry was staying!

'What's the second thing?' asked Berg, looking wimpy as he usually did.

'Very simply this,' continued our host, driving home his message. 'I deal in arms. All kinds of weapons. What I know about Nazi war criminals and their activities can be put in a thimble and lost.'

'Are you saying you can't help us?' I asked, beginning to feel anger rising within me. I didn't relish the idea of coming all the way to Munich on a wild-goose chase. Nor did it thrill me to think how I would have to justify the cost of two flight tickets to the administrator of expenses at the newspaper when the trip had been a complete waste of time.

Levenson held up his hand with a world of experience within him. 'Patience! Just have a little patience! Let's have some tea before you get indigestion! The world will wait until we've finished.'

'But will you help us?' I demanded.

Our host stared at me with his narrow eyes which seemed to burn with anger. 'Don't think I'm not sympathetic to you. I'm a Jew. Most of my family had numbers branded on their arms at concentration camps. Dachau isn't very far from here, in case you don't know your geography. But beware of your enemies. They're all around you. The followers of national socialism... the

Nazis... may have been defeated in war, but they exist in their hundreds of thousands in peacetime. I know what I'm talking about.' He drank deeply from his cup before continuing. 'I don't think it wise for people to be let loose in the world seeking out information. It's dangerous! I hope you've brought sufficient money for what you want.'

'How much are you asking?' I advanced, knowing we had little money on us.

Levenson shook his head from side to side. 'Not for me! I don't want your money!' He paused to look at us again. 'Well, you're both old enough to know what you're getting yourselves into, I suppose.' He fished a piece of paper from his shirt pocket. 'The name is Gunter Hausmann. He lives close to Berchtesgaden. Does that ring any bells with you? Hm... it doesn't seem to. Well... if you're as resourceful as you make out, you won't have any trouble finding him at this address.'

Berg took the piece of paper and stuffed it into his top jacket pocket. 'Thanks!' he said appreciatively. 'We owe you.'

The fat man burst into laughter. 'I like it. He owes me! What is that supposed to mean?'

'Well that's it,' continued The Rooter getting to his feet quickly. 'We got what we came for. We may as well go.'

'You mean you're giving up drinking tea at the Vier Jahreszeiten hotel when it's offered to you for nothing?'

'Yes. We haven't really time for all this. But I do owe you for the information.'

'Return the favour when you get to Heaven. I may need it there.' Our host was still laughing as we left the hotel.

I didn't like Levenson very much but I sympathised with him for Berg's strange attitude. 'When do you suggest we should contact Hausmann?' I asked as we walked away from the hotel.

'It's probably wiser to leave it until tomorrow,' he replied tiredly. 'I think we've done enough for one day... what with all the travelling.'

'Then how about going to a night-club to unwind,' I suggested.

He failed to reply and I assumed that wimps didn't frequent such places. They stayed at home and contented themselves with one boring hobby or another. As soon as we entered from the bright sunlight into the relative darkness of the apartment, I found myself staring into the face of an enormous man with a completely square head. Even his very short haircut had been shorn to look square. 'What in heaven's name...?' I began, staring in horror at the giant, trying to focus my eyes after the sudden change of light to shade. He pulled us both by the front of our shirts into the living-room and squared himself in the doorway to prevent any sudden departure. In the gloom, I could see another man laying full-length on the bed in the other room, with his hands behind his head in a relaxed pose.

'Strogoff!' I exclaimed in astonishment.

'How touching!' he replied. 'You actually remember my name!' His face broke into an ugly smile, continuing to resume its harsh skeletal structure.

'What the hell are you doing here?' I remonstrated.

'My dear old chap,' he laughed, clearly amused by my reaction. 'I came here to visit you. What kind of a host are you with such a bloody awful greeting? Life is so full of coincidences, don't you think? I mean, you attended my meeting in London at the People's Palace with that bitch of an Israeli agent. Now we meet again in this foreign country. Don't you consider that odd? By the way, my apologies for the rough way you were handled at the time, but you did become a nuisance. Oh, forgive me, I haven't introduced you to my friend, Karl. He's rather taken a liking to me.'

'How did you know we were here?' asked Berg, finding his tongue.

Strogoff stared at him closely. 'This is a face I have seen often. Tell me, why do I regard you as the enemy?'

'Never mind about me!' snapped Berg, without rising to the bait. 'What do you want?'

'I see, you're a man who likes to get to the heart of the matter quickly. That's a pity! I enjoy the play on words, the art of toying with a situation, the fun of innuendo. Still, if it pleases you, we'll get down to business. I understand you're here for information concerning secret lists of Nazi war criminals retained exclusively by various national countries. It was in my mind we might be of mutual assistance to each other.'

I stared at him with a puzzled expression on my face and then turned to Berg. 'What the hell's going on here?'

'Come now, gentlemen,' continued the Russian, with a grotesque grin on his face. 'Let's not be melodramatic! Just a little imagination and perhaps a token of friendship towards each other. I'd like that. I really would. If not, it all gets very dull. Very dull indeed!' He joined his hands across his chest, locking his fingers together tightly. Then he released them and rose from the bed. He muttered something in German to the other man who still blocked the front door. 'Now, I suggest we join forces in a little venture. In fact, I'm going to take you into my confidence by revealing a place some distance from here in the mountains. My fortress... my headquarters!'

'What for?' I asked, angry at being held captive. 'Why do you need us?'

'Sadly, I'm too well known. I have a reputation. Time has failed to release me from the bonds of the past. But, united, we can be a force to be reckoned with.'

'You're out of your mind,' I told him foolishly. 'Your plans are of no interest to us!'

'You were interested enough to come to my meeting in London!'

'Only for my own specific reasons!'

Strogoff laughed loudly, ending in a long-winded gasp. 'Do you hear that, Karl? Such innocence!' he mocked, gesticulating with his hands towards Heaven. His face suddenly hardened in a horrifying way and he leaned forward to stare closely at both of us. 'I'm surprised the two of you have teamed up together. Jack Berg, a man dedicated to rooting out Nazi war criminals, and Herr Erdbeer, the grandson of an SS Colonel. All right, this is the point where we stop playing games!' he hissed. 'We have work to do! I want two things from you. I need the information you seek from Gunter Hausmann. Money is no object and I can pay my way. After that, I want to meet Der Bankvorsteher.'

Berg laughed in his face. 'How the hell do we meet Der Bankvorsteher? I was right the first time. You're out of your mind!'

'Oh really!' replied Strogoff in a sinister manner. 'Well perhaps you ought to collaborate on a more equitable basis with your friend because he'll be meeting him in a few days' time.' He stared directly into my eyes. 'Isn't that so, Herr Erdbeer?'

'Where do you get your information, Strogoff?' I demanded, knowing it was a rhetorical question. He seemed to know everything as it happened, as though watching the developments of a play as they unfolded on the stage.

'I like the way you operate,' he countered. 'The grandson of an SS Colonel who's the senior executive of a private bank. You adopt the cover of a newspaper reporter who rarely writes a story very well. Quite brilliant really! But I'm wondering whether my information is slightly incorrect. You see, I take the view you might be Der Bankvorsteher in person yourself!'

'If that were the case,' I rattled, trying not to laugh at his ridiculous assumption, 'why am I here in Germany looking for Gunter Hausmann?'

'I don't know,' he replied calmly. 'But I'm working on it. I'll find out eventually. You can bet your life on it!' He paused for a moment. 'Why else would you be chased by Israeli agents through the London docks after you disposed of the body of an Israeli agent?'

'Carrie?'

'I believe that was her name. Carrie Fisher!' I stared at Berg, recalling how I'd been terrorised in the hunt through St. Katherine's Dock. 'Why else would Jack Berg try to kill you with a rifle at her funeral in Cheshunt, after he planted a bomb in her brother's car to blow him to smithereens?'

Berg looked very disconcerted as Strogoff reeled off the facts, and I considered the information slowly, trying to deduce why he should want to kill me. 'Is that the truth?' I asked Berg, as a tinge of anger welled-up inside me.

'He would love to deny it,' pressed the Russian, 'but he can't. Not while I'm here... because it is the truth!'

'I'll ask you once more,' I said calmly to Berg, beginning to seethe inside.

'It's true,' he replied lamely, 'but it's not the way he makes it sound. There were good reasons for my actions which I can explain.'

'I'm dying to hear the explanation,' muttered Strogoff in a low voice.

'What I have to say is to be said in private,' snapped Berg.

'Very well,' shrugged Strogoff casually. 'Your personal problems have nothing to do with me. I'm not really that interested!' He turned to me slowly. 'You should be more careful whom you choose as your friends, Herr Erdbeer!'

'What do you want me to do?' I asked the Russian, pretending to be so angry I was willing to switch allegiance to his side.

'I'm asking you to share the information you receive from Gunter Hausmann, that's all. I want a photocopy of the names and the details he sells you.'

'Very well,' I agreed. 'But I may call on you to help with the funding. Hausmann won't sell the information cheaply.'

'You can't agree to that!' intervened Berg in despair.

'Shut up!' I snapped. 'You're excluded from this deal until you offer me a satisfactory explanation why you tried to kill me!'

'Furthermore,' Strogoff continued, ignoring Berg's outburst, 'if you're not Der Bankvorsteher, I want to know his real identity and where he's located. That too is important!'

'I understand. But this is a quid pro quo situation. There's something I want in exchange. Firstly, a share of the treasure when we get hold of it. Secondly, sanctuary from my enemies in Israel and the Nazi party.'

'No problem, Herr Erdbeer. The treasure will be enough for all of us. As for sanctuary, you can stay at my fortress for as long as you wish.'

'As a prisoner... no thanks!' I retorted.

'Not as a prisoner. I'm forming a team to help me with my plans. You could have rank and power if you wanted them.'

'What do you have in mind?' intervened Berg wildly. 'King Strogoff or President Strogoff?'

The Russian muttered a few words to Karl. The giant moved forward to grasp Berg's arm, twisting it behind his back.

'Take it easy!' I called out, as Berg's face showed his agony. 'There's no need to get physical about this.'

The criminal nodded to his bodyguard who released him, and Berg rubbed his arm vigorously to ease the pain. 'You think you can conquer everyone by force!' he shouted, almost beside himself with anger.

'It seems to work,' returned Strogoff, with an evil smile on his face as he stood up.

'How do I get in touch with you?' I asked naively.

'At this stage of the game, I'm the one who gets in touch with you, Herr Erdbeer,' he told me coldly. 'Don't ring us, we'll ring you!' He laughed at his own joke, ending with the same gasping sound.

After he left the apartment with Karl, I poured myself a drink in the kitchen and stared at Berg. 'You've a lot of explaining to do, my friend!' I challenged fiercely. 'You'd better start talking fast!'

'If you knew anything about the situation, you'd realise I can't tell you anything at present,' he bleated, as though his personal problems excused him. 'Please don't ask me to explain.'

'I'm not asking you, you little weasel!' I snarled. 'I'm going to kill you if you don't tell me!'

He remained silent and I started to lose my temper. I warned him once again of the consequences if he refused to comply which still brought no response. Against my better judgement, I adopted a martial arts pose intimidatingly. He showed no emotion except to repress a smile at my ridiculous stance, believing I was bluffing. I was never going to be able to frighten him into submission. It left me with no alternative but to attack. He soon realised his mistake when I took hold of his arm and shoulder to bounce him off the chalky-white wall in the very small room. As he groaned and tried to get to his feet, I assailed him again. His threshold of pain was fused at a very low level and, if the truth were known, he was probably an even greater coward than myself. Ultimately, he screamed out to yield and I glowered at him fiercely.

'All right, all right! I'll tell you,' he conceded reluctantly, rubbing his shoulder tenderly as I relaxed and sat on a chair. 'But what I have to tell you is between the two of us. It has to remain a secret at all cost. If not, then years of painstaking work will go down the drain. Do I have your solemn promise?'

'Stop stalling and get on with it!' I commanded, determined to get to the bottom of it. 'If you think you can try to kill me and get away with it...'

'Of course I didn't try to kill you!' he interrupted, pausing to nurse his bruises. 'If I wanted to kill you nothing would have stopped me! I had to kill Carrie though. That was the sad part of it. She was an Israeli agent but she had to go. It was most regrettable because she was honest, loyal and industrious, and she worked well for her country. That was the problem... she was too good! A woman who was totally dedicated in her pursuit of Nazi war criminals, and she knew what was going on in International Three Thousand. Her life was at risk from both sides. Who could foretell her own countrymen would issue a death warrant? But that's the way it goes in espionage. You see, she concentrated all her efforts on Conrad Hayle, the Minister of Justice.'

'What was so wrong in that?'

'There's a secret file on him. His real identity is Isaac Czernovsky. He's an Israeli agent who infiltrated the higher ranks of the Nazis behind International Three Thousand. He was planted there. In that position, he's invaluable to us. I was the only person in Britain who knew anything about him. Carrie pressed too hard. She discovered a file on him which indicated he was the relative of a Nazi war criminal, which was the cover he'd been given, and she intended to expose him. She would have ruined two years' work. We had to stop her so I ransacked your apartment and carried out my orders to eliminate her.'

'What a lousy thing to do!' I gasped, filled with a mixture of anger and sorrow. 'And she was the woman you were going to marry at one time. What kind of scum are you, Berg?'

'Some of us place country first and personal life second. But perhaps you wouldn't understand that. When we tried to dispose of her body that night, we were followed by our own agents who tried to frighten you off the scent. In effect, they were trying to scare you enough so you'd give up. After all, you were implicated by being an accessory after the fact. It was a great disappointment to us when you turned up at her funeral. Carrie's brother, Hymie, was the next person on the hit-list. We didn't know how much she might have told him about Hayle. No one knew whether she confided in him. We couldn't take the chance. After the bomb went off, I fired at you a number of times with a rifle. I'm an excellent shot and made sure I missed you narrowly on each occasion. There was no intention to wound you... let alone kill you. We didn't want the police to start an investigation on the shooting of a newspaper reporter and open up another can of worms. There was only one problem which concerned me. I got Hayle to sign the recommendation for you to join International Three Thousand. On the night, he was forced to examine it in front of all the new recruits. You must have thought it strange he never questioned it.'

'It did pass through my mind a few times,' I replied attentively.

'Well, what could he say? He had to bluff his way out of it and hoped you'd go along with the idea too.'

I locked the door of the apartment and began to undress. 'I'll take the bed... you take the couch!' I muttered, scowling at him to show my disinterest in his welfare. 'We'll talk about this again tomorrow.'

'What about Strogoff?' he asked dolefully.

'We'll talk about him tomorrow as well! I've had enough for one day. I need to sleep!' I climbed into the bed and slid between the cool sheets thinking about the events of the day. The appearance of Strogoff was too much to cast to the back of my mind, while the revelations of Jack Berg needed a great deal of thought. The two men were making my life sheer hell and I had to do something about it! I lay churning it over in my head for what seemed like hours. It was some time well into the night when I finally gave up the struggle and fell asleep!

CHAPTER FOURTEEN

At first light, I made Berg hire a car and we drove to Berchtesgaden. We continued from Munich on the Alpine road which was the biggest tourist attraction of the eastern Bavarian Alps. The Berchtesgaden region was absolutely magnificent with its rugged giant mountains and its Alpine lakes of exquisite beauty. It took us thirty-five minutes to reach Ramsau, a superb mountain climbing base for the peak of Hochkalter which towered above it. Close by was the Hintersee, a small lake locked in steep slopes. We passed the tumultuous torrent raining down through the Wimbach Gorge which originated in the snowfields separating Hochkalter from the higher and wilder Waltzmann. Berchtesgaden was the centre of this area, known as an old market town. It was so densely wooded that only one sixth of it could be cleared for the erection of buildings. The main feature in the town was the castle-palace, an Augustinian abbey which belonged to the Wittelsbach family, the rulers of Bavaria. In modern times, it had been turned into a local museum. The views here were outstanding. We drove from the town up the Rossfeld mountain road running in a loop around the 4,900 foot Rossfeld which offered breathtaking vistas of the Berchtesgaden region and the Austrian mountains across the border. I had made a note to visit Kehlsteinhaus, the former Eagle's Nest of Adolf Hitler, normally reached from Obersalzberg by bus and elevator.

We soon found Gunter Hausmann's house. It was a built in typical Bavarian style and sported flowers which hung in buckets from the roof and lodged in barrels in the front garden. The temperature was lower out here... much cooler than in Munich ... but it was a delightful place to live. For some strange reason my mind floated back to the other informant I knew so well. Calvin would sit on his stool at the Dog and Duck, swinging his right arm mechanically to his mouth saying: "Comes to mind... comes to mind!" But he was dead now, and I would dearly love to see his murderer brought to justice.

Berg and I glanced at each other for a few moments and then I hammered on the door with my fist in the absence of any other means to attract attention. Shortly, Hausmann opened it and stared at us seriously. He bade us enter with a sweep of his hand and we shuffled into the dark hallway, unable to see anything once the front door had been closed; our eyes were still accustomed to the brilliant sunshine outside. He led us into the lounge and smiled.

'Good morning, gentlemen!' he welcomed in excellent English, although his accent was slightly clipped. 'I'm Gunter Hausmann. I welcome you to my home.' He was over six feet tall and very skinny. About fifty years of age, he was greying slightly at the temples, balding a little, and sported a goatee beard. He dressed very smartly in a light brown suit and a pure white shirt. There was a tie-pin attached to his contrasting tie and I took the view it might be a miniature camera. 'Let's have some refreshment and discuss matters relevant to all of us.'

We relaxed in comfortable chairs as Hausmann studied us closely in the dim light. Despite the fact the house was lodged in the mountains, the temperature in the room was quite high. Under the light above him, his face appeared slightly longer because of the absence of hair at the front of his head, while his salt-and-pepper goatee beard looked much darker. Hausmann had two obvious nervous habits. The first was to keep pulling at his beard with the thumb and index finger of his right hand as if it needed tidying every so often. The second involved blinking his eyes in a kind of nervous twitch which caused one to believe he was agreeing with them whenever it happened. Yet, despite these nervous traits, he carried an air of authority which commanded respect and his manner, although curt, was pleasant. Similarly to those people who enjoy taking their time to undertake business, it was apparent that Hausmann was in no hurry to launch the meeting, and he scanned our faces in his own time. Up in the mountains, everything took on a relaxed tone. There was no urgency, no hurry, to do anything in particular. After a short while, he stood up and went to a coffee-machine in the corner of the room and poured out cups of the hot liquid which he offered to us.

'I hope you like coffee,' he ventured. 'It's all I drink except at meals. Have you tried Enzian. It's a Bavarian spirit drink... like schnapps flavoured with the root of the yellow gentian. It goes well after having a large meal.' We took the cups of coffee and smiled weakly at him. 'You know, many people think we Germans are arrogant and warlike for the whole of our lives, but that's not the case at all. You will learn to love us... if you live that long!'

'What do you mean by that?' asked Berg with alarm.

Hausmann stroked his beard in his usual manner as he sat down. 'Information of the sensitive kind brings its own danger. The more sensitive it is, the more dangerous it becomes. We live in troubled times where the emphasis on intelligence is paramount. More wars in progress in the offices of secret service agencies in the world than were ever fought on any battlefield. You're two are amateurs with no protection or support. I can only presume you like to live dangerously.'

'You don't believe in pulling punches, do you?' muttered Berg, swallowing hard as he showed some degree of concern about his future.

'It depends on how much you value your life,' continued our host. There's an old Chinese saying: "Man with head in clouds get feet wet in puddle." I wouldn't like to hazard a guess as to how many eyes are focussed on the pair of you at this precise moment.'

I coughed slightly and glanced over my shoulder casually, pretending the words made no impact on me. Nonetheless, I began to feel distinctly uncomfortable. We were located in some misbegotten part of a strange town high up in the mountains in South Germany. Anything could happened to us here and no one would be the wiser. Who was this Gunter Hausmann anyway?

'I've been in this business a long time, gentlemen,' he went on. 'I know what it takes. The difficulty I face at the moment concerns the on-going use of the information if I let you have it. Naturally, it's available to anyone who wishes to pay the price, with certain exceptions. The exceptions make me reluctant to deal with you. For example, you may pass it on to undesirable parties.'

'What undesirable parties?' asked Berg naively.

'I know only too well about Strogoff and the deal he offered you,' he returned coolly.

Berg and I glanced at each other with the same thought passing through our minds. It was patently clear someone was either watching every movement we made, or more likely, they had planted some sort of bugging device somewhere in the apartment. How else could he know? It was astonishing that such information had travelled so far, so fast, to a person high up in the Bavarian Alps. 'If you know that, why don't you deal with him yourself?' I demanded boldly.

'Because he's the last person I would ever want to deal with. I know what he would do with the information. He'd blackmail every person on the list... bleed them to death.'

'You'd rather protect the war criminals of your country from him, would you?' Berg's question was very incisive.

'If you believe that you're crazy! Strogoff's a threat to everyone. You have no idea what he's up to!'

'Surprise me,' I challenged waspishly. 'What is he up to?'

'We're not dealing with a normal situation here... not where that man's concerned. Strogoff is devious. In the first place, he's trying to lay his hands on the money raised from Nazi war treasures.'

I shrugged my shoulder disconsolately. 'I doubt whether he would make many inroads on that ambition. But if he does succeed, what then?'

Hausmann blinked and twitched nervously before raising his coffee cup to his lips to sip the liquid noisily. 'In the second place, Strogoff's blackmailing many war criminals. He now has his own army in a fortress not far away from here... in the Zugspitze. It's Germany's highest peak, rising to nearly ten thousand feet. Most people think it's impossible to get about up there, but the Bavarian Alps are highly accessible. He has a fortress with helicopters and armoured cars, as well as about a hundred men and women in uniform.'

'Aren't the authorities aware of this?' I asked.

'Of course they are. There are spies everywhere. But the military have no wish to get involved in a costly private war on Germany's highest peak. And, anyway, he's causing no problems at the moment. Now, gentlemen, let's get down to business. Tell me exactly what you wish to know!'

'We want the lists of Nazi war criminals for each of the thirteen countries of the United Nations War Crimes Commission,' blurted Berg hopefully.

Hausmann shrugged, stroking his beard again thoughtfully. 'You realise, naturally, what you ask is impossible. However, I may be able to help you with regard to three countries. How much are you prepared to pay for the information?'

I emptied my coffee cup trying not to show my distaste for the ugly liquid and put it down beside me. 'How do we know the information is authentic?'

He bridled at the remark. 'The ability of my sources in the countries concerned is unquestioned. They are trusted people. The data I've provided over the past twenty years has always been authentic and accurate. Let's be clear about his! Anyone who provides false information is either out of business or dead within a very short time. There's no margin for error!' He moved towards the coffee-machine again as the door opened and a beautiful young woman entered the room. 'Ah, gentlemen! This is my daughter Helga!'

I stood up and bowed, leaving Berg firmly entrenched in his seat. Helga smiled at us and began to clear away the cups. She was a slender, beautiful young woman with short blonde hair, sparkling blue eyes, a retrousse nose, and high cheekbones. I was stunned by her natural beauty, forgetting in that instant my feelings for Tania. Even when she had left the room, the outline of her delicate face and lithe body lingered in my mind like a haunting refrain.

'Well, gentlemen,' continued our host. 'Let's negotiate for the three files you desire. If we reach an agreement, and I'm certain we will, there's something further we need to discuss... about availability.'

He reached into the pocket of his suit and produced a piece of paper on which he had written some figures. Berg leaned across and glanced at it before passing the slip to me. I stared at the figures with a dull expression on my face, ostensibly to show complete disinterest. Ted Flanders would fire me on the spot if I committed the newspaper to a sum of that magnitude.

'Out of the question!' I told him bluntly. 'Completely out of the question! You'll have to do better than that!'

He smiled casually and looked at the ceiling for a while as though the answer lay there or that the effluxion of time would resolve the problem. Shortly afterwards, he returned his gaze to us again. 'Write your own figure then?' he muttered. 'It'll save time. What do you think such information is worth?'

I opened the small briefcase I had brought with me and shuffled some papers around. It was simply a ploy to play for time. After a while, I produced a pen and halved the figure he had entered before handing the slip of paper back to him.

He stared at the figure benignly and his hand plundered a small dish of peanuts which he crunched noisily. 'With customers like you,' he said at length, 'I would be starving within a year. Don't you know the value of this information? Strogoff would pay me handsomely for it!'

'Oh, come on, Gunter!' responded Berg. 'You don't want to sell it to him. You're discussing it with us... not to sell it to him! If the Russian authorities found out you'd given him the means to develop an army, which might be used against them, they would cut you to pieces. It's common knowledge he blackmails war criminals and he's after the Nazi funds. You've got to keep well out of it where he's concerned or the KGB will destroy you and your family for a serious error of judgement. That's more like the truth, isn't it!'

Hausmann's face fell at the tirade which obviously struck home and he started blinking and twitching. From that moment onwards, he decided to ignore Berg and looked at me, as though I was a more reasonable man than my colleague. 'What do you say if we split the difference?' he suggested.

'If you accept half your original figure as I've suggested, I reckon we have a deal,' I replied excitedly, disregarding the ultimate confrontation with Ted Flanders and the way he would react when he discovered what I had done. 'But how do you know we won't sell the information to Strogoff at a higher price? He might use force against us, in which case we couldn't do anything about it.'

'I've thought about that one very carefully,' he countered quickly. 'The information is stored on microfilm. I'll give it to you when you bring the money. In the meantime, I've taken pains to arrange for another microfilm to be prepared which contains false information. You can take that one with you now. That's the one you give to Strogoff when he comes after you. And he will do so!'

'Thank you very much!' remonstrated Berg, with an anguished expression on his face. 'And what happens when Strogoff finds out it's false? He'll be after our hides like a shot! You're putting a pistol to our heads!'

'Why do you think you're getting this information so cheaply?' growled our host. 'Some agents would give their lives for it! How you deal with our mutual Russian enemy is your concern. I deal purely and solely in information!'

The atmosphere inside the room was becoming increasingly hostile and I wanted to get out of there as quickly as possible. 'All right, Gunter,' I said hastily. 'Let's have both the real and the false microfilm and we'll start the ball rolling. There's a lot to be done if I'm going to get the money sent to you from London.'

'You'll arrange for it to be paid in United States dollars,' he urged. He removed two buff envelopes from the inside pocket of his jacket and laid them on the table. 'The one with an 'X' marked on the front is the false one,' he told me. 'I hope you can resolve your problems.' He stroked his beard firmly as I rose and picked up the envelopes. Hausmann followed my example and led us to the front door before shepherding us out into the street where we adjusted our eyes to the bright sunlight.

Berg was furious at the new development. 'You're crazy even to consider we can outwit Strogoff!' he fumed, fearing his life had been placed in great danger. 'What's going to happen when he finds out?'

'One step at a time,' I told him calmly. 'One step at a time. We have to play the game by Hausmann's rules, otherwise we'll never get what we came for. Think about that for a while.'

We walked on a little until I heard the sound of someone calling to us. It was Helga urging us to stop, waving my briefcase aloft in her hand. Breathlessly, she reached us to give it to me and I grasped her hand instinctively.

'When can I see you again?' I asked quietly, staring directly into her eyes. 'I must see you... soon!'

'You can do that when you come to our house again,' she conveyed, her bosom heaving from the physical effort required to reach us.

'No, I mean tonight. I want to see you tonight!'

'You don't understand...'

'Tonight!' I pressed insistently. 'Please say you'll meet me!'

She paused to reflect for a moment, scanning my face closely. 'All right,' she agreed, with a tinge of hesitancy in her voice as though committing a transgression. 'I'll meet you at seven o'clock at Gastof Neuhaus in Marktplatz. It's a restaurant.'

'I released her hand and smiled. 'Seven o'clock at Gastof Neuhaus!' She ran off like the wind and I turned to Berg who stared at me and shook his head slowly. 'She's the most beautiful and exciting woman I have ever seen,' I told him. 'Did you notice the high cheek bones and those sparkling blue eyes?'

He showed his displeasure unremittingly. 'I never mix business with pleasure... especially with Germans! You should concentrate on what we've come to do... not chasing women! Steer clear of her. No good will come of it, I assure you!'

I considered him to be a very wet blanket and we drove back to Munich with very little to say to each other. When we returned to the apartment I opened one of the buff envelopes and took out the strips of microfilm, holding them up to the light to examine the details with a pocket magnifying glass. 'Hey!' I exclaimed angrily. We've been short-changed! The names of extend from A to M. He only gave us half the alphabet of war criminals. I wonder why?'

Berg appeared less than interested. 'He won't give you the rest until he receives payment,' he muttered dryly.

I hid the information in a drawer in the wardrobe. I decided to keep well away from him until leaving for Berchtesgaden again later in the day. I drove directly to Gastof Neuhaus in Marktplatz and sat patiently at a table to wait for her. Casting an eye over the passing crowd, I tried to spot her before she found me but the light was already gone which made the task impossible. Seven o'clock came and went but there was no sign of her. I made up excuses for her to dampen my disappointment, however there was little comfort in such deception. It seemed I had wasted my time. At eight-thirty I settled the bill and began to walk away. I had hardly taken a dozen steps when someone moved from the shadows and pulled at my arm. 'Helga!' I exclaimed, staring at her beautiful face in the moonlight. 'Where have you been?'

'It wasn't possible to get away earlier,' she explained.

'Do you want something to eat or drink?'

She shook her head. 'Let's walk and talk.'

I took her hand and we strolled for a while without speaking as the cool night breeze cutting in from the east. Eventually, I stopped and faced her squarely, rubbing one of my hands gently across her cheek affectionately. She leaned her face into it, clearly indicating her feelings.

'You're so beautiful...' I began passionately.

She placed the tips of her fingers to my lips to silence me. 'Don't say anything. Please! Tonight is merely a fleeting moment of time... a single second spent in the years of eternity.'

I stared at her in puzzlement, unable to follow her train of thought. 'What are you trying to say?' I asked apprehensively.

There was no immediate reply and we turned to walk a little further. 'I'm married,' she replied. 'I have a husband. But he's so very boring. It's funny, I married him because I was bored, now it's even worse. I want to feel like a real woman but it never happens with him.'

I was stunned at her revelation. 'What do you intend to do?' I asked.

'What do you intend to do?' she responded. She laughed at my expression. 'I hope you're not a fuddy-duddy as well!'

'On the contrary. I'm no fuddy-duddy!'

'Good! I've booked a room for us at the Stiftshotel in Bahnhofstrasse. I know I won't be disappointed.' She flung her arms around my neck and we entered into a long passionate kiss. 'Hm,' she cooed finally. 'I know I won't be disappointed!'

We reached the hotel and spent the next two hours in bed together in an exhilarating session of intimacy. Afterwards we dressed and some time later, just before we left the hotel, she handed me two buff envelopes... .one marked with an 'X' on the front.. 'What's this?' I asked.

'A parting gift from me. It's the other half of the microfilm... from N to Z. Goodbye, Herr Erdbeer! At last I feel like a real woman. I'll never forget you!'

I drove back to the apartment in Munich and decided to cheer myself up by drinking the best part of a small bottle of whisky which I purchased on the way. Berg was nowhere to be seen. It was rather pleased not to have to gaze at his miserable face. I took the buff envelopes which Helga had given me and put them in the tea-caddy in the kitchen for safety. It was just as well, for a little while later the door opened without warning and I found myself staring at Karl who burst into the room. He brandished a pistol to ensure the place was empty in case his master was in any danger. Then Strogoff entered, closed the door behind him, and limped into the living-room. He rested a black executive case on the table and sat down in a chair. 'So!' he began, opening the case to show me it was full of United States dollars packed in neat little bundles. 'Here's the money! Now... I think you have something to give me.'

'Go to hell!' I shouted, as the whisky filled me with Dutch courage.

'Don't play games!' he warned menacingly. 'Give me the microfilm!'

The spirit caused me to giggle and he quickly tired of my attitude, making a sideways movement with his head to the bodyguard. Karl took hold of my shoulders, heaved me off the chair, and dragged me roughly into the kitchen. He forced my head under the tap in the sink and turned on the cold water, holding me in a fixed position so that I couldn't move. I felt I was drowning and yelled when I was unable to stand the torture any longer. He released me, throwing a tea-towel over my head, not as a measure of good faith but to prepare me for the next onslaught. My head felt as large as a giant football but before I could feel sorry for myself I was propelled back into the living-room and pushed roughly into a chair.

'Do we have to go on like this?' demanded Strogoff. 'Violence always wins in the end if one is prepared to use it indiscriminately. Now... where's the microfilm?'

The man was right! The meek would never inherit the earth! It was the revolutionaries, the dictators, the tyrants and the despots who controlled it. Karl grabbed me by the collar and started to slap my face until I yielded like a coward. I went to the tiny wardrobe in the bedroom and produced one of the buff envelopes... the one marked with the letter 'X' on the front... .which I passed to Strogoff.

'You should keep away from the bottle,' he advised. 'It impairs your judgement.' He opened the envelope and took out the strips of microfilm which he held up to the light. He screwed up one eye to focus accurately. 'What's this?' he demanded angrily. 'This film has been cut. It shows only the names of those criminals with surnames beginning from A to M. What happened to the rest of it?' I staggered over to the executive case with a pain throbbing through my head at each heartbeat, and examined the money. 'What happened to the rest of this?'

'You're not that drunk then!' grunted the Russian. 'The rest of the money's in a safe place. It's my insurance you'll give me the information I need.'

'Well keeping half the microfilm is my insurance that I'll get paid.' I started to laugh, which had the effect of setting him off as well.

'I like it, Herr Erdbeer,' he roared. 'We're two people from the same mould. I'll pay you the balance when you deliver the rest of the information.'

'Tell me?' I asked, still slurring my words. 'How did you know what the cost of the information would be?'

'I don't think you need to know that,' he replied austerely. 'The rest of the money's at my fortress. It'll be a good opportunity for you to visit me in my domain in the Zugspitze.'

'Where exactly is this place?' I asked suspiciously.

'All you have to do is to start making your way up the mountain. My troops will see you coming and direct you to the right place. However, I'm returning there tomorrow by helicopter. Both you and your friend can ride with me. I'll be here at ten o'clock in the morning.

Make certain you have the rest of the information.' He uttered a brief order in German to his henchman and, by the time I had collected my wits, they had gone.

I spent the next twenty minutes drinking coffee to bring myself back to normality. Once I had sobered up a little, I checked the money in the executive case which was practically the same amount I had agreed with Hausmann. How Strogoff knew what Hausmann would ask was a complete mystery to me. I drove all the way back to Berchtesgaden without delay. Hausmann must have known what had happened but he didn't blink an eyebrow. How could I have possibly secured so much money in such a short time? And why was I bringing it to him at such a late hour? He must have known! He examined the money carefully and blinked and twitched a few times as though recognising the Russian's fingerprints on the soft leather top of the case. Then he handed me a white envelope which he said contained the rest of the true microfilm. I wasted no time and returned to Munich, going directly to the British Embassy.

They were not too pleased with my presence at that time of the morning but they acted effectively in the knowledge I was acting under the direct instructions of the Prime Minister of Britain. We undertook the official procedures with regard to security, which involved my signature on a number of documents, and both the buff envelope containing the right microfilm and the white envelope were eventually locked away in a secure place. It was the only way I could be sure Berg wouldn't steal it. When I arrived back at the apartment it was four o'clock in the morning. Berg was waiting for me and I could see he was agitated.

'Where have you been?' he demanded.

'Why? What's happened?'

'Nothing. I was concerned about you, that's all!'

'That must be the overstatement of the year,' I laughed.

He looked at me strangely. 'Something happened, didn't it? Other than with Hausmann's daughter! Furthermore, I can't find the envelope with the microfilm. Have you any idea where it is?'

He pressed for further information but I withheld the events of the night. 'Tomorrow!' I told him, unwilling to discuss anything in the early hours of the morning. 'I'll tell you all about it tomorrow!'

'For your information,' he riposted, 'it is tomorrow!'

I laughed at his comment. For a change the boot was on the other foot. He had no idea I had received a visit and money from Strogoff. Nor did he realise I had paid Hausmann and taken receipt of the rest of the microfilm. Now he was the one who would have to wait for details! Gradually, the success and achievement of the trip filtered through my tired brain. What a coup! I had obtained the information... and got it for nothing too! Ted Flanders would simply grunt ungratefully when i told him the story, but there was no doubt about it being a highly-prized coup! Needless to say, the end was in sight and I was extremely please with myself. However, I was a long way from home and there was always the possibility of danger in store ... especially when Strogoff was around.

The next day, Karl called at ten o'clock. I looked through the window to see Strogoff sitting in the back seat of the car and nodded quietly to myself. 'You're going to his fortress to pick up the money,' I told Berg bluntly, much to his surprise, as I removed the second buff envelope with the letter 'X' marked on the front from the tea-caddy. 'He has half the microfilm. Here's the rest of it.' I stuffed the envelope into his hand as he started to protest, but I refused to let him have his own way. 'Get back as soon as possible with the money,' I lied, 'and we'll go back to Hausmann and collect the real microfilm.'

I indicated to Karl that Berg was going with him and held my breath in case he insisted that I went along too. The car waited for about half-a-minute and then moved off, leaving me to heave a sigh of relief. Strogoff had obviously asked Berg whether he had the rest of the information. When The Rooter responded affirmatively, the Russian decided there was no point in waiting for me. He could track me down whenever he wanted to. If I discovered the identity of Der Bankvorsteher, Strogoff would find some way to compensate me providing I divulged the details to him. No doubt some fiendish plan was working its way through his evil mind in that direction. I considered coldly it might be the last time I ever saw Jack Berg. The money promised by the Russian was simply a ruse. After landing in his own realm, he would take the buff envelope from Berg and tell Karl to get rid of him. Berg was expendable. He would never know I had the true microfilm in my possession all the time. I disliked being deceitful to a fellow human-being, but someone had changed the ground rules again and we were all fighting for survival! I didn't even dare to think what Strogoff would do when he discovered the information was false. After all, the truth would emerge sooner or later. I hoped it might be later, for everyone's sake... especially when it came to my own!

CHAPTER FIFTEEN

I spent the following day at a leisurely pace, walking along the gentler grassy slopes near the hotel. There was a carefree feeling within my bones I was on vacation again, away from all the worries, the cares and the problems of a troubled world. I ambled along trying not to think of Berg, or International Three Thousand, or about Nazi war criminals. Everything here seemed so remote from the exigencies of civilisation. I ought to have packed and arranged for my return flight to Britain yet I remained, held by the invisible grip of destiny for a reason far beyond my understanding. For a while, I lay on a grassy slope with my eyes closed enjoying the pleasant breeze. At the back of my mind I dwelt on how long I should wait before taking a taxi to the British Embassy to collect the microfilm and report back to the Prime Minister.

In the real world, it was essential to follow that plan without delay, but I allowed the hours to pass by unrewardingly using them for my personal pleasure. Ted Flanders would have had a fit if he could see me stretched out here in this mountain paradise. But why should he grumble? I had accomplished a great deal for the newspaper in a very short space of time. If the assignment had been given to someone else, it was unlikely they would have reached this point for months... maybe even longer! Not that the editor had time for that kind of logic. He simply wanted results! In his rule book there were many whippings and extremely few carrots!

Berg never returned that day. At least he hadn't come back by five o'clock. I decided it would be dangerous to spend another night at the apartment so I booked a seat on the next flight to London. There wasn't much time left for comfort before departure and I hastened to the British Embassy to collect the microfilm and continue speedily to the airport. Before boarding the aircraft, I started to wonder about Berg again, and I rang the apartment with forlorn hope but there was no reply. It was almost certain that Strogoff had carried out his mischievous plan to kill him once he laid his hands on the other part of the microfilm. If Hausmann hadn't been sharp enough to divide it into separate parts, my demise would have been imminent as well. Furthermore, I was glad not to have been forced physically to join the Russian in his helicopter flight to his mountain retreat. If that had happened, the world would never know the truth!

It was customary for me to become agitated at the commencement of a long journey to get home. My blood always raced with impatience and excitement. I could hardly wait to enjoy the comfort of climbing into my own bed. On this occasion, however, sleep was uppermost in my mind and, after landing at London airport, I decided to rent a room for the night at a nearby hotel. Once again fate took a hand. When I returned to my apartment the following morning, there were two police cars outside and uniformed men and detectives crawling over the place. It didn't take someone with the instincts of Sherlock Holmes to realise something serious had happened. I pushed my way through the crowd of inquisitive on-lookers, racing upstairs until I came face to face with a posse of plain-clothed and uniformed police. Once again, the apartment had been wrecked, but this time the damage was total. The intruder had pulled every piece of furniture apart, ripping through all the soft furnishings with a knife, clearly searching for something important. The flash of the police photographer's camera reflected off the white walls of the bedroom and I pushed a policeman aside to find Tania's body on the bed covered with a sheet. I lifted it to stare at her. She lay pale and inert, with blood seeping from a corner of her mouth. There was no doubt she had passed from this world to the next. I noticed the handiwork well. Her appearance and the position in which she had been left was identical to the one in which I had found Carrie on the night she was murdered. I was hustled quickly out of the bedroom and a police inspector started to interrogate me.

'The tenant of this apartment is a person called James Savage. Are you that man?'

'I am.'

'Where were you between the hours of eight and ten o'clock last night?' he began firmly, looking for any signs in my face which might give him a clue to her death.

'I was thirty thousand feet in the air, on my way back from Germany,' I told him, as the shock of Tania's death filtered through my mind to become reality.

'How well did you know this woman?'

'She was a colleague. A fellow newspaper reporter. She was staying here for a while. How was she killed?'

'Who said she was killed?' he riposted suspiciously.

'Look, inspector. She was a young woman, ambitious and happy with life. She wouldn't have taken her own life. Don't play games with me! She was murdered!'

'Then you'll be surprised if I told you she died from an overdose of amphetamines administered between eight and ten o'clock last night. What do you say about that?'

'There's blood seeping from a corner of her mouth. An overdose of tablets wouldn't do a thing like that!' I was angry, almost to the point of insolence. 'I tell you there was no reason for her to take her own life! She wouldn't have done it! We were on an assignment together. If she took tablets, someone forced her to swallow them. That's why there's blood seeping from her mouth! Are there any other marks on her body?'

He refused to answer the question and there was a momentary silence. Then he inhaled deeply and stared directly into my eyes giving me a piercing look. 'I'd like to know more about this assignment of yours, Mr. Savage.' he went on slowly. 'But first, let me ask you... do you follow any kind of a cult?'

'Cult? What are you talking about?'

'Some kind of pursuit you indulged in together perhaps? Something a little out of the ordinary?'

'You've lost me. I don't know what you're talking about.'

He moved to a corner of the room and picked up a black leather case laying on its side. I had never seen it before. I could only presume it belonged to Tania. He opened it and tipped out the contents on the badly-damaged settee for me to examine. It contained a number of Nazi artefacts which could be readily identified by a small flag bearing the insignia of a swastika and a large book with a coloured fylfot on the cover. 'Do you collect souvenirs from World War Two as a hobby?' he asked gruffly.

I was too upset to play games with him, deciding to call a halt to the interrogation. 'Before you pursue any lines of enquiry,' I advised him, much to his astonishment, 'you'll have to contact the Prime Minister. The assignment in which we were engaged is one of the utmost secrecy and of national importance. I can't answer any questions without breaching the Official Secrets Act. If you contact Mr. Maitland, the Personal Assistant to the Prime Minister, he'll advise you accordingly.'

The inspector stared at me tiredly for a few moments, weighing up the situation and then reached for the cordless telephone which lay on the floor. As he dialled the police station to ask them to verify the situation, I looked at some of the artefacts. They were the normal run-of-the-mill collectors' items from Germany in World War Two, comprising an Iron Cross, a steel dagger, some ribbons and medals, an automatic pistol, and a few other incidental items, but it was the book which took my interest. On the cover, below the fylfot, emblazoned in gold, the initials P.C. had been branded, which meant little to me. I opened the tome to realise it represented a family album containing a great deal of text written in neat copperplate handwriting in German and many photographs. While waiting for the inspector to finish the telephone call, I flipped over the pages swiftly, extremely impressed by the painstaking effort of the originator of the volume, scanning the photographs of a high-ranking German officer who had served in both major World Wars. The face was familiar although I couldn't place it, and I went on to look at the pictures of his son as he grew up. I couldn't recognise the boy's face and ended up with some degree of frustration for my ignorance. Remembering the names of people I met had always been one of my weaknesses. There were so many actors in films whose names I couldn't recall when they appeared on the screen, and I often let the problem roll round in my mind for days. Sometimes, in the middle of the night, I would wake to remember who they were, by which time I had forgotten the name of the film in which they had acted. As I closed the cover of the book, I knew that the personal filing cabinet in my brain would start to search the data stored there thoroughly. How long it would take for me to discover the identity of the man, and what use it was likely to be, I had no idea. But it had meant something to Tania or she wouldn't have given her life for it.

'Who found her?' I asked the police inspector, who was still holding the telephone, waiting for a reply.

'Your next door neighbour, Mrs. Fanshaw, called us half an hour ago to say that someone had broken in and was smashing up the place '

'It's obvious, isn't it,' I told him point-blank. 'Whoever killed her wanted these artefacts. That's why they pulled this place apart after she was murdered.'

'What's it all about?' asked the inspector sharply, trying to get me to render information meaningful to him.

'You'll have to ask the Prime Minister,' I insisted, refusing to tell him anything at all.

At that moment, a man in plain clothes emerged from the bedroom and crossed to the inspector to whisper in his ear. My interrogator's lips appeared to tighten as he nodded. Then a voice sounded in the telephone receiver and he grunted before placing it down gently on the ripped settee. 'Well,' he told me, with disappointment in his voice, 'it looks like you're one of the untouchables. I can't ask you anything at all, which leaves the police hanging out on a limb as usual. I wish people in high places would confide in us occasionally. It would certainly help. I don't know how they expect us to fight crime if they refuse to tell us anything and handcuff us at the same time!' He paused for a few moments before imparting the rest of the information. 'By the way,' he went on, 'you may be interested to learn it wasn't an overdose of tablets but the administration of a deadly poison which takes about fifteen seconds to cause death. If it helps, the body shows signs of bruising around the stomach and the ribs. At least three ribs were broken. Who are these people you're involved with?'

'You know I can't answer that, inspector,' I replied, feeling anger welling-up inside me. I was furious to hear that Tania had to suffer being beaten-up before she was killed. I would have liked five minutes alone with her murderer to avenge my dear friend. But it would never happen. The telephone rang and I picked up the instrument. 'Savage!' I snarled into the mouthpiece.

'Mr. Savage,' responded the woman at the other end of the line. 'I'm calling on behalf of Mr. Kirk. He mentioned the other day you would be interested in coming here again... to meet with one of his colleagues. Is it still your wish to attend?'

My anger subsided quickly at the invitation and I took a deep breath to quell my excitement. 'Yes, I wish to attend,' I uttered quietly as my heart pounded strongly in my chest. At last I was to meet Der Bankvorsteher! 'When is the meeting to be held?'

'I'm afraid it's very short notice. Can you be here at four o'clock this afternoon?'

'I'll be there. At four o'clock. Do I need to bring anything with me?' The line went dead without warning and I turned to the inspector coldly. 'I have to leave,' I told him, 'but you can contact me at the newspaper office if you need me.' I gave him one of my business cards and shuddered at the state of the apartment as I glanced round before leaving. The administrator of expenses at the newspaper would never believe me if I submitted another claim for the damage. I had no idea what the loss-adjuster of the insurance company would say when he saw the debacle. The police inspector was very unhappy at my departure as he had intended to question me further. However, after confirmation of my immunity by the spokesman at the House of Commons there was little he could do about it. I was very surprised Maitland had made any comment at all. The Prime Minister expressed a view I was on my own if there was ever any trouble. It was the first time in my life the government had ever been on my side, except just before the General Election when prospective candidates tried to get me to vote for them.

I took a taxi to the newspaper office and went immediately to see Ted Flanders, knowing exactly how he would react when he saw me. He was sitting in a smoke-filled office with a cigar burning brightly between his lips poring over an edition of the newspaper. As I entered, he glanced up and sat back in his chair, staring at me as though I had forgotten to spray on my deodorant.

'Where the bloody hell have you been?' he demanded in his usual off-beat manner. 'You must think you're still on holiday! Did you forget we employ you... pay your wages! You go beetling off on some spree without telling a single soul and then crawl back in here expecting sympathy. Just who do you think you are? More to the point, when are you going to get down to some decent work? Do you know who gets the ulcers round here? I do... because I'm responsible for everything that happens! I'm the one who has to bear the cross! And what do you do? Go out on some bender without so much as 'by your leave'.' He looked at me in mock fury. 'What have you got this time... or are you asking for more research to be done to get you off the hook?'

I waved my hand forwards and backwards across the gloom. 'You need a smoke extractor in here, Ted,' I muttered. 'Otherwise you'll suffocate to death!' I began to laugh loudly. 'But don't worry, if that happens most of the staff will chip in to buy you a wreath. I'm sure of it!'

'Funny!' he snapped sarcastically. 'Very funny!'

'Has Research come up with anything yet?' I asked, anticipating another onslaught with much richer language this time.

'They're still working on it!' he rattled, counter to my expectations.

'I've been very successful,' I boasted calmly. 'Very successful. You'll be pleased to know my trip cost absolutely nothing... except for two airline tickets, but more people have died. The last one in my apartment. It's getting real rough out there.' He failed to show any interest in my remarks but it was clear he wanted me to continue. 'I bought the files of Nazi war criminals relating to three countries. France, Czechoslovakia and Greece.'

His ears pricked up quickly. 'You what? I thought you said it cost you nothing except for the airline tickets!'

'That's right. It didn't cost the newspaper a cent.' His body relaxed with a sigh of relief. I placed the white envelope on his desk with some degree of pride. 'These sets of microfilm tell us all we want to know about the war criminals in those countries and I want hard copies made of them. Three sets should be sufficient.'

'What do you intend to do with them?'

'One set will remain here. I'll take two to the House of Commons. I think we ought to keep the originals in a safe place, don't you? More important is a meeting I'm going to this afternoon. I hope to meet Der Bankvorsteher... the man who's in charge of all the Nazi funds in the world. Naturally, I have to go alone but I want to carry a clever mechanical device which can't be detected to take a photograph of him.'

For the first time in my life Ted Flanders showed an interest in my welfare. 'Jimmy, boy!' he began, with a worried expression on his face, causing all his wrinkles to show. 'I know the game is rough but I'm really worried about you. Take care... don't take any foolish chances!'

'Why, Ted!' I returned with a smile on my face. 'Don't say you're showing traits of humanity in your old age! Perhaps I should tell you there's a Russian criminal on the loose who'll be after my blood shortly. He doesn't mince words or actions. He might even take it to mind to liquidate you as well. After all, I'm only the reporter... you're the editor!'

He paled at the comment and decided to move on to other matters quickly. 'We can set you up with a special camera. It looks like a typical tie-pin and it's very easy to operate. In addition, I think you ought to take a mini tape-recorder with you. It's not the conversation I'm interested in but a voice-print which might be useful at a later stage. What do you think?'

'If you say so. Just hope and pray they don't search me, that's all, otherwise I'm a dead duck. What's the newspaper going to do with its copy of the microfilm?'

'I'll have to take it to the big banana for his decision,' related the editor. 'It could be dynamite!' He almost bit his tongue for allowing his enthusiasm to erupt to the surface. 'I'd better wait until you get back. There might be something more. Who knows? This thing gets bigger every day!'

I nodded dolefully. 'I must have a session with the Financial editor. If I'm going to meet a man controlling billions of U.S. dollars, I ought to know something about finance. I'm supposed to be the senior executive of a private bank, you know.'

He puffed deeply on his cigar, polluting the atmosphere even further, and I decided it was time to leave the office to let him choke himself to death in peace. It would serve him right! Strangely enough, if anything happened to him I would miss that miserable character more than I care to think. I walked down the stairs to the Financial Department... a place rarely visited by a spendthrift like myself. I didn't have a clue about financial matters because I always spent every penny I earned, which meant there was nothing left to invest. Nonetheless, I knew Glen Palmer and recognised him to be a man at the top of his profession. He achieved miracles with a very small staff.

'What do you know about forfaiting?' he asked casually to test my financial acumen.

'Not a thing,' I responded candidly. 'Never even heard of the word. What the heck is forfaiting?'

He smiled and proceeded to cover the area of finance. 'Would I be wasting my time asking you about discounted cash-flow, off-balance sheet finance, zero-based budgeting, or ratio analysis?'

'All Chinese to me!' I replied, with an uncomfortable feeling in the pit of my stomach that I was doomed to failure.

'Well how about the Eurocurrency market, the commodity market, project financing, equity investment, LIFFE, or negotiable instruments?'

'Glen, my old buddy,' I laughed in reaction, to compensate for my appalling lack of knowledge. 'I haven't a clue what you're talking about! Look, I've got thirty minutes to get up to scratch. What can you teach me in that time?'

It was going to be a real challenge for both of us, but I had the greatest confidence in the man as his teaching ability matched his prowess in the field of finance. He knew exactly how to treat my situation, starting off by handing me a pen and a sheet of paper. His course of action was to force me to learn numerous terms by means of mnemonics and jot them down on paper. Half an hour later, the perspiration ran from my temples down both sides of my face. I began to despair in case I lost my sanity. All kinds of letters and strange terms fluttered around my brain. It was only the beginning, however, because he increased the pressure for a further thirty minutes, and I felt like sleeping for a week. I groaned inwardly as the shackles of responsibility of this assignment became extremely onerous! They were becoming too tight for a simple soul like myself! However, editors tended to be short on sensitivity in relation to newspaper reporters. I just had to grin and bear it! In due course, I went to lunch in the main canteen with my mind buzzing like an electric saw. I was so engrossed in Glen Palmer's advice I hardly knew what I was eating. There were so many things to do... to know. Firstly, I had to get a tie-pin camera, and then a miniature tape-recorder. The use of such equipment was not without its problems. The administrator of expenses didn't trust anyone... especially when it concerned useful electronic goods which could be easily borrowed and never returned. Ultimately, I had to go through the procedure of signing a number of forms to guarantee the safe return of the equipment before being allowed to borrow it. The tie-pin camera was very neat and easy to fit. The tape-recorder had to be strapped tightly to my right arm with a tiny pearl-coloured microphone fitted on to the button of my shirt. In the space of a few minutes, I was ready for action. It was no help to advise me I had to use caution. If I was discovered with this equipment, my life wouldn't be worth a fig! Equally, if I made a serious error during the discussion on finance, Kirk would be alerted immediately.

I drove to Epping Forest and approached the house with trepidation. Each visit here was a trial in itself and the odds were starting to stack up against me. I couldn't continue indefinitely without ever putting a foot wrong. Today was an occasion when I could easily find myself sinking into the quicksand. There was an expert at the helm in the guise of Der Bankvorsteher. It would be impossible to fool him. In my impecunious state of life, I couldn't even visualise what fifty billion United States dollars looked like, let alone talk about how such a fortune could be administered. So I hesitated on the threshold of the lion's den, with my heart sounding like a steam-hammer in my ears, before making my presence known with the giant door-knocker which bore a grotesque face that seemed to mock me. My mind whirled with financial details. I could only hope I would get the mnemonics in the right order and remember what each letter or syllable represented. Kirk opened the door himself, still wearing his black uniform, and he greeted me before ushering me into the library.

'I'd like you to me Der Bankvorsteher,' he said, introducing me to a dapper middle-aged man who sat in one of the armchairs, with a hand resting on a large black leather case by his side.

He stood up to shake hands with me, allowing a gentle smile to touch the edges of his lips, although his eyes never left mine. 'So,' he ventured with a cultured American drawl as he returned to his seat, 'you're the man I've heard so much about. How do you feel about assisting me in the function of my important duty?' I was about to respond but he continued irrespectively. 'At last I meet a banker of some repute who truly belongs to the cause. I heard a lot about you. That deal in Switzerland with three hundred million in gold. The timber forest transaction in Canada... especially with that little trick of taxation rollover. The control of monies deposited by the Jews in the early part of the war. It's doubtful whether any of them are still alive... but you have the money. Your reputation goes before you!'

I froze and smiled weakly. I had no idea what the newspaper had actually issued on the grapevine about me in financial circles. Clearly, they did me proud! In my haste to learn as much as possible from Glen Palmer, I had forgotten to check what I was supposed to have done in the sphere of banking through the dummy company owned by the newspaper. 'Some of it was elementary,' I boasted falsely, pretending to be modest. I could only hope he wasn't trying to trip me up with some false claim to test my honesty. If that was the case, I had already fallen into the pit. 'By the way, what do I call you?'

'For our present purpose, Herr Erdbeer,' intervened Kirk sharply, 'it would be better to retain anonymity for a while. If you wish to be informal, why not use the name Hans. Der Bankvorsteher is a good fellow. He won't really mind!'

'If you say so,' I agreed, trying not to show my disappointment. I had no option but to rely on the two devices I had brought with me, otherwise the identity of the man would remain a mystery. I touched my arm gently to start the miniature tape-recorder, but my courage failed me with regard to the tie-pin camera. I had an uncomfortable feeling that any action from the front would appear too obvious. The last thing I wanted to do was to commit professional suicide. It was prudent to wait a little longer until everyone's attention was diverted.

'We're here to ascertain your suitability to assist Hans,' continued Kirk officiously. He turned to the banker. 'But I'm in the way here. I'm sure you both prefer to continue your discussion in private. I'll leave you to your own devices.' He clicked his heels smartly and left the room.

After he had gone, Hans and I stared at each other without speaking to the point of embarrassment, until I decided to break the silence. 'I'm surprised you handle the whole fund on your own... without help from anyone else.'

'Why should you think that?' he replied. The brief smile no longer touched his lips. 'Ah, most probably you've been conditioned in terms of management profit. That doesn't apply with me. Administration is simple in general terms. The funds are deposited in various money markets, bonds, stocks and shares, and other methods throughout the world. I don't have to be on the ball the whole time. We don't have shareholders breathing down our necks for extra profit or dividends. There's no Chairman leaning on me if one area makes a small loss at any point in time. The most important thing is not to draw attention to our activities, so we never manipulate markets or participate openly in take-over bids or mergers. Our main intention is to ensure our funds grow at a reasonable rate, but it must always be possible to liquidate them at a moment's notice as the overall plan requires.'

'What about the art treasures? Have all the sales been completed?'

'Practically. There are still a few more paintings to go. Sales had to be accomplished slowly over the years in order not to flood the market or bring attention to ourselves. Art has been a very profitable area. The longer we waited, the greater the return.'

'I presume you retain substantial holdings in gold in case of the collapse of currencies and stock markets.' I was digging deep down into the depths of the instruction given to me by Glen Palmer.

'Of course. That's why no person can breathe down the neck of Der Bankvorsteher. The gold price is relatively low at present but, in the event of the collapse of stock markets worldwide, it would rocket. Our plan would not be compromised by the collapse, in fact we would be that much richer.'

'Do you mean you wouldn't have to wait until Die Stunde arrived.' I realised too late I was playing a trump card too early in the game.

His eyelids flickered for a moment as though he didn't expect me to have known about Die Stunde. He recovered quickly to reply to my question calmly. However, in that moment, I knew something was terribly wrong. Why shouldn't I know about Die Stunde, Many people were aware of it. Miss Grayson, for example... and my dear departed contact, Calvin, but then he was an exceptional person dealing in information on a major scale... and me! How did Miss Grayson find out about it? Was the computer disk in her drawer given to her by someone with an elevated rank in the movement, or had she written it herself? No... what was I thinking of! She wore a Star of David. A Jewish person wouldn't join the ranks of the Nazis, would they? Not after the trauma of Belsen, Dachau, Auschwitz and numerous other concentration camps! She couldn't possibly have switched sides! Then the scales fell from my eyes and I realised what a fool I'd been. I had been treating everyone in this assignment like normal human-beings. The concept was counter to the name of the game... especially with the assassinations and attempted killings! Most of them were agents, double agents, spies and international crooks, more cunning than foxes; more devious than Machiavelli! Anyone could buy a Star of David from a jewellery shop. It didn't prove one was Jewish! Miss Grayson knew that one day some astute person would invade her privacy somewhere along the line to determine her identity. She had to be prepared for it and made certain of her cover by having a photograph taken of her with a Star of David round her neck to throw pursuers off the scent. It was cleverly done to hide the photograph in a locket. In my opinion, Miss Grayson was probably a descendant of a Nazi officer. I was more concerned that she had managed to stand by the side of the Prime Minister without being detected. It was amazing that a mere hesitation by Der Bankvorsteher relating to Die Stunde had placed another piece of the jig-saw puzzle into position.

'Die Stunde is the benchmark,' he drawled, staring directly into my eyes. 'No one can bring the benchmark forward!'

I laughed easily, feeling completely the opposite inside. 'Forgive my foolishness. One becomes over-anxious sometimes to move the plan forward.'

He nodded casually with the lines in his face creasing deeply. 'I like a man with character... someone willing to admit to foolishness. Let's face it, we all show human weaknesses and failure at one time or another. You must tell me about the deal you made with that German chemical giant... the one involving six different currencies.'

The wheels of my mind began to grind into motion and my poker brain recognised the request had been baited like a gin-trap. If I answered affirmatively, I would be unmasked as an imposter immediately. 'I fear you're confusing me with another banker,' I told him point-blank. If I got it right, my riposte would be solid. If I got it wrong, I would subside quickly but courageously.

He stared at me for a few moment while I hung in space, and the smile returned to his face. Fortunately, I had gambled correctly. 'Yes,' he said quietly. 'I must be confusing you with someone else.'

'May I ask you some questions about the funds in particular?' I asked, ignoring his feeble excuse which was obviously false. 'Would you tell me more about the distribution of the funds?'

'Of course,' he replied, ostensibly unruffled by my inquisitiveness. 'Thirty per cent in gold. Ten per cent in currencies. Thirty per cent in gilt-edge stocks and equities. Twenty-five per cent in money markets, and five per cent in cash.'

He rattled off the percentages so smartly I sensed that he failed to move the funds often. 'In which country is the main concentration of funds?' It was my intention to put him under pressure until he told me something of value. At the same time, my questions might prove to him I was a real professional in the banking sphere.

'An emphasis in the United States, Britain and Europe in general,' he told me in the same soft manner as before. 'There are some investments in Asia.'

He was telling me very little. Anyone who managed substantial funds or a large portfolio would have related exactly the same thing. We both knew it but I decided to play along with him for a while. 'Herr Kirk told me you were arriving here from America. Where are you based there?'

'Denver, Colorado.'

I mistrusted his reply continuing my onslaught regardlessly. 'And you administer all the principal activities from an office there I suppose. Admirable!'

'As you know, one needs only a telephone and a facsimile machine to do what I have to do.'

'Do I ever get to see the accounts?' I ventured, looking at the black leather case by his side. At that moment, my courage moved to its highest peak and I took his photograph with the tie-pin camera, coughing lightly to hide any slight noise it might make.

'Not at this stage, Herr Erdbeer.' His hand moved to the case as if to protect its contents. 'Perhaps the next time we meet.'

'When will that be? I'm anxious to get working!'

'Herr Kirk has his own methods of checking people out. As you know, in banking we have to be a little more prudent. Don't get me wrong! You're probably as genuine as twenty carat gold... pure gold... but I have to check you out to my own satisfaction.'

To his surprise, I started to laugh at his comment. 'I hope you check me out thoroughly,' I told him lightly, 'but please stop trying to use traps to catch me out. It gets boring. You don't have to be a banker to know there's no such thing as twenty carat gold. Pure gold is twenty-four carats. Of course another thought crosses my mind. Perhaps I ought to check you out. You talk of prudence in banking but I don't know your real name or anything else about you.' I took another photograph with the tie-pin camera, at the same time easing the knot of my tie to make the movement seem authentic. 'Isn't it time we were frank with each other?'

He began to look a little queasy and started to hold his stomach. 'I think I ate something on the plane that doesn't agree with me,' he griped, showing signs of real discomfort.

I wasn't certain whether he was putting on an act or not. However, he began to moan and groan, rubbing his stomach gently. After a short while, I went to the door to call for help. Kirk came quickly and I pointed to the stricken man before we helped him from the room. We took him to the bathroom and Kirk waved me away, indicating he could cope with the situation. I wondered whether Der Bankvorsteher had something important to impart to him about me, but I couldn't hear anything through the door except the sound of the man wretching. Perhaps he was really ill after all. Whatever the reason for his departure, it was a golden opportunity for me to examine the contents of the black leather case he had brought with him. I bounded into the library and closed the door before reaching for the case to open it. My heart sank for it had been fitted with a combination lock comprised of four wheels bearing the numbers zero to nine. I could spend a whole day trying to find the right four digits. Then a brilliant thought struck me. Die Stunde! The first of June. One, six, zero, zero! My fingers moved the wheels until they fell into the correct places and I closed my eyes as I pressed the catches. It opened like a dream! I moved the papers in the case near to the window to gain the benefit of the light. I wanted to use the tie-pin camera to its fullest ability. Without delay, I began to photograph everything I could lay my hands on with great speed. Of paramount importance, however, was a list of accounts held in numerous countries which would prove invaluable to the British government. All the time my heart beat like a drum for fear of discovery. It only needed someone to open the door and look inside and my existence would be in jeopardy. After a few minutes, which seemed like a lifetime, I returned the papers to the case in the same order and closed it accordingly, making sure the wheels were returned to the same numbers at which they had been left before I moved them. Then I returned the case to its original position, wiped it quickly with my handkerchief to erase my fingerprints, and sat back in my chair as though butter wouldn't melt in my mouth. It was only just in time because thirty seconds later Kirk returned.

'I'm sorry,' he apologised, 'but Hans is extremely unwell. I think he has food poisoning.'

'Does this mean he doesn't want to consider me for the job?' I asked directly. 'If he doesn't, I'll understand.'

'Not at all,' he replied. 'He really is ill. I'm afraid he won't be able to continue the discussion. He needs medical treatment. Would you be prepared to fly to the United States next week to meet him there?'

I nodded slowly, with an uncomfortable feeling in the pit of my stomach. 'Yes, I can do that. You can telephone me at the bank or at my home. You have my card.'

He led me to the front door and offered his apologies again. I was vexed the meeting had been so short. On the other hand, I couldn't wait to get back to the office, having secured a mass of data with the camera. I climbed into my car full of doubts and suspicions about the brief visit. What had really happened there? Why was I left alone in the library with such important material in the black leather case for so long? And why didn't Der Bankvorsteher return? Kirk explained that the man was ill, but was that the real truth? It was going to be a mystery that might never be resolved. Not in the short term anyway. As I stared at the closed front door with the grotesque door-knocker, I noticed the insipid Nazi youth, whom I had angered at Hayle's party, leaning against the outside wall idly as though he was a permanent sentinel. He stood perfectly still with his arms crossed, glowering at me with the same stare of vengeance I had seen in his eyes before. I started the engine and drove to the top of the hill. Once I had turned the corner, I stopped the car on a patch of waste ground at the edge of the forest, opening the window to look back on the house and its acres behind it. The martial arts combat squad was practising once more and Lieutenant-Colonel Topham stood watching them. A dozen thoughts plagued my mind and I tried to sort them out logically. It was an ordinary person's nightmare, but a poker player's dream, so I decided to adopt the attitude of the latter to make a final deduction. The man called Hans knew all about Herr Erdbeer... the banker. He had tried to trap me in very modest ways, which didn't work, and then left before I realised the truth. But what was the truth? There was only one conclusion to reach. The man himself was a fraud! Kirk had set up the meeting to test me. He had provided a man with an American drawl who had a good knowledge of finance. After a while, Hans would pretend to fall ill and be taken from the room, leaving me with the black leather case. They knew that if I was an imposter, I would be astute enough to open it and microfilm the documents. What an idiot I had been! The man I met wasn't Der Bankvorsteher; the information in the case was almost certainly false. At least I believed it to be false! As soon as the first enquiry was made on any of those accounts, my cover would be blown. Kirk would know I was an imposter!

As these thought raced through my mind in the stillness of the afternoon, I reacted sharply as a shot rang out close to me, and a flock of birds flew out of the trees in panic. I ducked down in my seat, ostensibly to protect myself, wondering what to do next. Eventually, I raised my head in curiosity to find the large frame of Gates, the chauffeur, leaning on the window frame of the car, looking down at me. He smiled at the fear in my eyes as I noticed the rifle in his hand, and he opened the hatchback window to throw it into the boot. Then he walked to the other side of the car, opened the door, and climbed inside.

'Oh, no!' I complained bitterly. 'You're not going to abduct me again, are you?'

'No, I'm not going to abduct you,' he laughed. 'I only came here to assassinate Lieutenant-Colonel Topham!'

I looked hard towards the back of the house where the martial arts squad was poring over Topham's body. Gates didn't mince words... that was certain! And if he said he had assassinated Topham... the man was surely dead!

CHAPTER SIXTEEN

The profession of newspaper reporting often involves a flurry of activity because that is the nature of the business. It's the job of every newshound to make sure they're always at the heart of the action. However, the activities which had taken place during the short term of this assignment had been too savage and outrageous for words. I considered the ultimate had been reached when Gates... a man I believed to be a servant of the State... killed a senior ranking officer at the Ministry of Defence and smiled at me as if he had accomplished a task which was of great service to his country. At first it was difficult to accept what had happened, but a final glance at Topham's body was enough. I watched the martial arts squad carry it slowly from the field of combat. The situation was very serious indeed. It was not my place to pass judgement on my peers but was it right for people to take the lives of others without anyone demanding the need or the objectivity? Was there any point in such death-dealing activities whereby everyone's life was in danger? Worst still, the assassin was sitting right next to me!

I was surprised that there was no pursuit from the mansion. No wild, exciting car chase as often happens in films shown in the cinema or on television. No act of vengeance by a stray guard within the vicinity. Death was an accepted part of the life of these people. They knew it was always carried out by a professional killer. Consequently, there was little point in allowing one's emotions to erupt. Nothing could be done until the tables were turned.

'Drive on and let's get out of here!' ordered Gates in a gruff, determined voice. His attitude was completely clinical towards the act he had just committed, lacking even the slightest twinge of conscience. I started the motor and drove away as quickly as possible. 'I suppose you're wondering why the Prime Minister brought you into the viper's nest,' he went on, his tone becoming much softer.

I glanced at him briefly before turning my attention to the road again. 'It crossed my mind a few time, Mr. Gates. It crossed my mind! After all, the government has all kinds of agencies and powers to call to its aid if it wanted to resolve a particular kind of problem. Why pick on an innocent newspaper reporter when there are so many professionals? They're far better equipped for the job!'

'That's the crux of the matter,' he explained. 'Once professionals are enlisted, some miserable mole puts out the word and every enemy agent is alerted. And believe me, they infiltrate everywhere. You see, if MI5 or another agency was called in, the bad guys known to us would melt away into the distance to be replaced by another set whom we don't know. We wouldn't know the new ones or where to find them. How then could we keep track of what was going on? It's the old adage: "Better the Devil you know than the Devil you don't know". When we learned you'd been given the assignment by your newspaper... which was at the top of our priority list... we decided to run with you; use you as bait. It was a gift from heaven! I should imagine you feel angry about it, but that's the truth. If they followed your trail, you would lead them off the real scent. Unfortunately, you're too good at your job which led everyone into all sorts of trouble. State Security knew some eminent men and women were involved with International Three Thousand. It stands to reason. There are certain people in high-ranking positions who would do anything for a greater share of power. And there it was! The United States of Europe looming ahead... to be funded by money raised from the sale of Nazi war treasures The descendants of Nazi war criminals were determined to continue where their ancestors left off... in effect to control Europe. You might say it was reaching for the moon. Not so! The integration of the European Community has been anything but smooth. Each nation is jealous of every other one. They fight like cats and dogs for different advantages. How easy it could be for a well-organised machine to infiltrate and take over. During the transition period, all opposition would be removed. How can this happen? Well, we're too soft, that's why. We forget too easily and over-indulge in mercy. World War Two ended so long ago it's hardly worth remembering the bad parts any more. Parts like the extermination of millions of people... mass murder! One of the men with ideas far above his station was Lieutenant-Colonel Topham. He was retired actually, but we offered him the job of rooting out the villains of the piece. He was known to be involved with International Three Thousand, so by appointing him to our elite committee we could keep an eye on him.'

I sighed with relief to realise that Gates was on my side, and I continued to drive into London. 'That's why Topham wasn't in the military lists!' I muttered, fitting another piece of the jig-saw into place. 'He'd retired, so his name wouldn't appear on the serving register.'

'In actual fact, he got himself in a fix trying to use both sides at once. You met him at Kirk's house by accident, which caused us a big headache. In the end, we had to eliminate him to save your skin. He was much too much of a liability.'

'Tell me about State Security!' I pressed him to reveal a little more.

'State Security, MI5, what's the difference? They're all pretty much the same the world over!'

'I think the public ought to be aware of unlisted agencies and unlisted civil servants or police.'

'Don't be naive, Savage!' he growled, scaring me a little by the quickness of his temper. 'What good would it do? It would tie our hands. We'd have to be accountable for everything we did. Within six months, Britain would be infiltrated with Communists, Fascists and anarchists. By then the public would be screaming for someone to protect them. All in all, I think we do a pretty good job. If my agency was listed and I had to play the game according to the rules, you wouldn't be alive today. Now there's something for you to think about!'

I glanced at him briefly. 'How do you make that out?'

'When Kirk discovered Tania was a newspaper reporter it actually helped you. I mean, no newspaper would put two journalists on the same story and have them join the same movement together. Also, reporters from competitive newspapers would never work together on the same assignment. It was too far-fetched. They came to the conclusion she'd got her hooks into you and it was in the best interests of International Three Thousand to eliminate you. Do you remember the car which tried to run you down in the car park near her apartment... the one which ended up on the rockery? They thought they could run you into the ground.'

'So you're the one who put a bullet through the front tyre,' I blurted out, as the answers to some of the questions began to unfold.

'I saved your life although it was a close-run thing. While the heavy mob were employed to kill you, their colleagues were trying to find out what Tania knew. It was quite a surprise when you appeared and turned the tables on them. You're quite handy at times when action's required, aren't you? After that, you fooled them with that story about your grandfather being a Colonel in the SS. It was a good move because it took the heat off you. They changed their minds about killing you.'

'Do you know who killed Calvin?' I asked, not expecting him to offer me an answer.

'Calvin... the fat man at the Dog and Duck in Backchurch Lane?' he replied casually. 'Yes... I killed him.'

I jerked slightly at the shock of his revelation. 'You killed him... with a metal stake? What did you do that for?'

He was beginning to accumulate a lot of information of a highly secret nature. If released, it would have been against the public interest. Some people have a greater love of money than loyalty to their country, you know. He knew everything about you. It was simply a matter of time before someone paid him to reveal your true identity. We couldn't afford that. I would have shot him with a pistol but it jammed. There was a metal stake leaning against the wall which they used to lever up a manhole in the toilet. I had no alternative but to use that.'

There was no point in condemning the man for his actions. He was charged with undertaking many unpleasant duties for his country. Who was I to take him to task when he had saved my life on more than one occasion? 'You do know that Miss Grayson is probably one of them too. I enlarged the photograph in a locket which showed she wore a Star of David. But, in my opinion, she's a senior member of the movement.'

'Very good, Mr. Savage!' he lauded. 'You fathomed it out well. Miss Grayson was the grand-daughter of Willy Graz, an officer on the list of those advising Adolf Hitler during the war. She was arrested at her office this afternoon.'

'Was the grand-daughter? Why the past tense?'

'She duped us a short while after her arrest... reminiscent of the old Nazis who refused to be captured. She committed suicide by biting on a cyanide capsule hidden in a cavity in one of her teeth. Her capture and death is a closely-guarded secret at this stage. You see, the whole thing is going down!'

'Going down?' I asked with mixed emotions, recalling briefly the night I spent with the woman after the incident in the shower cubicle. It proved to me how ephemeral were such alliances. For many of them, there was no tomorrow! I also recognised I was a death-wish to all women who slept with me. None of them ever survived very long afterwards!

'Yes, we're ready to wrap-up the whole thing soon... all over Europe, partly thanks to your help. If we can push Die Stunde back for a hundred years, posterity can take care of the rest. But it will never end, you know. The Germans have a national pride which won't be quenched. You can split their country, expose their arrogance and belligerence one decade after another, crush them time and time again in battle, but they'll still come back to try and conquer the world and create a Master race. The development of the European Community is the ideal instrument at the present time. If they're thwarted now it'll really set them back!'

I was relieved to hear the pressure of the assignment would end shortly, reflecting that the next task set for me by Ted Flanders would pale into insignificance against it. I would be delighted to investigate some banal story closer home to normality. 'How soon do you think it will take you to wrap it up?' I prayed inwardly that he would respond with an early date.

'A couple of days,' he replied. 'There's one big fish we have to catch yet. It's only a matter of time. For your part, you'd better carry on until further advised.'

A big fish! My mind wandered to the Prime Minister and raced with a dozen thoughts flashing through my head. No... it couldn't be the Prime Minister... that would be too much! I pestered Gates for further information but he sat back with his eyes closed.

'I'll leave the rifle in the boot,' he told me, squeezing the bulk of his body out of the door in the East End. 'Cover it up with a rug or something. You'll be going to the House of Commons tomorrow to submit your next report. You can let me have it then.'

Three uncomfortable thoughts lodged at the back of my mind. Firstly, how did he know I would be visiting the House of Commons tomorrow? I didn't know it myself. Secondly, what was the point of going there if Lieutenant-Colonel Topham and Miss Grayson were dead? Thirdly, was Gates setting me up? The rifle had been used to kill a man. If the police discovered the body and they were informed that the rifle lay in the boot of my car, I would have an awful lot of explaining to do. Gates wouldn't support me... no one would believe my story. As I dwelt on these matters, Gates disappeared into one of the alleys and I had to live on with my fears.

I drove on to the car park of the newspaper office and then wandered into a nearby cafe to consider the affairs of the day. It had been counter to my expectations in some ways, yet successful in others. I still didn't know the identity of Der Bankvorsteher; he was probably located anywhere but in Denver, Colorado. Yet I had taken his photograph and his voice-print, and secured photographs of the documents in his case. There was a vain hope they were genuine although I recognised the level of operation was beginning to escalate way beyond my control. It was moving too fast and I had insufficient information to proceed with confidence. It was some time later when I entered Ted Flanders's office to find him still incarcerated in his smoke-filled room. The stench of cigar smoke was now becoming foul and I sat facing him uncomfortably.

'What have you got, Jimmy?' he asked bluntly, looking at me with tired eyes as he flicked the ash off his cigar.

I placed the tie-pin camera carefully on the desk and undid the miniature tape-recorder from my arm. 'A lot... and not much, Ted,' I told him, feeling a wave of fatigue sweep over me which may have been caused by the lack of oxygen in the room. 'You have his photograph, the sound of his voice but, if my gut feeling is correct, the man was just as much an imposter as myself. This camera contains film of the documents he brought with him. Apart from individual letters and papers, there's a list of accounts relating to funds in various countries. If it's genuine, we may be able to sequestrate all the Nazi funds and removed the sting from the tail of the bee.'

The editor's eyebrows inched up at the comment and he leaned back in his chair. 'We may have a real scoop here in that alone,' he said excitedly.

'I don't think so,' I returned, dashing his aspirations arbitrarily. 'If the man was an imposter, then all the documents are false. I think they want us to start asking questions and making accusations. Once that happens, they'll be alerted to the fact I'm a fraud as well. In other words, they're checking up on me. It was a set up... one big trap!'

He stared up at the ceiling as if the answer lay there, puffing on the short stub of a cigar vigorously. 'Are you telling me this was all a waste of time? That none of this is for real?'

'I don't know,' I answered candidly. 'It looks as though I might have put my head in the lion's mouth for nothing. We'll need to check it out to learn the truth.'

'And where do you go from here?'

I stood up and opened the office door to release some of the pollution. 'I hoped you might have some idea about that. I'm going to see the Prime Minister again tomorrow, to advise him of the latest developments. But I've been told it's all going down shortly.'

His eyebrows shot up again. 'Who told you that?'

'Someone called Gates, of State Security. He killed Lieutenant-Colonel Topham this afternoon with a rifle he left in the back of my car. We drove back to London together.'

'Jesus Christ!' he blasphemed. 'Gates of State Security? That's the organisation which doesn't exist.'

'The very same. He reckons that after I meet with the Prime Minister tomorrow certain things will start to happen. There's a big fish they want to catch yet.'

'Who's that?'

I could see the excitement mounting in his eyes as another scoop loomed on the horizon. If he could only be in at the kill, the newspaper would carry a large photograph and a giant headline exposing the story to the world. Ted would cover himself with glory! 'I don't know,' I said simply.

'You don't know much, do you?' he snapped. 'How the hell can I run a newspaper if you can't get me the facts? I send you out on assignment which most reporters would give their right arm for, and what do you do? You come back with a weird tale of a man who isn't what he's supposed to be, photographs which are probably useless, and nothing for me to get into print. I could get a copy boy to do your job and get better results!'

'Oh, shut up, Ted!' I shouted, surprised at my own vehemence. The man was beginning to get on my nerves and I reacted accordingly. 'I've been shot at by a rifle, nearly mown down by a car. I risked my neck here there and everywhere ... what more do you want?' I was so angry I couldn't talk to him any more, so I stormed out of the office and sat at my own desk to sulk.

After a while, I heard a movement from his office before a plastic cup filled with coffee was placed on the desk beside my arm. I looked up to see the smiling face of Ted Flanders. He stared at me with the expression that butter wouldn't melt in his mouth. 'You mustn't get upset, Jimmy,' he told me, in the form of an apology. 'This is a rough business and we often give people a piece of our mind through the pressure causing us all that frustration. But there's never any harm in what we say to each other. Once it's off our chest, it's forgotten. Come on, drink your coffee and let's have an end to it. There's no point in holding a grudge.'

I stared up at him and relented reluctantly. 'You've no idea what it's been like this past week,' I told him. 'Apart from the attempts on my life, people all around me have been killed, and my nerves are frayed like bare electric wires. Gates told me Miss Grayson was arrested this afternoon. I don't know what for. She was the grand-daughter of a German officer called Willy Graz. Apparently, she committed suicide by biting on a cyanide capsule lodged in the cavity of one of her teeth. Can you imagine what courage and dedication is

184

required to do that rather than give information on a cause to the authorities? Tania was killed in my flat because she was a newspaper reporter and they found out...'

'A newspaper reporter!' he echoed, with a note of horror in his voice at the possibility of losing the scoop. 'Don't tell me someone else has this assignment! Someone from another newspaper!'

'Not any longer,' I growled. 'The police took her body to the morgue this morning They had to contact the House of Commons to get me off the hook or I may have been charged with her murder.'

'That's all very well,' he stormed, 'but what if she kept her editor fully informed? Feeding off your information! What then? We'll find ourselves reading all about it in someone else's editions!'

I stared at him as though he had just crawled out from under a stone. 'You miserable creep!' I snarled, sweeping my arm across the table to send the cup of coffee speeding towards the far wall where it disgorged its contents. 'Don't you have any feelings at all? A newspaper reporter is dead... killed in pursuit of an assignment... and all you do is to gripe you might lose the scoop. Well let me tell you this straight, Flanders! To hell with the story and to hell with you!' I stood up and walked to the other side of the room, striking my hand against the wall fiercely without feeling any pain. 'Tania was a young... pretty... lively person, and I had strong feelings for her! Those bastards broke her ribs and forced her to swallow a cyanide tablet... and she couldn't do anything about it. Why, dammit, why? Because she stole a case which was important to her newspaper!' I paused as I thought about the book and the artefacts in the case. The volume bore the initials P.C. and the photographs reminded me of someone... but I still couldn't fathom whom it might be. The filing index in my brain had failed to come up with a solution!

Flanders stared at me, seemingly at a loss for words. 'What you say is perfectly true, Jimmy,' he said confidentially, revealing part of his innate nature. 'I don't relate to human emotions any more. I don't know how to show sympathy or to distinguish between sorrow or happiness. It all looks alike to me.' He seemed genuinely sad and, ostensibly, it hurt him to reveal his innermost feelings. 'After my wife died, and my daughter was killed in that tragic car accident, I buried myself in my work here at the newspaper. Do you know how many stories I've read throughout the past twenty years alone. Thousands. Thousands! About life, about death, on perverts and pimps, on the brilliant and the stupid, on corruption, sex, crime... you name it, someone's done it in this rotten stinking world. I've read them all but they mean nothing to me. A person can be in the middle of the biggest city in the world and still find himself alone in more senses than one. Perhaps I've seen too much of it. Maybe I've had it! I ought to give it all up and hand the reins over to someone else with wider vision, more drive, and youth on their side!'

His change of attitude evoked empathy in me and I shrugged my shoulders disconsolately. 'I didn't know your daughter was killed in a car accident,' I returned, with hallowed tones as a token of respect for his loss. 'And as far as resigning, that would be stupid. You have your ways, but the newspaper holds your judgement in high esteem. We need you here, Ted! I hate to be the one to say it, but we do need you here.'

'Jimmy,' he ventured solemnly. 'If I'm ever reincarnated and have to come back to this world again, I don't want to return as a newspaperman. I want to be a cat. Then I can just sit on the window-ledge in the sun all day long, get fed regularly by someone who keeps talking to me as though I don't understand a word, and have nothing more productive to do than purr away on her lap. By the way, I've got the copies of that microfilm for you on my desk. Which reminds me, I must get the copyboy to take the other film you gave me with the tie-pin to the photolab.'

He wandered off to his office leaving me nursing my thoughts. Poor Ted was over-conditioned to the profession and a very lonely man. There were many people widowed, but to lose a daughter as well was sad. I regretted having released all my frustration on him in that bitter interlude, and then I screwed up my face in a grimace as I realised what he had done. Ted Flanders didn't have a daughter! He made it up to win my sympathy! And he would never resign from the newspaper... not in a million years! It would take wild horses to remove him from that nauseating, smoke-filled, office. He had upset me and didn't know how to get round me, so he concocted a story to turn the tables. And like a fool, I fell for it. He must have thought me to be an outright idiot! I picked up the telephone and contacted Maitland. He was ready with the information I needed. Apparently, the Prime Minister had asked about my health and requested I should join him for tea on the terrace at the House of Commons at three o'clock the next day. I sat in my chair feeling extremely fatigued feeling worn out but I couldn't sleep. Ted Flanders came over and prodded me in the ribs to start a new discussion.

'I've been thinking about the Russian you saw in Germany. The one who might be after my hide. His name was... ' He snapped his fingers a few times

186

to jog his memory. 'Strog something or other! Do you think he might come here to threaten me... or do something worse? Only you know what these fanatics are like. They'd no more look at you than shoot you!'

'Strogoff!' I reminded him, smiling inwardly. It was my vengeful way of achieving mild revenge. He was getting the jitters about someone who didn't even know he existed. I wondered how Flanders would have fared had he been in the front line over the past week. The words of Romeo in Shakespeare's play came to mind in relation to the editor: "He jests at scars that never felt a wound!" I reckoned the Bard had summed it up in a nutshell. 'Don't worry, Ted,' I told him quietly. 'If anything happens to you, we'll see you get a decent burial. Interred with the latest editions of the newspaper, cigars, and all!' I burst into laughter but he didn't see the humour and returned to his office to brood over the problem. After that, I settled down to doze off in an uncomfortable pose. I awoke sharply at three o'clock in the morning with a sudden start. No one else was in the office; the place was completely silent. It was the index file in my brain which had summoned me to wake. Of course, the initials P.C. emblazoned on the case stolen by Tania belonged to Sir Peter Cavenham... or was that too much to accept. It was full of Nazi regalia! I thought about the photographs and made comparisons in my mind regarding the likeness of the boy. There was no doubt about it. Sir Peter was a man of ambition who sought greater power beyond his present role. He was an important man in International Three Thousand... a high-ranking officer in the Fascist regime designed to annihilate the government to whom he had pledged his loyalty and allegiance. I remembered the actual phrase he had used at the first meeting in the House of Commons when I complained about my abduction. "Life doesn't always fit into little square boxes, you know," he had fired at me. Well I would make sure he fitted into one of them when I met the Prime Minister! He could count on that! I could stomach many things in life but personal violence and treason were abominations!

I managed to doze off again and woke up with the hustle and bustle of newspaper people carrying out their regular routines. As I sat up to shake the sleep from my head, Ted Flanders came over to me with a cup of coffee in his hand.

I hope you're not going to throw this one all over the wall and carpet,' he ventured as a greeting.

I sat up rubbing my eyes, brushing my hand through my hair. I was feeling very tired following a restless night and I took the cup, grimacing at the awful taste as I sipped the liquid.

'You did very well yesterday,' he complimented, and I could only presume he had taken credit for the breakthrough at an early meeting with the Chief editor. 'The photographs of the man you met came out well, and the information on those documents looks interesting. When you're ready, come to my office and we'll talk about it. I want confirmation of a comment you made last night... the one where you thought an enquiry would set off an alarm.'

He left me trying to shrug off the mantle of sleep as I recalled the incident in the night when I realised the initials P.C. related to Sir Peter Cavenham. As I shook my weary head, a further thought struck a chord in my mind and I went to the bookshelf to examine a copy of the latest edition of Who's Who. "Sir Peter Cavenham, son of Brigadier Peter McNeill Cavenham and Joan Elizabeth Cavenham (nee Kenyon) Educated at Winchester College and Trinity College, Cambridge. Married Vanessa Holmes. One son and two daughters. Joined Accountancy firm Archibald Selley & Co, and then Petrey Velos and Co. Special Consultant to the Treasury. Consultant on Prices and Consumer Protection. Assistant Chairman, the Committee on Invisible Exports. Parliamentary Under-Secretary to the Treasury. Home Office ... " The entries ran on but they were of no interest to me. When a person was knighted, the editor of the publication Who's Who sent a form to the new knight to be completed. It covered the whole compass of a person's curriculum vitae. The recipient could enter anything they cared to on the form if it suited their purpose. Son of Brigadier Peter McNeill Cavenham... a likely story! I had seen the volume of text and photographs to prove the truth to be quite different. Yet the son had been awarded a knighthood. It led me to believe that other Nazis located in eminent places in Britain were looking after their own. The rest of the data was likely to hold true. An accountant with two fairly large firms, and a number of posts connected with the Treasury and large-scale financial funds. Even the Committee on Invisible Exports related to international banking, insurance, tourism, shipping and air transport. What a fantastic discovery I had made! I was searching high and low to determine the true identity of Der Bankvorsteher and he had been staring at me in the face. It was still only a hunch. I might be way off beam but in my bones I considered I had found the man at last!

I dwelt on the matter facing the mirror in the washroom. Suddenly, I was beginning to look older, with odd creases appearing under my eyes and at the edges of my mouth. My career in the newspaper profession had started to age me, especially with someone like Ted Flanders pushing from behind all the time. After a while, I ventured into the editor's office and sat down holding yet another cup of bitter coffee in my hand. The room was clear of cigar smoke at this time of the morning but the undeniable stench clung relentlessly to the walls, the curtains and the furniture.

'You think the information on the film you took is false,' began Flanders, holding up the first enlarged photographs in front of his eyes as he glanced at the details. 'It all looks pretty good to me!'

'No, Ted,' I told him tiredly, emitting a long woeful yawn. 'It was all too easy... too much of a charade. I'm in a room with vital information which the other man had in his case. There's just the two of us. Then, suddenly he goes down with a chronic attack of food poisoning, and I'm left alone with all that valuable data.'

'What kind of lock did the case have?'

'It had a combination lock with four wheels on each side. I took a chance that the date was Die Stunde... one, six, zero, zero. It seemed a likely code and it worked perfectly. Too well!'

'Clever boy!' he congratulated, nodding his recognition of my astuteness at a time when I was clearly under pressure. 'How could they possibly know you'd find the right combination?'

'They didn't. But something was wrong. As soon as I mentioned Die Stunde, the other man tensed up. I think my rank, as a mere recruit, was far too much down the line for me to know anything about it... unless I'd been making enquiries. They gave me plenty of time to open the case. If I didn't nothing was lost. If I did... and made enquiries... they would know immediately I was an imposter. If so, they would eliminate me because I knew too much.'

'It's all assumption, Jimmy boy! All assumption!'

I stared at him wearily. 'In the newspaper business, Ted, experience teaches that you have to fight like a dog for this kind of stuff. No one throws it into your lap for nothing. Yet it went as smooth as greased lightning. I thought at the time I was risking my life. They may have had me under surveillance for all I know. Anyhow, whatever you do, don't make enquiries about those accounts until I've seen the Prime Minister!'

He stared directly into my eyes. 'I'm afraid it's out of my hands, laddie!' responded the editor firmly. 'I had a word with our lord and master who decided, in his wisdom, to press on. Enquiries have already been made on the international network. If your hunch is right, a lot of people will be racing for cover... and the first one may be you!'

Although I was holding the cup of coffee in my hand, I slammed it down on his desk, spilling the liquid everywhere, but mostly over his trousers. 'Damn you, Ted Flanders!' I shouted angrily. 'This is my assignment and I strongly resent people taking control at a critical stage without my permission! Do you realise what you've done? You've let all those people escape the net and lost us every advantage we had! Of all the stupid things to do!' He stood up wiping the coffee off his trousers and I stormed out of his office in disgust leaving him to mop up the mess.

It was difficult to believe the man could be so ham-fisted on such a delicate matter. He had tried to pull the wool over my eyes with his comment: "I've had a word with our lord and master who decided, in his wisdom, to press on!' Bullshit! It was his way of laying the blame at someone else's door. In all probability he had taken the decision himself to act upon it without asking for authority from anyone in the newspaper hierarchy. Well the damage had been done now; there was nothing I could do to repair it. For once, I hoped I was wrong, in which case Ted would have gained us some lead time. Alternatively, he had started the clock on a time-bomb which was likely to explode in our faces.

On my way to the House of Commons, I thought about the options carefully. Assuming I was right... that the documents I had photographed were false... it was necessary to focus attention on Sir Peter Cavenham. If he was Der Bankvorsteher, he was the key to the whole problem. The authorities ought to search his home and office for clues to identify the location of Nazi funds as quickly as possible. When I arrived, Maitland showed me to the same room as before and made pleasant comments as I waited for the Prime Minister. After a few minutes, the door opened and, to my surprise, Sir Peter Cavenham entered. I tried to show no emotion at his presence as he sat opposite me and we stared at each other calmly.

'The Prime Minister is delayed at present,' he informed me benignly. 'He sent me along in his place. What do you wish to convey to him at this time?'

I weighed up the situation carefully before replying, pretending I was one of the major players in a big poker-game. The odds were that the Prime Minister hadn't sent him at all. He simply wanted to find out whether his cover had been blown... to decide whether or not to flee the coop. 'I'm Herr

Erdbeer,' I said quietly, looking about the room as if to check we were alone. 'It's my honour to meet Der Bankvorsteher at last!' He stared at me coldly for a while without speaking and I could almost see the cogs of his brain working at tremendous speed. 'The photograph album of your father and yourself... the one stolen by the newspaper reporter... is being held by the police. Do you want me to retrieve it for you?'

'You took copies of the documents at Kirk's house yesterday!' he accused. 'Your editor decided to start checking the details this morning. It triggered off an alarm signal in every area of banking and finance involving the organisation. The funds are being switched to alternative sources worldwide as we speak. You will not alter the final Anschluss!'

'I have no doubts about that,' I replied casually, cursing Flanders for his blunder. 'But tell me, why didn't you inform your sources I was a newspaper reporter making enquiries into International Three Thousand? Why didn't you alert them.'

'There's a lot you have to learn in this business, Mr. Savage,' he went on. 'An awful lot. The winners are those in control of the information. I must say you threw everyone off the scent by pretending to be the son of an SS Colonel, calling yourself Herr Erdbeer. However, that's all in the past.'

'What business do you have with me now?' I asked in trepidation.

Without warning, he drew a pistol from his pocket and pointed it at his head. 'I understand you have certain information on microfilm. A list of names of some of my compatriots who have settled in a number of different countries. You came here to give it to the Prime Minister. Instead, it would be appreciated if you would hand the microfilm to me. If the United Nations War Crimes Commission refuses to reveal the data, I don't think the British authorities should possess such secret details.'

'And if I refuse to hand it over?'

He laughed loudly. 'Do you think you could stand in our way? We have a plan for the Fourth, Fifth and Sixth Reich over the next thousand years. You are merely a straw in the wind!'

'You know where you went wrong,' I ventured, playing for time. 'You recruited too fast. The organisation should have developed its hierarchy and some of its operations more fully before it stepped up its recruitment campaign. But then you Krauts always get it wrong, don't you!'

'The microfilm!' he ordered, angered at my words. 'You have ten seconds before I pull the trigger!'

It was the longest ten seconds of my life but I didn't move an inch. There were some people afterwards who, when they heard the story, hailed me as a hero for standing my ground against the enemy, but the truth was that I stared down the nozzle of the pistol and froze. I couldn't lift a finger to save my life. At the end of ten seconds, his finger squeezed the trigger and a shot rang out. I sat still for a few moments wondering why I was still breathing, without feeling any pain, and then I saw Cavenham laying on the floor with blood seeping out of a wound at the side of his head. Gates pushed open the door widely, holding a revolver in his hand, and he stared at the inert body.

'That's another life you owe me,' he muttered, which I took to be a humorous remark although I didn't appreciate it at the time.

Maitland appeared at the door and took me by the arm, almost lifting me to my feet. 'The Prime Minister will see you now,' he told me, disregarding the body. I felt as though all the blood had been drained from my system. Both he and Gates assisted me to the terrace overlooking the Thames where I watched the river flow swiftly by. Gates decided to postpone his immediate plans and he sat with me for a while, realising I was in a state of shock.

'Are you okay now?' he asked sincerely, after a short period of time had elapsed.

I looked at him but all I could see was a vision of the nozzle of the pistol which had been pointed directly at my head. Then it vanished and I began to return to normality. 'Yes, I'm feeling a bit better now,' I replied, still shaking slightly. 'I wish you hadn't killed him... he was a very important man in International Three Thousand.'

'We knew him to be the Der Bankvorsteher but, like the old saying goes, the Krauts aren't stupid enough to put all their eggs in one basket. After a while, we discovered that no single individual holds the title. There are something like twenty of them, each one managing a fair parcel of the Nazi funds. So, if one is captured or dies, the system lives on. Sir Peter Cavenham was one of those bankers. Another one was here recently... an American who lives in Denver, Colorado. I think you might have met him at Kirk's house.'

'Yes, I did. He went under the pseudonym of "Hans", but he still had false information in his case.

'That was merely to test you out. If you'd played ball, they would have set you a number of further tests. Once passing those, Herr Erdbeer would have been appointed another Bankvorsteher. You see, they want to spread it around so that no single banker can filter off the funds for himself. It appears that each

Bankvorsteher has the telephone numbers of two others to contact in case of emergency. In that way, no conspiracies can be hatched. When the balloon went up this morning, after your editor started to make enquiries, a chain reaction began, culminating into a sharp diversion of funds into different areas and accounts. Just to be on the safe side.'

'But the information they gave me was false!'

'Perhaps not all of it. Certainly there were a number of movements in the money markets indicating changes of large sums for investment.'

Does that mean you can locate where the funds are invested?' I asked hopefully, although I knew exactly what he would reply.

'I don't think so. We can only make assumptions. Most of the accounts will be in the names of nominee companies. It's a lifetime's work unless one is on the inside with the information to hand. There's no means by which to sequestrate the funds worldwide.'

At that point he left me and I sat watching the river running by, with the sun playing on the ripples as the current swept past. I wondered how State Security would explain away the death of Sir Peter Cavenham. He had a wife and two children: what would happen to them? Perhaps they intended to continue with the cause. Many thoughts plagued my troubled mind for the next five minutes, then the Prime Minister arrived and sat at the table.

'Isn't it a beautiful day, Mr. Savage!' he greeted amiably. 'I've been looking forward to meeting you again. I understand you have some valuable information following your trip to Germany.'

I handed him the white envelope containing the microfilm I had received from Gunter Hausmann. He passed it to an aide who was hovering nearby and turned to face me with interest. 'All right, Mr. Savage, what have you to tell me?'

'Well, Prime Minister... ' I began, deciding to unfold the whole story from start to finish. After all, this time we were having tea on the terrace of the House of Commons and he was a captive audience. I wasn't certain whether he was any wiser at the end of it all. His committee had been annihilated. Sir Peter Cavenham was dead... his body still warm in the other room. Miss Grayson had committed suicide. Lieutenant-Colonel Topham had been assassinated. The only one left was Henry Jacobs. I had no idea what his fate might be.

'If you're free, I have an exciting day outlined for you,' the Prime Minister told me eventually.

'What do you want me to do?' I asked suspiciously.

'There's nothing for you to do,' he answered quietly. 'I simply want you to observe. After all your efforts, I think you should be privileged to be present at the final reckoning.

I shrugged and nodded at the same time. 'Yes,' I told him, 'I'd like that.' I had no idea what he was talking about but it sounded like a good idea to stay with him for a while under the protection of his security men. He seemed certain it would be the final reckoning but I had my doubts and, as a poker player, I knew I was right. He was a politician having reached the exalted rank of Prime Minister, but I, from the experience of a life-time, mistrusted all politicians. Of that I was certain!

CHAPTER SEVENTEEN

After we had finished tea on the terrace of the House of Commons, the Prime Minister left for an urgent meeting. I wondered what motivation he could have for rushing to different meetings at a moment's notice at his age, to face difficult problems of State day after day. The answer seemed to lie in the fact that the pursuit of power tended to corrupt reason and, once on the treadmill, it was difficult to review the direction of life except in retrospect. We all suffered from the same dilemma in a way. For myself, it was a life-long intention to read the classics like Mill on the Floss, the books of Charles Dickens, Tom Jones, Far from the Madding Crowd, and many others, but I knew in my heart I knew that I would never get down to the task. Life was too short; discipline too weak! Well, it was the Prime Minister's concern how he wanted to conduct his life. If the man wished to dedicate himself to the nation by devoting all his time and energy to the effort, it was his privilege to do so. It left me with the feeling that none of us were masters of our own destiny. In effect, we all had some role to play in our span of life on earth. No doubt, if it came to the pinch, he would question my reason for having become a newspaper reporter. For what it was worth, I could challenge myself on that decision.

I continued to watch the Thames flow by in solitude, allowing the anxiety to seep gradually from my mind, sensing the current of the river was carrying away all the tension. How soothing it was to let one's problems float gently into the distance with the tide. If only it could happen that way all the time! Eventually, my attention was arrested by a young man in the uniform of an army officer who marched swiftly to my table and stopped. He smiled at me under a thick moustache before sticking out his hand which I shook.

'I'm Captain Watson,' he announced loudly. 'Would you mind coming with me, sir? The Prime Minister has asked for you to be present.'

I got to my feet and followed him as he marched off at regulation pace. 'Where does he want me to be present?' I gasped, trying to keep up with him.

The Captain continued without speaking until we arrived at a set of lift doors. 'In the Operations Room, sir. You may recall that Sir Winston Churchill had a similar room elsewhere in which he co-ordinated activities during World War Two. It enabled him to focus his attention on operations and make decisions quickly and effectively. Well, we have such a room downstairs, although we rarely use it. This is quite a momentous occasion. In my opinion, sir, you're rather lucky to be part of it!'

As far as I was concerned, he was talking gibberish. However, I had no option but to wait for the lift to arrive and descend in it with him. He led me out across the flagstone floors of the basement and took me to a door which he opened. Indeed, it was an Operations Room, fitted out to display an enormous table on which had been overlaid with a giant board outlining all the countries of Europe in bright colours. A number of men and women in military uniforms stood around holding croupier's rods, capable of pushing small black arrows mounted on blocks of wood... each one representing the location of activity in the European theatre of war. On one side of the room sat five men and women in service uniforms, each with two telephones in from of them. They were assisted by small computers with monitors by which they could keep track of developments. At the far end of the room, a wooden dais had been elevated at a vantage point where the Prime Minister sat in a comfortable chair and watched with interest. Captain Watson led me to the chair next to him and I sat down to witness the proceedings.

'At first light this morning,' the Captain informed me, 'we attacked a fortress on the Zugspitze in the Bavarian Alps. The German and Austrian governments co-operated with us on the mission allowing SAS commandos to land their aircraft and helicopters and storm it successfully. The man known as Strogoff was captured and we have advised the Russian authorities who are making speedy arrangements for his repatriation. His welcome will be chilly in more ways than one I should imagine. We managed to prevent him from destroying a large amount of information held on microfilm... some of it being the false information on the three countries you passed to him... but he managed to obtain microfilm of Nazis in five other European countries. You had the lists for France, Czechosolovakia and Greece. The others are Belgium, Luxemburg, Denmark, Norway and the Netherlands. It looks like we can start operations initially in eight countries.'

I felt a great deal of relief that Strogoff was no longer a threat. The man had no conscience and he was quite capable of carrying out the most devious destructive plans. However, through circumstances beyond his control, he became caught in a giant spider's web and suffered being taken back forcibly to his own country as an escaped prisoner. Of all people, Ted Flanders would be most delighted to hear the news! At least he would be able to sleep easily in his bed at night... even if it constituted an executive chair in his smoke-filled office!

The Prime Minister turned to me in the intermediate silence to enlarge on the possible developments of the day. I listened to him with interest. 'In view of the serious threat from International Three Thousand, which has been exposed to other European countries today, albeit some of them were already keeping track of their development, we have asked for their support and co-operation whether they're members of the United Nations War Crimes Commission or not. I believe there's a distinct possibility they will all become involved.'

'Have you any information concerning a man called Jack Berg after the attack on Strogoff's fortress?' I asked, still not fully understanding the nature of the Operation's Room.

'A report will be submitted to us later,' confirmed the Captain sombrely. 'It was a surprise attack against troops which had received only elementary training, so casualties ought to be light.'

'Tell me,' I ventured impatiently, 'what's going to happen here today? Why are we watching this map of Europe?'

The Prime Minister looked at me as though I ought to have known better than to ask such a question, 'We can no longer tolerate the evil elements in Europe and those who control International Three Thousand for their own purpose. A United States of Europe would be a wonderful event in the history of mankind if it were negotiated successfully... although I believe it will take a millennium before it can be achieved properly. It's a concept in which we all believe but we have to allow the development to take place in its own time. The foundation has already been established. It's taken us since 1963, the Treaty of Rome, to get to this point. How can a group of people dare think they can fulfil the plan by the first of June? With regard to the sons and grandsons of the Nazis who wish to take control, well the situation by necessity must be corrected without delay.'

'But how can you deal with all those people at once and hold them for questioning and trial?' I asked naively, without giving the matter too much thought. 'The task is practically impossible! Not only that, but it might attract support for a United States of Europe, in which case the general public would be out of accord with your government's policies.'

'Exactly!' replied Captain Watson, coming to the aid of his superior. 'We can't afford to publicise the facts. The Prime Minister had a secret meeting this morning with the Cabinet where a unanimous decision was made to seek out and destroy... as we did with Strogoff!'

'Seek out and destroy?' I turned my head to stare at both of them. 'Do you mean you've sent out squads... like the SAS ... to hunt down the leading Nazis and their families, to assassinate them where they are.'

'Can you suggest another way to deal with the problem?' asked the Captain coldly. 'We're willing to listen to any reasonable suggestions.'

I had to admit I had no clever solution, but then it wasn't really up to me to decide what needed to be done. If Berg had been here, he would have danced with joy at the co-ordinated effort being made to fulfil his life's work. Nonetheless, killing people in cold blood didn't appeal to me at all. 'What about the families of Nazi or military officers who have no intention of pursuing the Nazi cause? What if they're listed on the microfilm? You'll be killing innocent people!'

'Really?' responded the Captain, with a tinge of sarcasm in his voice. 'I'd like to reply to that argument on a personal basis, i.e. nothing to do with rank, uniform or politics, if I may. Firstly, as a Jew who's family was murdered by these butchers in two different concentration camps, I can tell you with conviction that the only good Nazi is a dead one! Secondly, if you examine the history books and read how they experimented on defenceless human-beings, tortured them and murdered them... and we're talking of a total of some eight or nine million people... you'll realise that if we don't act immediately the same thing will happen again... perhaps on an even more grotesque scale. They want to turn Europe into a Fascist state and maintain full control for themselves. I think my conscience can bear the responsibility of the demise of a few innocent descendants of such a race if my efforts save the world from despotic rule and millions of deaths in the future.'

'Come now, Captain Watson,' scolded the Prime Minister, although his reproach was not meant to be real. 'Aren't you being a little harsh on our capable ally here? He's a newspaper reporter... not Jewish... and not a military man. It's part of his job to safeguard the public interest... to tell them what's going on.'

'Exactly so, Prime Minister,' declared the Captain. 'That's why I'm explaining it to him in such detail!'

'I can't report a story of such unbelievable depths to an unsuspecting public!' I complained. 'It wouldn't be acceptable. Anyway, you'd put a "D" notice on it to prevent it from being published.'

The Prime Minister nodded slowly. 'I'm afraid the true story would run counter to the public interest. If people learned the Nazis intended to rise within our midst by the time Die Stunde arrived, it would be an excellent advertising campaign influencing many people to support, if not join, International Three Thousand. The situation would breed on itself, especially as many would fail to realise the evil side of the development, ignoring the fact they would lose their freedom and their rights as citizens under the new regime. We would play directly into the hands of those enemies we hope to destroy. Indeed, Mr. Savage, we' have no option but to issue "D" notices to your newspaper and all the other newspapers for that matter, to prevent publication of the story at the present time.'

I could imagine Ted Flanders in his office dancing with rage as he puffed deeply on one of his pungent cigars. He would demand to see me the moment I returned, swearing and ranting in his usual manner, insisting I find an angle by which he could print the story. In the present circumstances, there was little I could say or do... and even less to write! At that moment, one of the telephones rang and everyone waited expectantly with baited breath.

'It's the Belgian authorities,' related a female army sergeant answering the call, holding the receiver tightly to her ear. 'Belgian storm-troops are operating in five major Belgian cities... Brussels, Antwerp, Liege, Bruges and Mons.'

Two of the service staff in the centre of the room moved wooden black arrows around the board with their croupier rods to the location of the towns.

'It all starts now,' declared the Prime Minister, as though sitting on a bench at the edge of a football pitch to watch a cup-tie. 'I had a long conversation with an official called Hendrickx in Brussels this morning. He seemed pretty keen to join in the action.'

The shock of the cold-bloodedness of the operation still chilled my veins. Then I pulled myself together to reason with reality. It wasn't possible to take sides in this issue, or to judge with fairness. We had entered into a war during a period of peace where, at some time or another, there had to be casualties and death. It was them or us... and they couldn't be allowed to win. Therefore, like it or not, the decision taken by the authorities had to be decisive under the circumstances... even if it was horrendous and savage.

'Tell me,' I asked Captain Watson, whose eyes began to gleam at the commencement of hostilities, 'how many people are involved roughly in each country, and how are the storm troops, police, or the military going to deal with them?'

'Well you've put your finger right on the button, Mr. Savage,' he replied candidly. 'We assess there are about five thousand people in each country descended directly from Nazis. Even if split into five or six towns, the numbers are relatively large. The Belgians have two old disused prisons and a detention centre, all of which are located deep into the countryside. They're using ambulances, police vehicles, and military transport to take them there. Each person will be interrogated carefully to determine their background, ideals, and so on. But we really know the key people involved. However, you must bear in mind that many will have slipped the net before we get to them... very much like the situation at the end of World War Two when many Nazi criminals managed to escape. We recognise it's impossible to achieve a one hundred per cent success rate. It's a fact of life. What we intend to do is to put Die Stunde back fifty years or more.'

'It sounds as though you're doing the same thing to them as they did to the Jews in World War Two!' I retorted. 'Carrying them off without giving them a reason!'

The Captain bridled at the remark but he kept his cool. 'I don't think so, sir. You see, the Jews were the scapegoats of the Nazis who turned the whole German nation against them. They had their shops, their jobs, their public appointments, and their possessions seized from them without reason. Each one was forced to wear a yellow Star of David as a sign that he or she was inferior; a sub-classified citizen to be mocked or bullied at anyone's whim. We're speaking of educated people in business and commerce, academics, intellectuals, and the like. We're talking of a race of people, totally innocent of any crime, whom the Nazis tried to eliminate without mercy. The annihilation of a race of people on earth! No, Mr. Savage, this is not the same thing at all! These people are the bad seed. Their history proves them to be a warring nation with a strong taste for world domination. They have this desire racing through their blood like a virus. In modern times, a soft-hearted world forgave them for the butchery in World War One. Millions of people died yet still the Germans were forgiven. And what happened? They started another world war, without provocation, and killed millions more. Now they want to take over Europe in its current throes. How long can we go on letting them perpetrate these crimes before someone cries out: "Enough!"'

He was a tough man to quarrel with because he felt such conviction. 'The saddest thing of all,' I responded, retreating somewhat into my shell, 'is that not all the countries in the United Nations War Crimes Commission will play ball. Australia agreed to let Israel examine their files and so has China. Their co-operation is more of a token of willingness than anything else. But the United States, New Zealand, Poland, the factions which make up Yugoslavia, and Britain... what about them?'

'You've no need to concern yourself about Britain,' replied the Captain firmly. 'We've been weeding our own garden in the past without fuss or direction from the Press or other watchful eyes. We considered it was far better that way. But the problem is not only in Europe. There are Nazis hiding in comparative safety in many South American countries, as well as in South Africa. The Israelis have agents there but it's hard work finding the real culprits. They've hidden themselves away, adopting different identities which remain well-guarded by bribes to certain officials in the respective countries. If I read your mind correctly, there's no way anyone can flush them out to end the threat once and for all. They teach their children and grandchildren the ways of national socialism... the Nazi ways. I fear we shall have to learn to live with the problem forever!'

The tactics employed by the authorities against the bad seed nauseated me, but I liked Captain Watson's reply even less. The world had defeated the belligerent Germans twice during the first half of the twentieth century. It had been divided into two separate countries, managed by different political regimes, and the Nazis had fled for their lives to different countries throughout the world. And yet here we were still fighting to keep them at bay... fearing for the safety of our children and grandchildren in the future. Why? Because of an element of people with a national spirit of overgrown proportions and Fascist ideals who would never stop until they ruled the world! Worse still, we helped them by allowing reunification of Germany to take place. Another telephone rang, and the call was answered instantly by an eager member of the Royal Air Force.

'France!' he called out. 'The French police have descended on Paris, Marseilles, Lyon, Toulouse and Bordeaux!'

The croupiers were back in action again, moving the black arrows across the table towards the respective cities, but I was not inspired by the action. Certainly the exercise was likely to set Die Stunde back for a while... perhaps even fifty years... but for me it wasn't enough. No one could rest easily until every Nazi, and the family of every Nazi, was removed from the face of the earth... otherwise the whole world would remain under threat for eternity, or at least until the Nazis had achieved world domination! Suddenly, the whole issue came into perspective as the words of Captain Watson reached deeply into my mind. The Nazis had escaped to many countries to avoid paying the penalty for their cruelty to mankind, and yet here we were still fighting for our lives and the freedom of our future against them. They had sold off all the treasures looted during the war and now had substantial funds to support them in any action they wished to take. It was incredible but true! I stood up with the intention of leaving, becoming tired of the proceedings.

'I'm sorry, Prime Minister,' I apologised, 'But I haven't the stomach for this sort of thing. I leave you to your own devices.'

To his surprise, I walked towards the door. 'I would have liked to arrange for some award to be given to you for your efforts,' he called out, 'but in view of the nature of the situation I'm sure you'll understand my reluctance to do so.'

I nodded with a sad expression on my face, although I couldn't really have cared less about an award or medal. I left with Captain Watson racing after me to ensure I reached the front door of the House of Commons safely. Once away from the building, I stood watching the Thames flow swiftly from a different angle and I breathed in fresh air to help me clear my mind. I doubted that an international operation of the kind planned would escape the notice of the public for very long. However, after a period of two or three weeks, lack of information by the media would cause interest to lapse. One thing I had learned well in the newspaper business was the fact that the public had a very short memory. The campaign was nonsense really. How many real Nazis, in positions of power or otherwise, would storm-troops or police or the military catch in their net? And what about the offspring? The children and grandchildren! How could anyone prove whether they still carried Fascism in their hearts and minds and intended to do something sinister about it? On the other hand, how far did one have to go to stamp out the concept of Nazism? It was a question I had failed to pose to the eloquent Captain Watson, but it was too late to determine the solution now. The Nazis had been famous for delivering lorry loads of people to concentration camps. Now the boot was on the other foot. I wondered how they would like it?

I returned to the newspaper building and walked tiredly into Ted Flander's office. He was on the telephone, puffing away at a large cigar and I sat down until he finished the call. When he replaced the receiver, he glowered at me as though I had opened Pandora's Box to bring all the ills of the world upon him. 'They've issued us with bloody "D" notices!' he shouted, as if I was the person to blame. 'Bloody "D" notices! We come up with a story to shake a nation... to shake the world... and what does the bloody government do? They won't let us print it! Do you realise the government's guilty of suppression of material facts which the public should know about! They to run this country as a secret society like tyrants and despots. We can't let it happen without a fight! I mean it! We've got to fight!'

I yawned with little interest, rubbing a hand over my face. 'What are you going to do about it?' I taunted him, because I knew that he was powerless to do anything.

He sat back on his haunches allowing his temper to subside. 'There's damn all anyone can do... and you know it!' he muttered puffing fiercely at his cigar before embarking on a chronic bout of coughing. 'Remind me to give these up, will you?' he went on, once he had regained his breath. 'Smoking can damage your health, you know.' He ignored my gales of laughter as the humour of his remark sank home.

'Anyhow it's not all bad news, Ted. Strogoff, the man who's after your blood, is on his way back to Russia,' I revealed eventually. 'He's been arrested and I'm afraid it'll be the last you ever see of him again.'

'Afraid?' he challenged vehemently. 'Thank God they got him!' He puffed strongly on the cigar again, causing great clouds of smoke to pollute the office further. 'Okay, let's get down to business! We can't publish the story of your assignment but there's more ways of killing a cat than banging its head against the wall. What side issues are there? Something we might be able to sneak in without getting slapped on the wrist by the authorities! There must be something of great news value in this assignment somewhere!' He looked up at the ceiling. 'Come on, God of newspapers! Give me something to work on!'

I shrugged my shoulders aimlessly. 'I've just come from the House of Commons. There's a witch-hunt going on in European countries to root out the Nazis and their families. Don't ask me to give you further details because it isn't worth the aggravation thinking about it.'

'Come on, Jimmy!' he urged. 'Give me an angle... any angle! I've got the boss in the penthouse on my back, and a public's hungry for news outside. What do I do?'

I waved the smoke away from my face with a sweep of my hand and stood up to leave. 'Why can't you print the story about Strogoff? A Russian criminal who escaped across the icy wastes of Siberia to start a movement in this country to avenge himself against his captors. You could say he then discovered a number of Nazis living in hiding, and blackmailed them to help him build a fortress near Berchtesgaden... near the Eagle's Nest... one of Hitler's favourite retreats. It sounds pretty good to me. Your blessed public will love it. Not only that... but it doesn't have a "D" notice slapped on it. You can print what you like!'

A gleam came into his eyes as he realised he had a story after all. 'Write it for me, Jimmy!' he pressed. 'Make it a two-column item with a two inch header on the front page, plus a three-part story for the Sundays!'

'Go write it your bloody self!' I swore in contempt. 'I'm going home to get some sleep... even though my mattress has been cut to ribbons!'

'Ah, you're always going home to sleep. What's the matter with you? Low blood-pressure or something? Don't worry, I'll get someone else to look through your notes and write it... but you won't get the credit. You won't get the by-line!'

'Before you blow a gasket with your rotten threats, Ted,' I informed him frankly. 'There are no notes. It's all up here in my head! But, for the sake of my job, I'll start writing it in the morning.'

'Good, lad!' he called out as I left his office. 'I'm glad I thought of using it as a story! You know, sometimes I get these brilliant ideas! You're lucky to have an editor of my calibre. Someone who can lead this newspaper successfully!'

The situation was too pathetic to contemplate. I had offered him the idea as a joke. Now he claimed it to have been his own. It wasn't worth arguing the point with him, to reduce myself down to his level. What did it matter whose idea it was anyway? When I arrived back at my apartment, I stared at the damage woefully. This sort of thing didn't happen to journalists in the ordinary line of duty, yet the apartment had been smashed up twice within a very short time. I lay back on the damaged settee and rested my head on the arm. The nightmare was over at last! Kirk and the Glazers would have been arrested by now... if they hadn't escaped... and the house near Epping Forest closed completely. There would be no more combat sessions or classes in economics, international law, or government. At the same time, there would be no more Israeli agents like Carrie, no more Nazi hunters like Berg, no Nazi torch-bearers resembling Miss Grayson, no saviours such as Gates, and no dangerous outside elements in the form of Igor Strogoff. The assignment had ended!

I poured myself a drink and dwelt on the assignment in slow motion. It was different reviewing it in retrospect... reflecting the incidents in comfort without feeling the pain. After a while, the tiredness drifted from my body and I decided to visit one of my favourite haunts for a late lunch. As soon as I closed the front door, I sensed that something was wrong but I couldn't fathom the danger. Someone from another world was trying to force me to recognise a premonition but I was too ignorant to make the connection. About two hundred metres from the apartment, I turned to discover the Nazi youth I had angered at Hayle's party. He was dressed in ordinary clothes this time and he moved in for the kill with an ugly-looking knife in his right hand. I had no idea whether he knew of the action being taken against his colleagues by the government of Europe, but I became swiftly aware he was determined to take vengeance on me for the way I had treated him. I turned and parried the initial thrust, pushing him lightly into a set of railings. He rallied and came at me again like a bull in the ring against a matador. I adopted a martial arts pose by habit and used his weight to help me, sending him to the pavement some distance behind me. He grasped the dagger more tightly and hurled himself at me in blind desperation. I managed to send the knife spinning from his hand, and we fell to the ground together grappling fiercely. The public watched without interference as we rolled forwards and backwards across the pavement, trying to batter each other senseless. Eventually, we broke free and stood like two animals ready to lock horns. He glanced towards the middle of the road where the knife lay glistening in the sunlight. I followed his gaze, estimating that we were both about the same distance away from the weapon. My brain told me I couldn't afford to let him reach it first. Obviously, he read my thoughts for we dashed at tremendous speed into the road, both aiming to get there first. I recalled vaguely hearing the sound of a car horn and some kind of commotion and, suddenly, everything went black.

It was some time later when I recovered my senses to find myself in a ward at the local hospital. My leg was covered in plaster which was supported by a wire from aloft, while Barnaby sat in a wheelchair beside the bed. He was playing patience with a pack of cards.

'Welcome back to the land of the living, Jimmy, boy!' he greeted with a smile on his face.

I tried to shift my position but it caused indescribable pain. 'What happened?' I asked, trying to focus my mind on the fight with the Nazi youth.

'It would seem you were fighting someone in the street and the two of you ran into the road for a knife that was there. He was hit directly by a car coming your way and killed outright. You were struck by a glancing blow by a vehicle going the other way. Lucky you didn't get to the knife first!'

I shrugged sadly at my predicament, although relieved at having escaped the wrath of the young Nazi. Barnaby pressed me to tell him what happened and I related the story of the assignment to him. Sometimes he interrupted with short spurts of laughter. At other times, he came in with hoots of derision as though I was unfolding a modern tale of the Arabian nights. I was hardly surprised by his reaction, for he was probably jealous so many interesting incidents had taken place. After all, if he hadn't broken his leg he would have been handling the assignment. When I finished, he became sombre and silent, thinking about the dangers I had faced. Most likely he was thinking to himself: "There, but for the grace of God, go I!" In my opinion, if he had been fit enough to carry out the assignment, he wouldn't have survived.

We developed a new conversation in due course, complaining to each other about the fate of innocent trouble-shooting reporters whose efforts often demanded actions and decisions above and beyond the call of duty, and the faults of newspaper management to recognise the value of front-line reporters. Then the door opened and Ted Flanders entered with a smile on his face, as though he had just accepted the divine appointment to be our Fairy Godfather. However, the image was ruined by the fact that he wore a faded creased blue raincoat and chewed on the butt of an old cigar which fitted incongruously between his yellow teeth.

'How are my boys today?' he called to us cheerfully, stopping to light the cigar without showing any interest in our responses.

Barnaby and I glanced at each other coldly, neither of us willing to offer any comment. We both knew that if the editor was in such a good-natured mood it meant he wanted something to be done urgently.

'We're running a story on Igor Strogoff that looks great!' he went on enthusiastically, turning towards me. 'You sly old devil! You did write up those notes on him! We found them in your desk drawer!' He brought his hand down on the bed playfully which caused me to wince. I wasn't sure whether he did it deliberately as a token of revenge because I had lied to him. But then it could have been accidental for the man had no empathy at all for other people. 'I've got another assignment for one of you. How about it, Barnaby? You've been in here for a week. You're the one nearest to recovery. The newspaper doesn't care too much for malingerers, you know!'

Barnaby stared at him icily and then pointed to the door. 'Out!' he shouted angrily. 'Out! Out!' I began to join him, repeating the same word in a chant, until a staff nurse weighing nearly two hundred pounds stormed through the doorway to investigate the disturbance.

'What on earth is going on here?' she demanded, sizing up the situation quickly, staring hard at the editor before attacking him vehemently. 'Take that filthy cigar out of your mouth! This is a clinical hospital ward! Put it out this instant! And then get out! You're upsetting my patients!'

Ted searched for an ash-tray to stub out the cigar, under the harsh gaze of the fearless nurse, before deciding to cut his losses and run. 'Out!' she repeated as he headed for the door. 'Out!'

He turned as if to reason with her but, as he looked into her eyes, she took a step forward menacingly and he retreated swiftly, running out of the door as fast as his legs would carry him. He had met his match! It was such a funny sight that Barnaby and I were unable to stop laughing. The gales of mirth caused me to suffer extreme pain but I never regretted a moment of it. The vision of the editor being thrown out of the hospital by a belligerent staff nurse, as he tried to hide the butt of a burning cigar in his hand, was an unforgettable incident I would cherish until my dying day.

When Barnaby had gone back to his own room, I was given a sleeping-tablet and the lights were turned off for the night. I couldn't sleep and lay in bed as my body throbbed with every beat of my heart. I kept thinking the forces of evil were at play at that very moment, embarking ceaselessly on a silent march. My mind, in torment, visualised row upon row of white crosses set out neatly in cemeteries designated for war graves. Although I had never visited any of them, it seemed to me that I spent the hours of the night counting the cost of human lives. I was naive enough to be disappointed that pernicious subversive elements existed in modern civilisation. Why was it necessary for the people of one particular nations, like the Nazis, to create their own Aryan race... a Master race... and view themselves a cut above everyone else? Why did they need to aim for the control of Europe, and then the rest of the world? Was it the desire for power, rank, possession, or simply to attain over-riding authority over every other human-being? It was something I would never truly understand and I doubted whether I was alone in that consideration. The only way I could reason with it was by analysing the existing facts. The world was filled with pockets of Nazis, their children and grandchildren and their followers, years after they had been crushed in a merciless war. The funds derived from the plunder and looting of gold vaults, art galleries and museums in Europe was increasing each year by means of investments in international markets. How many Nazis, their descendants and followers existed worldwide? The Prime Minister was perfectly correct when he suggested the public would become paranoid if they discovered the truth. I felt the same way by simply thinking about the danger to mankind from such evil predators... a section of society which murdered millions of others and brought the world to its knees because of its greed for power and domination. I looked across the room, out of the window, into the clear starlit night. The enemy was at large. They had the national spirit which burned fiercely within them. They had their followers who sought change. They had the funds by which to undertake a war during a time of peace. As for myself, despite the dangers, I had emerged unscathed. As Berg once told me: "One of the rules of the game is that you never do anything unless you're absolutely positive you're not going to get caught." In my case, it proved to be more by luck than judgement. But there was another thing Berg had said which I considered far more important. "We must remember never to forget." It was clear to me now that if we failed to do so, they would come at us again and again until we were conquered... and then the freedom we know and enjoy will exist no more!

THE END

Lightning Source UK Ltd.
Milton Keynes UK
UKOW02f1724180516

274532UK00001B/103/P